P9-CSV-531

"I didn't know you were Waylon's guardian."

Abram stared at her. "If you think about it, you'll see I was merely in the wrong place at the wrong time."

"Don't tell me what to think," Lou said, somewhat peevishly. This was the worst possible situation. She'd finally met someone she could really like and he was completely off-limits.

"It's policy at the college not to sweep anything under the rug." He propped his hands on his hips. "I'll give full disclosure, though it's likely they will be in touch with you. Just tell them the truth."

No way would she reveal how well they got to know each other. She didn't think Abram would be willing to do so either. They met, they danced once and they shared a drink. Period. End of story.

Both she and the too-delicious-to-have-even-contemplated-in-the-first-place coach had screwed up...and the innocent might end up suffering because she wanted to play Cinderella.

Why had she even entertained a different ending for herself last night?

Hadn't she learned nothing in life was easy?

Dear Reader,

As a Southern girl I learned early that if you can't ignore 'em, you join them. The *them* referred to here are college football fans, and all across the nation on Saturdays you will find them throwing up tents, wearing their jerseys and firing up generators. In my neck of the woods, college football is a religion. You must worship at the purple-and-gold altar, make a burnt offering and drink the proverbial, ahem, beer. If you're not with us…you're tiger bait. Plain and simple. I cannot describe Saturday night in Tiger Stadium—the sheer intensity of over 90,000 fans under the influence of gumbo, bourbon and dreams of grandeur. It's definitely something to see.

So when the idea of writing about a recruiting scandal struck me, I knew the best place to set the book. Of course, the college in this book is not Louisiana State University and there are no Bonnet Creek Owls. But if you dig deep enough, you'll see the foundation for the story.

Want to see several thousand grown men gathered around the TV as if it's the finale of *The Bachelor*? Tune in to ESPN on the first Tuesday of February—you may even see tears. College football is big business, and National Signing Day is the sorority rush of the sport and the perfect place to launch a story about want, desire and love under the lights.

Hope you enjoy Lou and Abram's journey to love. And *Geaux*, Tigers!

Happy reading,

Liz Talley

PS—I love to hear from readers. You can reach me through my website, www.LizTalleyBooks.com.

Under the Autumn Sky

LIZ TALLEY

TORONTO NEW YORK LONDON
AMSTERDAM PARIS SYDNEY HAMBURG
STOCKHOLM ATHENS TOKYO MILAN MADRID
PRAGUE WARSAW BUDAPEST AUCKLAND

If you purchased this book without a cover you should be aware that this book is stolen property. It was reported as "unsold and destroyed" to the publisher, and neither the author nor the publisher has received any payment for this "stripped book."

Recycling programs
for this product may
not exist in your area.

ISBN-13: 978-0-373-71788-0

UNDER THE AUTUMN SKY

Copyright © 2012 by Amy R. Talley

All rights reserved. Except for use in any review, the reproduction or utilization of this work in whole or in part in any form by any electronic, mechanical or other means, now known or hereafter invented, including xerography, photocopying and recording, or in any information storage or retrieval system, is forbidden without the written permission of the publisher, Harlequin Enterprises Limited, 225 Duncan Mill Road, Don Mills, Ontario, Canada M3B 3K9.

This is a work of fiction. Names, characters, places and incidents are either the product of the author's imagination or are used fictitiously, and any resemblance to actual persons, living or dead, business establishments, events or locales is entirely coincidental.

This edition published by arrangement with Harlequin Books S.A.

For questions and comments about the quality of this book please contact us at Customer_eCare@Harlequin.ca.

® and TM are trademarks of the publisher. Trademarks indicated with ® are registered in the United States Patent and Trademark Office, the Canadian Trade Marks Office and in other countries.

www.Harlequin.com

Printed in U.S.A.

ABOUT THE AUTHOR

From devouring the Harlequin Superromance novels on the shelf of her aunt's used bookstore to swiping her grandmother's medical romances, Liz Talley has always loved a good romance. So it was no surprise to anyone when she started writing a book one day while her infant napped. She soon found writing more exciting than scrubbing hardened cereal off the love seat. Underneath Liz's baby-food-stained clothes, a dream stirred. She followed that dream, and after a foray into historical romance and a Golden Heart final, she started her first contemporary romance on the same day she met her editor. Coincidence? She prefers to call it fate.

Currently Liz lives in north Louisiana with her high-school sweetheart, two beautiful children and a passel of animals. Liz loves watching her boys play baseball, shopping for bargains and going out for lunch. When not writing contemporary romances for the Harlequin Superromance line, she can be found doing laundry, feeding kids or playing on Facebook.

Books by Liz Talley

HARLEQUIN SUPERROMANCE

1639—VEGAS TWO-STEP
1675—THE WAY TO TEXAS
1680—A LITTLE TEXAS
1705—A TASTE OF TEXAS
1738—A TOUCH OF SCARLET
1770—WATERS RUN DEEP*

*The Boys of Bayou Bridge

Other titles by this author are available in ebook format.

Don't miss any of our special offers. Write to us at the following address for information on our newest releases.

Harlequin Reader Service
U.S.: 3010 Walden Ave., P.O. Box 1325, Buffalo, NY 14269
Canadian: P.O. Box 609, Fort Erie, Ont. L2A 5X3

This book is dedicated to the fans of college football everywhere for wearing the colors and loving the sport.

Special thanks go to Louisiana State University coach Sam Nader and his son Breaux for teaching me about the fascinating process of recruiting; to Coach Jerry Byrd for suffering my questions; and to my boys, Jake and Gabe, who make me proud *every* day.

CHAPTER ONE

April, 2011

ABRAM DUFRENE HADN'T wanted to cover Daryll Moreland's recruiting area any more than he wanted to lick
a donkey's butt, but there was no choice in the matter. Louisiana University's head football coach Leonard
Holt's word was law, so Abram sucked it up, grabbed
a coffee and hit the road in his quest for the next best
wide-out or bone-cruncher for the Panthers.

Pulling Abram from his old recruiting area covering
Mississippi through Florida didn't bother Coach Holt.
He didn't have a mother living west of Baton Rouge in
the new recruiting area, did he? No, his mother was far,
far away in his native state of Ohio. Didn't Holt know
Abram couldn't pass his birthplace of Beau Soleil and
not stop in? His mother had eyes and ears all over the
state of Louisiana. Somehow she'd know and the guilt
trip would start. Abram had never been able to get away
with anything. His mother always found out.

Not that he was a momma's boy or anything.

No, quite the opposite, but Picou Dufrene was like
the hurricanes that often ravage the Louisiana coast-
line—she hit with a fury leaving a person standing
among rubble blinking up at the sparkling sun wondering what the hell had happened. She killed with a
smile…and an assload of guilt.

So he'd stopped by the home place, a near-to-crumbling Greek revival plantation several miles from I-10 between Lafayette and Baton Rouge, gulped down chicory coffee and some of the housekeeper Lucille's buttermilk pie, and listened to his mother prattle about his brothers—and his sister, who'd recently been reconciled to the family after having spent years presumed dead. Sally was always part of the conversation.

"You are coming to my birthday dinner on Friday?" his mother had asked when they stepped out onto the veranda. It wasn't a question. It was a reminder.

"Of course. I should be there."

Picou's blue eyes narrowed even as she smiled. Which was hard to do, but the woman mastered challenges. "Should?"

"Will," he said, shuffling his travel schedule in his mind. He'd totally forgotten her 60th-ish birthday. His future sister-in-law, Annie, had sent him an email reminder last week, but he'd skimmed over it. Lots more in his inbox that needed attention.

"That's my sweet Abram," his mother said, giving him a kiss on the cheek goodbye, making him feel like he was a seven-year-old child. How did mothers always do that?

The side trip to Beau Soleil had put him off schedule by a good two hours, but as he neared the small town harboring the state's best prospect at tight end, Abram's focus shifted to his job. He was confident he could land this kid.

Yawning, Abram studied the straight dark highway ahead of him before switching off the heat and turning up Better than Ezra on the radio.

He was dog-tired.

The spring game had revealed the need to pad the

roster at tight end, and as much as he needed rest from the marathon recruiting season and the grueling spring practice schedule, he knew he had work to do. Always work to do when one coached a top-tiered Division I football team. Even on vacation, he worked.

But it was what he wanted.

What he'd wanted since the day he'd hung up his own cleats—to coach at his alma mater.

So he shut up and put up, and did whatever it took to do his job and do it well. He was the youngest position coach on the University of Louisiana, Baton Rouge, staff and he was still hungry.

Which was why he was currently headed up Interstate 49 toward the small town of Bonnet Creek, a dot on the map, but current home of Waylon Boyd. Boyd was a big drink of water at six foot five inches, two hundred thirty-five pounds. Good hands, nice physicality and covered major ground on his runs. He reminded Abram of Jeremy Witten, so he'd kept his eye on Waylon ever since he'd seen tape on him last October.

When the boy had shown up for Junior Day on the ULBR campus, Abram had taken a special interest in the prospect. A nice 4.63 on the 40-yard dash combined with marked improvement on his quickness, meant Abram wanted Waylon on the Panthers' roster come 2012. Tomorrow began the period in which he could make his first call to Waylon, but he never discounted the importance of contact with a recruit's head coach. Some things were better done in person.

The exit to Ville Platte materialized in the vacant landscape, and Abram, stuck on the left of an eighteen-wheeler, blew by it.

Damn it.

He looked at the empty water bottle in the cup holder

and groaned. Maybe he shouldn't have drunk the entire thing on top of the coffee. He ignored his full bladder and charged forth. He'd take the next exit for Chicot State Park and head back toward Ville Platte, where he had a room for the night since there was no motel in Bonnet Creek. Sleepy Town Inn. He'd stayed in worse, he supposed, but he wasn't looking forward to a lumpy bed and *King of the Hill* reruns. Maybe he could find a place to wet his whistle close by so he could wind down.

And like a wish bestowed, a large rambling honky-tonk appeared ahead of him on the right.

Rendezvous.

Normally he wasn't spontaneous, but he had to take a leak. And a beer would help him sleep. He jerked the steering wheel, sending his big F250 into the gravel lot off the cedar-clad, tin-roofed building, taking the last spot.

Music spilled out into the cool air, raucous and inviting. This wasn't a simple bar and grill where one sat alone watching an NBA game while nursing a long-neck. No, this sounded like Ladies' Night at a college bar. He glanced around. The lot was full for a Wednesday, filled with big trucks like his, many with camouflage accessories and most with ULBR license plate holders and decals.

Abram looked down at his purple sweater vest with the ULBR logo over the breast.

No freaking way.

He'd be swarmed by the ULBR faithful as soon as they saw the businesslike athletic department moniker on the breast of the sweater. They'd know he was part of the program, and after a less than impressive spring game shown on ESPNU, he'd not be able to find any anonymity in the out-of-the-way dive.

He pulled the sweater vest over his head, leaving his white oxford button-down, thankfully clean of logos. He squinted at himself in the rearview mirror and smoothed the light brown hair that stuck up from the static in the sweater. Not bad.

He climbed out, sliding his keys in the front pocket of his jeans and his wallet in the back.

One beer, then he'd be off to Ville Platte.

No harm in that.

Lou Boyd tripped over a stone surrounding the sign proclaiming Rendezvous as Home of the Legendary Cooter Gilbeau, which she thought was quite a reach since Cooter had only been a percussionist for the Charlie Daniels Band for one year. But whatever. She guessed old Cooter was proud of his cowbell days. She frowned down at the red stilettos her friend insisted she borrow. Hell of a shoe to wear when walking through a loose-gravel parking lot.

"Hurry up, Louise," Mary Belle Prudhomme called, swishing toward the broad steps of the honky-tonk in her own too-tight jeans and a skimpy top. "I told Bear I'd be here over an hour ago. He's probably got some little slut in his lap already."

"You mean other than you?" Brittney Wade, the bookkeeper for Forcet Construction drawled, stopping to wait on Lou. The more practical Brittney had planned the evening and volunteered to be the designated driver, which was good considering Lou felt woozy from the mojitos the girls had made for Lou's twenty-seventh birthday gala. Lou celebrated the small victory in Mary Belle letting her take off the silly tiara the woman had bought her. The shoes were bad enough.

Mary Belle paused to flip Brittney off. Brit laughed. "Kidding. Just kidding."

Lou made it up the wooden plank steps, blinking at the flashing beer signs and advertisements for bands playing the honky-tonk soon. She didn't think this was such a good idea. Rendezvous wasn't the kind of place she belonged in...or at least hadn't for a long time. "It's been fun already, girls. We don't have to stay out all night. We have work tomorrow and Waylon and Lori have school tomorrow and—"

"Not another word," Brenda Pierpont warned with one finger. "You're twenty-seven years old and never go out. This is our treat. Don't ruin it for us, 'kay?"

Lou gave the older woman who ran the construction office a pained smile.

"Okay, then," Brenda said, smoothing her orangey hair back and the shirt over her poochy belly. Brenda had been the one who insisted Lou wear makeup tonight and had indulged her own desire to be the host of *What Not to Wear* by outfitting Lou in her daughter Jillian's wardrobe, namely a too-tight T-shirt that was low-cut and blinged-out with colored sequins. Lou looked like a rainbow had vomited on her.

Lou tackled the last step, praying she'd mastered walking in the shoes that were already rubbing blisters. This was why she loved her steel-toed work boots. But she could do this. For her friends' sake.

Mary Belle turned and swept her with her bright eyes. "You don't look like Lou Boyd. No one is going to even recognize you. Get ready, baby, men are about to be on you like flies on cow shit."

Lou winced. She'd let them kidnap her, and truss her up with tight clothes, makeup and dangly earrings—all with the ultimate intent of taking her to Rendezvous for Ladies' Night to celebrate her birthday.

In all honesty, Lou would have rather eaten chocolate pudding and watched some Netflix, but her coworkers had gone to such trouble and seemed almost giddy about taking her out for fun. "I'm not looking for a man, Mary. Well, not for a while anyway. I can't really date with two kids to—"

"Um, they're in high school now, Lou. And they're not your kids. You're entitled to a life, so stop being a martyr. No one likes a martyr," Brit said, jerking her head toward the entrance to the honky-tonk. "So get your ass in gear, Louise."

Trapped. And she didn't appreciate being criticized just because taking care of two teenagers didn't lend itself to a carefree lifestyle. After all, she had to get her brother up for a Fellowship of Christian Athletes meeting tomorrow, and her day at the construction company started at 7:00 a.m. She had a family to tend to. No matter what Brit said.

There was reality and then there was Lou's reality. The reality of no life. No love. Oh, sure, she'd tried. She'd dated, but no matter. No man wanted a woman with two kids to raise—even if they were her brother and sister.

Lou had learned long ago to wish differently didn't do one damn bit of good. She wasn't a martyr—just doing what had to be done by taking care of Waylon and Lori the only way she knew how. Fairness wasn't up for consideration.

But she was here, shellacked with makeup and too tipsy to drive herself home. Might as well try to act her age. Which was younger than she felt. At the very least, she'd have a drink, watch Mary Belle act a fool over Bear Rodrigue, and then proclaim a headache. She could be home before—she looked at her watch—eleven o'clock easy.

Oh, come on, Lou. Let go a little. Flirt with being more than what you are for just one night.

Point made, voice in her head. "Okay. Ass in gear."

Brenda pulled open the door to the bar. "In the words of Shania Twain, 'let's go, girls.'"

Lou smiled back. "Sure. No harm in that."

ABRAM WATCHED THE BAND from his perch at the end of the bar. They were good, especially the drummer. Probably barely eighteen, but she could lay a lick.

The place rocked with rowdy rednecks and coonasses. He wasn't much of a partier—tended to be a nose to grindstone sort—but he enjoyed watching others pass a good time. It was something easy to find in Louisiana. From Shreveport to New Orleans and every town in between, the natives liked a reason to get together and indulge in fun.

The patrons at Rendezvous were no exception. The dance floor was large, surrounded by tables with two bars anchoring each side of the stage. He'd chosen the bar closest to the bathrooms only because it was the first stool he'd spied after exiting the john. He nursed the icy Blue Moon and pretended to be an anthropologist studying the local wildlife.

His eyes moved over the crowd as they ebbed and flowed onto the dance floor. Several women tried catching his eye, but he looked past them, refusing to open himself to any conversation. Mostly, everyone left him alone, only occasionally eyeballing him curiously, before going about the business of getting drunk or getting lucky.

The door opened and four women entered.

The last one made him swallow. Hard.

Damn, she was gorgeous with straight blond hair, high full breasts and long, long legs. He watched as she crowded into the woman in front of her, who by his estimate was forty pounds too heavy to be wearing the clothes she wore. He watched the blonde—and so did almost every other man in the room.

If this were the ball, then Cinderella had just walked in.

He lifted his beer and took the last swig. He'd told himself he would leave when the bottle was empty. He glanced over at the bartender who'd raised himself onto the balls of his boots to get a look at the beauty. He raised his eyebrows and whistled in admiration.

"Can I get another one over here?" Abram called.

So much for an early night.

The bartender flung a towel over his shoulder. "Same?"

"Why not," Abram said, moving his gaze back to the woman. He couldn't find her, mostly because several rowdy-looking rednecks had blocked his view. Followed by a few more. Then a few more.

The bartender used a church key, cracking open the beer with a practiced motion, and setting it on the bar. "Wanna tab?"

Abram shook his head and placed a ten on the bar. "This will be my last. Keep the change."

The man nodded his thanks. "She's a beauty, ain't she?"

So he'd seen him notice Cinderella. Figured. Bartenders didn't miss a thing. "Yeah. Is she your local beauty queen?"

"Ain't never seen her in my life. Must be a stranger. Like you."

There was a subtle question in the statement. An invitation to state his business. He ignored it. "Maybe I'll buy her a drink."

"Better get in line."

The bartender went back to work, mostly because money was being waggled at him. Lots of thirsty customers at Rendezvous. And Abram went back to watching the beauty dodge the advances of the men surrounding her and her friends. She looked like a dog he'd once seen trapped by animal control. Caught and not happy about it.

"I haven't seen you here before." The voice came from his left. He turned to find one of the women who'd walked in with Cinderella. She looked kind of pissy. Definitely mad.

"First timer," he said, toasting her with the fresh beer. "Can I buy you one?"

Her gaze was fastened on someone behind him. He turned and saw the man she was trying to burn a hole through with her poisonous eyes. He stood in line for Cinderella. She looked back at Abram. "Well, honey, you're the best-looking man in this place. Think I'm gonna turn that down?"

He smiled.

She smiled in return, but it didn't reach her blue eyes.

"I'm Mary," she said, elbowing the man next to him off his stool. "Move, Eddie. Can't you see I'm a lady and I need to sit down?"

"That's stretchin' it by a mile," the man said, but he grinned fondly at the woman who settled her rather plump butt on the bar stool. "How's it going, Mary Belle?"

"It's goin'," she said, motioning the bartender over.

"Hey, Butch, get me an Abita amber and put it on this fellow's tab."

Butch glanced over. "He ain't gotta tab."

She looked at Abram, who pulled out his wallet. "So whatcha doing here? We don't get too many visitors. You with Wildlife and Fisheries? Over at Chicot?"

"Nah," he said, sliding a bill toward the bartender. "Just traveling through."

"Oh." She turned to look at her friend and her bevy of admirers, including the Wrangler-clad guy she'd shot daggers at earlier. "Well, then you're perfect to do me a little favor, aren't you?"

Alarm bells clanged. He started shaking his head.

She grabbed the elbow of his shirt. "It's easy as long as you aren't married. You ain't married, are you? I didn't see a ring, but some guys don't wear 'em, you know."

"I'm not married, but I'm about to head out."

"Won't take long. I just need you to pretend to be my friend's date."

"Date?"

"Yeah, Louise over there. I didn't realize the ruckus she'd cause. She's pretty."

That was an understatement. The woman she pointed at wasn't merely pretty. She was sensationally gorgeous. "So I see."

"You and every other man. It's her birthday and I wanted her to come out with us and have a little fun, you know? But damn ol' Bear Rodrigue don't even know I'm in the room. He's standing over there by her like a rutting buck." She turned her blue eyes back to him. "And he's supposed to be ruttin' me."

He didn't know why or how this woman had found

him in the sea of people stomping around Rendezvous, but she had. With a plan in mind.

"I'm not sure this is a good idea."

"Of course it is. You think she wants all those dumbass men tripping over themselves like that? She is clearly drowning in 'em. All you have to do is pretend to be her date. I'll introduce you as my cousin. Come on."

She pulled on his arm. Insistently.

He shook his head. "I've got to be going."

She looked down at her watch. "Give me thirty minutes to help a stranger out. What's your name?"

"Abram." He sighed. Well, he'd wanted to buy Cinderella a drink, hadn't he? This would be his chance. Plus, poor Mary Belle needed someone to help her, too. He rose, picking up his fresh beer, and allowed the crazy woman to pull him toward the center of Rendezvous' universe for the moment.

Cinderella had pasted a fake smile on her gorgeous mouth. She nodded and darted desperate glances at her two remaining friends. Yeah, she needed some help.

He'd pretend to be her date for the next half hour.

Surely there was no harm in that.

CHAPTER TWO

LOU PEERED OVER the shoulder of Sid Lattier, which was easy to do since he barely came to her nose thanks to the four-inch heels she balanced in. She needed to be rescued and didn't see the one person who could move these men out of her way. Mary Belle had disappeared into the thick of the crowd after seeing her man ogling Lou's breasts.

Mary was pissed. Oh, she wasn't mad at Lou, but Bear might as well stretch out his palms because his ass was about to be handed to him. Mary Belle didn't shoot marbles.

"Excuse me, guys," Lou said, stepping past a man she vaguely recalled spraying her house for bugs once. Or was he the guy who cleaned their ancient chimney? She wasn't sure, but she didn't plan to find out. "Hey, Brit, find a table?"

"You can sit with us," Lloyd Day said, jabbing a thick finger at a tiny table where two guys with huge beer bellies ate peanuts out of a bowl. "Plenty of room."

"No, thank you, Mr. Day. I'm here with my girl-friends."

Brenda waved her toward a table in the back where Brit had dropped her purse. Lou tried to shuffle through the men, but they didn't want to move. She truly felt like she was in some crazy movie. She knew these guys. She'd worked with half of them and they'd never treated her this way before. Her grandmother's words came back to her. *A little powder, a little paint, will make you what you ain't.*

"You look mighty good tonight, Lou," Bear drawled, his pretty hazel eyes moving over her body.

"Thanks, Bear. That means a lot coming from Mary Belle's boyfriend." Lou frowned at him as he tried to give her a seductive smile. Lord, help him. It wasn't going to work. Was he dumb as a brick? Wait, she shouldn't answer that. She'd gone to high school with him and knew the answer.

"Boyfriend? I don't know if I'd go as far to—"

"Here he is!" Mary Belle interrupted, dragging a man behind her. As if Lou needed another one. "He was waiting at the bar just like I told him to."

Eight pairs of eyes turned toward the man standing behind Mary Belle.

He was easily six foot two or three with light brown hair cut military short. His eyes were a bemused soft green and his jaw was nice and lean. He moved with a loose-limbed elegance, like her brother. Like an athlete. His white oxford shirt was open at the throat and rolled up at the sleeves, giving him a sort of Abercrombie-ish look. Breezy and totally gorgeous.

"Who was where?" Bear asked, stiffening like an old dog guarding a bone.

"My cousin Abram. He's Louise's date tonight, so all you fellas can just back it on up now. She's taken for the evening."

"Date?" Lou chirped, looking around for Brenda as if the older woman could save her. She couldn't have been party to setting Lou up on a blind date, could she? That would be, well, plain mean.

"What cousin is this?" Bear demanded, crossing his

arms across his broad chest and once-overing the guy Mary Belle clutched.

"From Baton Rouge. On her daddy's side," the stranger said, nodding at Mary Belle. "She sometimes forgets about us over there."

Mary Belle punched his arm. "Oh, you know we love you guys. See? Here's Louise. Didn't I tell you she's the prettiest thing this side of the Mississippi?" She gestured to Lou as if she were a prized heifer.

Lou felt her hackles rise. What in the hell was Mary Belle thinking? "I don't need—"

"Of course, you do." The man answered for her, sliding his hand to her elbow and pulling her to his side. He leaned down, dropping his voice into her ear. She felt a bit shivery when the warmth of his breath caressed her neck. "I've driven all this way to meet you, Cinderella. Mary Belle said you'd be perfect for me and we should never argue with Mary Belle. At least let me buy you a drink."

His touch was firm. And hot on her skin. She watched as he lifted a hand, Moses-style, and parted the men standing between them and the bar on the far side of the room. They stacked up to either side of them like obedient soldiers. If they had saluted, Lou wouldn't have been surprised.

Like an idiot, she let him escort her around the perimeter of the dance floor toward the bar.

He pulled out a stool and gestured. She folded her arms and stood. "I'm not prepared for a date. I don't know what Mary told you but this is not—"

"   a date," he finished, a twinkle in his eyes. "I know. Though I must say when I saw you come in I thought the idea had merit, but I can see now you're a stubborn sort of girl."

Lou narrowed her eyes. "Stubborn?"

He smiled and sank onto another stool. "I'm guessing, but I'm pretty good at reading people. And it's not an insult. Stubborn people are some of my favorite people."

She uncrossed her arms. "Who are you? Mary Belle doesn't have people in Baton Rouge."

"That you know of."

She tilted her head. "That I know of, but she talks about everyone in her family. Great-Aunt Velma who's still canning tomatoes at age ninety-three. Her niece Kaley who won a twirling competition in Lafayette last week. And she's never mentioned a hot cousin in Baton Rouge."

"Thanks," he said.

"For what?"

"The 'hot' compliment."

Lou hadn't realized she'd even loaned an adjective to him. Damn the mojitos. They'd made her fuzzy. "I didn't mean to say that."

He smirked in a pleasant way. "No take-backs."

Lou shrugged, uncrossed her arms and used her foot to pull the empty stool to her. She sat down. "Seriously, who are you?"

He glanced at the bartender and lifted a finger. The man immediately appeared in front of him. "I need a drink for the lady." He turned to her with a lifted eyebrow.

She shouldn't have anything else. The clock over the bar read 10:15 p.m. She had maybe thirty more minutes before she could talk Brit into taking her back to Bonnet Creek and the patched-up ranch-style house on Turtle Bay Road. "Um, a rum and Coke."

The bartender nodded and grabbed a highball and a bottle of Captain Morgan.

"My name truly is Abram and I actually live in Baton Rouge. However, I met Mary Belle about ten minutes ago. She slipped me a twenty to be your date."

"She paid you?"

He laughed and something plinked in her tummy. He had a good laugh. Deep, rich and filling like a good piece of chocolate cake. "No. She twisted my arm a little, but I could see very plainly you needed rescuing."

"I don't need rescuing." She nodded at the bartender and lifted the glass he'd set in front of her to her lips. He'd been generous with the spicy rum and it burned a hot trail down her throat. "I've been seeing after myself for quite a while. I certainly don't need a man doing it for me."

"Oh, you're one of those women." His eyes laughed at her and she saw he liked to tease.

"What women? Just because I don't need a man—"

"I didn't realize you were a feminist, but I'll buy your drink anyway."

She laughed. "I'm not a feminist. Much. And you're a tease."

At this he smiled again. She felt his smile. Like really felt his smile. "I'm not a tease. I like to deliver the goods, lady."

She sobered. "I'm not taking deliveries."

But even as she uttered the words, an idea formed in her mind. *What if. What if.*

He lifted his eyebrows. "Okay, no deliveries, but will you dance?"

She looked out at the dance floor, at the couples joining hands, wrapping arms around waists, swaying to the slower rhythm of a misty-eyed country song and a long-buried urge slammed her. "Sure."

Lou downed the last of her drink, telling herself she needed liquid courage. She hadn't been held in a man's arms on the dance floor since her senior prom, and Ben Braud hadn't qualified as a man at seventeen. She set the empty glass down and took Abram's hand.

Ten steps later, he gathered her in his arms, leading her with a smooth glide around the worn boards. For a moment, Lou forgot to breathe. It was that wonderful.

"I don't remember the last time I danced," Abram murmured, meeting her gaze with a shadowed one of his own.

"I do," she said. "April 16, 2003."

He stiffened. "Seriously? You haven't danced in almost ten years?"

"Well, I've danced around my kitchen. Does that count?"

He shook his head. "I'm feeling the pressure. We've got to make this count."

He spun her away from him then reeled her back in, tugging her closer to his body, before sliding left then right. Her hair fanned out behind her as they whirled around the floor. She felt his hardness against the soft parts of her body, and all her good intentions for getting home early enough to watch the *Iron Chef* episode she'd DVR'd earlier in the week flew right out the front door of Rendezvous.

Then and there whirling around the dance floor in the arms of a mysterious stranger, Louise Kay Boyd thought about getting a little bit of what she'd not gotten the chance to do after her daddy crashed his plane into the Ouachita National Forest, leaving her and her siblings without parents. Her days of irresponsible, selfish, wanton behavior had disappeared before she'd had the chance to use even one of them. Gone was her freshman year at Ole Miss—cramming for tests, trying pot, drinking too much and going all the way with a Kappa Sig she'd met at a kegger. Gone were the days of little responsibility and lots of spare time. They'd vanished in a whirl of funeral preparation, a looming mortgage payment, and the tear-streaked faces of her six- and seven-year-old brother and sister.

So would it be wrong to grab a little bit back?

The drinks and this sexy stranger had unwittingly unleashed pinings no one could possibly know anything about.

She didn't know him.

He didn't know her.

So what would it hurt to pretend to be someone other than who she was?

She was already halfway there, looking like some honky-tonk angel. No, he'd called her Cinderella. A honky-tonk Cinderella. What would it hurt to pretend herself into a fantasy for a few hours? Maybe this was her time to cut loose. Maybe this was her time to lose the monkey riding on her back.

The song ended and the band launched into a rendition of an old Kenny Chesney song mixed with something that sounded like reggae. Abram stopped and looked down at her. "You wanna go again?"

She shook her head. "Let's get another drink."

He nodded and curved an arm around her waist, making her feel gooey inside. Like melting caramel. She sank a little bit into him And he tightened his hand on her hip, an almost caress. Her mind said *Don't. Do. This.*

But her bratty, whiny, life's-not-fair voice said, *Get*

jiggy with it, sister. You've missed out on too much. You need this.

Abram slid a hand under her elbow as she dropped onto the scarred wooden stool. Definitely a caress. Definitely revving something in her blood she'd locked away ever since her last boyfriend had unhooked her bra and slid one hand down her panties the night before he told her he was seeing someone else. She decided to give whiny, not-fair inner voice some headway.

She smiled at him and felt his reaction. He didn't flare his nostrils or anything like some of the heroes did in those novels she kept stacked by the bed, but he got the message in her smile.

Abram beckoned the bartender again. And again the man flew to do his bidding. A rum and Coke sat before her not two minutes later joined by an ice water for Abram. "He's bustin' his hump for you."

"I'm tipping him more than twenty percent. I learned long ago to treat bartenders well." He watched her as she raised the glass to her lips. She returned his measure. He really was too good-looking. Sweet temptation swirled around her and she wondered about what it would be like to taste him. Was he good at kissing? She stared at his lips as he lifted the glass of water and drank. Was drinking supposed to be sexy?

"Hey, how's the date going?" Mary Belle poked at her back.

"Huh?"

"The date with my cousin here," Mary Belle said, a devilish twinkle in her eye. Lou swung around. Brenda and Brit stood behind her.

"He's not your cousin," Lou said, sipping the cool drink, keeping one eye on her pretend date. "And our date is going fine."

"Yeah, we saw you dancin'," Mary Belle said, taking the drink from Lou's hand and taking a sip. "Brenda thinks she has food poisoning or something, so she needs to go home."

Lou looked at Brenda who bit her lip. She did look a little pale and sweaty. "Oh, no. Sure. Let's go."

Mary Belle pressed her back onto the stool. "No, you stay. I'll come back for you in an hour or so."

"You can't. You've been drinking. A lot. So I'm going with Brit."

"I'm good, I tell ya," Mary Belle slurred.

"Uh, no. I don't have a death wish." Lou slid from the stool.

"I'll be glad to give her a ride home. I'm fine to drive," Abram said, winking at her friends. "I am, after all, her date."

"Perfect!" Mary Belle said, glowing in a liquor-haze.

"That's not necessary," Lou said, giving Brenda a concerned look. "You think it was the fajita meat, Brenda? We all had that."

Brenda made a face. "I don't know, but I can't stay. I'm so sorry, baby, ruining your birthday like this. I was going to teach you that new line dance."

"We'll live," Brit said, giving Brenda a smile before looking hard at Abram. "How do we know we can trust you with our friend? You could be a serial killer for all we know."

"I'm not a serial killer."

"Like a serial killer would admit to being one." Brit crossed her arms and studied him. "You're good-looking, but one of those guys was good-looking, too. Which one? Um, Gacy?"

"Ted Bundy," Abram said, taking another sip of water. He looked so cool, like nothing would faze him.

Like he dealt with all kinds of crazy all day long. Maybe he was a psychiatrist. Or a postal worker.

"See? He knows his serial killers," Brit said.

"I'm going with y'all," Lou said, sliding from the stool. Time to end this charade. The dance was fun. The flirting even better. But reality always intruded, no matter what Lou wished. She'd left fairy tales behind long ago. "No worries."

Mary Belle frowned. "You're having fun, though. Just because Bear is a shit and Brenda's faking, shouldn't affect you. Stay with Abram. He looks like a stand-up guy. Dance. Drink. And don't think about anything else."

"I'm not faking," Brenda huffed, but Lou wasn't paying attention to any of her friends. Abram's finger stroked her inner wrist. It caused loopy loops in her stomach.

"Stay with me, Cinderella. I'll make sure you get home from the ball." He gave her a Prince Charming grin, kind of lopsided like the one a small boy gives when he's got a frog behind his back. The one where a girl knows she should run, but can't possibly pick up her feet. That exact grin.

"Okay, as long as you don't turn into a pumpkin at midnight."

And that settled it.

For a few more hours, Lou was going to play the part of maid-turned-princess. And she wasn't going to have regrets.

She looked back at her friends. "Thanks, friends, for making my birthday so much fun."

She gave hugs all around and the ladies she worked with at the construction company took their leave. She spun toward her prince for the night. "So, what shall we do first?"

Abram didn't say anything. Just looked at her for a few moments, his eyes bright but guarded. Then his eyes slid down to the red stilettos she'd hooked on the bottom of the stool. "Those don't look like glass slippers."

She pulled one free and wiggled it. "No, and they're not too comfortable. I think I'd rather go barefoot."

"A barefoot Cinderella?"

She laughed. "Suits me better."

"Well, in that case, follow me."

Lou watched him rise from the stool, all six foot whatever of chiseled, handsome male, and grabbed her half-finished drink. She needed courage because tonight she was Louise, Cinderella, whoever, as long as she was a girl who threw caution to the wind and grabbed fantasy tight to her.

And because she'd made up her mind. Tonight on her twenty-seventh birthday, she would lose her virginity to the handsome stranger with the green eyes and magic touch.

CHAPTER THREE

ABRAM TOOK LOUISE'S hand and led her through the throng of people carousing in the bar. He didn't fail to miss the curious glances, and occasionally envious stares, tossed their way. He also didn't fail to hear the voice in his head saying, *Don't do anything stupid, Coach.*

It sounded like Coach Holt's voice and should have stopped him cold, but, for once, he didn't want to listen to anyone who would talk him out of something more with Louise.

So he'd taken the wrong exit and ended up with a cold beer and a hot woman? How was that anything other than incredibly lucky?

No harm. No foul. No problem.

"Where are we going?" she asked, as he pushed open the front door, whisking them into the cool night air.

"Just somewhere a bit more private."

She stopped and looked around. "But we're in the middle of nowhere."

He glanced around. "I don't plan well."

She laughed and his balls tightened. He could suggest going back to the motel, but it didn't seem right. Too fast. Too obvious. And she didn't seem like that kind of girl. Even if she had a body made for sin and a face made for salvation.

She pointed behind him. "If I remember correctly,

there's a pier over there. It goes out to the lake. We could take a moonlit walk. That's date-appropriate, right?"

"It's perfect."

They linked hands and started through the high grass toward the nearly hidden pier. Thick, tangled brush grew unchecked and he wondered how she knew the pier sat nearby. He pulled at some vines, clearing the path. The vines gave and he caught his breath. The length of the old wood jutted out onto Lake Chicot, opening to a brilliant star-studded velvet sky.

"It looks like it's steady enough," Louise said, testing the wooden stairs with one red high heel.

He placed his weight on the wood. "Yeah, it's fine."

Louise bent down, slid her shoes off and set them on the bottom step. Her unpolished toes wiggled as she flexed them. "Ah, feels good. Besides, I don't want to end up in the water. Too cold tonight."

For the first time since they'd slipped out of Rendezvous, he noticed the chill in the air. "It is cool. Are you okay with being out here?"

Louise gave him what he thought was an unpracticed siren's smile. "As long as you keep me warm."

His body tightened and he grew erect. Hell. It had been a while since he'd been with a woman. His on-again, off-again playmate Alison was currently in off mode and he rarely went to bars looking for temporary comfort. He spent most of his time in the athletic facility surrounded by men. And he never picked up chicks on the road. This was a first for him.

"I can handle that," he heard himself say. Which surprised him because his body had obviously gone into auto sex pilot.

"Good."

He curved an arm around her shoulders, dropping

his hand to her waist, which he stroked lightly. She sank into him as they climbed the steps leading to a sky of stars. The lake smelled earthy and primal, and the sound of cicadas along with the gentle lap of the water struggled to be heard over the music spilling from the honky-tonk they'd left moments ago. Altogether, Abram couldn't have designed a more romantic spot.

They didn't speak. Merely strolled to the end of the pier and stared out at the black water.

Louise glanced up. "Beautiful, isn't it?"

He looked at her. "Yeah, you are."

She jerked her gaze to him. Her eyes were a stormy blue, deep like the glittering stones his mother sometimes wore. He forgot the name of them, but they were just the color of Louise's eyes.

He wanted to kiss her.

So he did.

Dipped his head and caught her pretty pink lips.

She sighed before turning into him. He felt her breasts rise as she pressed her soft flesh into his chest. Something struck inside him, flaring, heating. He slid a hand to cup her cheek, noting how smooth her skin was, tilting his head so he could deepen the kiss.

She accommodated him, opening her mouth, giving him a taste of the spicy rum she'd had earlier. She tasted like sheer heaven, sheer molten heaven.

He pulled back and studied her. "You taste good."

She pressed a hand to her lips. "Do I?"

He pulled her down so they sat on the edge of the pier. She snuggled next to him, dropping her legs so they dangled next to his.

"This is like a fairy tale," she said, glancing at him. The shadows had pulled back into the night, leaving her face luminescent in the moonlight. Her skin glowed against the ripeness of her lips, against the depths of her eyes. Her blond hair shone like a curtain on either side of her face. He was fairly certain he'd never seen a woman so delicate and lovely. "I feel like a fairy princess. It's strange."

"It probably sounds like a cheesy pickup line, but I think this is some crazy fate thing."

"Fate disguised as magic," she said.

"I took the wrong exit, you know."

"What?"

"I missed my turn and took the exit for Chicot State Park thinking to wind my way back to Ville Platte. But I saw Rendezvous and decided to stop for a beer."

"So fate brought me a Prince Charming. For one night only."

"For one night only," he repeated.

She took a breath, almost like a steadying breath. "Can we dance?"

"Out here?"

She nodded. "It's been so long, and it was so nice to be held in your arms. We can hear the music from Cooter's. Listen. It's George Strait."

He cocked an ear in the direction of the honky-tonk. "So it is." He held out a hand with a questioning crook of an eyebrow.

She took his hand. Her reflective smile looked slightly sheepish, as if she knew they were acting silly. Okay, they were. But so the hell what?

She melted into his arms and under the night sky, he held her close, drawing in the silky scent of something flowery, and swayed to the faint sounds of the steel guitar. She fit him well, her head tucking under his chin, her breasts hitting him right at his solar plexus, her hips brushing the rising result of being so close.

She hummed along to the music, stroking her hands over his back, as if she knew that drove him crazy, taking him to the place he wanted to go, but was afraid to say aloud.

The song ended but still they swayed, their footfalls barely rising as they shuffled over the worn boards.

"My feet are cold," she murmured into his shoulder.

He raised his head from where he'd been contemplating the delicateness of her ear. "We should go."

"No," she breathed. "I don't want this to end. Not yet. It's not midnight."

He laughed. "Fine, but let's go back. We can sit in my truck and I'll put the heater on your toes."

She shook her head. "I'd rather have cold toes. It's too perfect here."

He pulled her down, crossing his legs and settling her into his lap. She curled into him and he wrapped his arms around her. "I was right. You're stubborn."

Her laugh was light, but she didn't respond to his comment. Just tucked her cold toes beneath the hem of her too-long jeans and settled against him. He could feel the beat of her heart, the rise of her breath, and was struck at how absolutely strange this moment was.

Who was this man cradling a woman he'd met an hour ago on an old rickety pier in the cool Louisiana night in a place he neither knew nor intended to find?

Not the man most would recognize as the unyielding Abram Dufrene.

She linked her arms behind his head and looked up at him. "Kiss me again?"

Why had he gone so long with his lips away from hers? Really. Should she have to ask?

He lowered his head and gave her what she asked for.

And did it so well, it left them both breathless.

"You are a good kisser," she breathed, dotting small kisses on the scruff of his jaw. Each tiny brush of her lips inflamed him.

"Not bad yourself," he muttered, running his hands down her back to her hip, stroking the curve through the denim. He really wanted to see her breasts. They were likely works of art, rounded, pink-tipped with angel kisses, so he started kissing his way down her neck, knowing his thoughts were absurdly poetic. This was what the night had created in him.

Louise's head fell back, spreading her golden hair across his thigh. He groaned his approval as he reached her collarbone and tugged the fabric of her shirt aside to reveal a serviceable white bra.

It made him smile.

This woman, as lovely as she was, appreciated comfort. He didn't need the allure of lace, not when what lay beneath was much more valuable. He tugged the strap, but nothing popped free. He tugged again. Same result.

"Here," she said, wiggling and reaching behind her back. One grunt and the bra fell loose.

"Thanks," he said, returning to his pillaging. He slid the neck of the blouse aside and was rewarded with a perfect plump pink-tipped breast. He wasted no time laying claim to it, and noted self-satisfactorily her hiss of pleasure when he closed his mouth over her hard nipple.

For a moment, he simply nuzzled her, sucking her into his mouth while stroking her into a fever. She unfurled her long legs, turned and wrapped them around his waist, allowing her bottom to cradle his erection, giving sweet friction to them both. He groaned and lifted his head from her breast and looked down at her cradled in his arms, cold toes forgotten, eyes closed, breathing like she'd finished a wind sprint.

"We can't do this," he said, sinking his head down to rest at the top of her breast.

She jerked, opened her eyes and struggled to lift her head. "Why not?"

"We're strangers."

"So?"

He shook his head. He knew most men wouldn't have stopped, but something prodded him. His upbringing. His common sense. The fact he didn't have a condom.

"So you're okay with just one night?" He tried to sound playful. Most women wanted dinner, movies, talk of swapping keys before a willingness to fade away into a memory. He'd never in all his thirty-one years had a one-night stand. Not even in college. "No woman wants that."

"This woman does."

AND SHE MEANT IT.

She'd gone far too long without having the real deal. It was beyond time to uncork the champagne of her sexuality. In fact she was approaching epic spinster-hood. She needed to get laid and what better way to do that than with a handsome, sexy, no-strings-attached stranger?

He wouldn't meet her eyes at the grocery store and then turn away.

He wouldn't show up on her doorstep with flowers and a DVD she had no interest in watching.

He wouldn't marry one of her friends and cause her to have one of those I-know-what-your-husband-looks-like-naked moments.

It was perfect.

A gift from fate. For one night only.

"I'm serious. I don't expect anything other than this

little magic moment." She licked her lips as insurance. The romance books beside her bed seemed to indicate that licking her lips would inflame a man beyond reason.

He shook his head. "This is crazy."

"You don't want me?" She knew he did. Could feel the evidence against her bottom. She glanced down, caught the time in the glow of the waxing moon. 11:13 p.m. She had less than an hour. Okay, she had more than an hour, but for the sake of the whole magic fate thing, she'd rather it be tonight. On her birthday. With him.

"Of course I want you," he said. "Too much."

"Then shut up and kiss me," she said, hooking his neck and bringing him down so she could kiss him.

His lips met hers and her pulse went wild.

This was what she'd been missing, not counting that time with Bud Hargon when he'd prematurely ejaculated before getting the job done or the time when she'd layered her bed with rose petals and had just gotten naked with Cole Lanier when Waylon had come in with a busted lip, wailing like a banshee.

Until tonight, Louise Boyd had been a virgin.

But she wasn't missing another opportunity for deflowering.

"I don't have a condom, Louise," Abram said, nibbling her lower lip. "But we can please each other in other ways."

She shook her head. "No, I want the real deal. The whole shebang. That's what I need. That's what it's gotta be."

He stilled. "You make it sound like—"

He lifted his head and searched her gaze. Something

dawned on him. He understood. "For crap's sake, Louise, you're not telling me you're a—you're a—virgin?"

She didn't blink. Was that really any of his business? No. It was hers. And when he said it out loud like that it made her feel pathetic. "You make it sound like a crime."

He lifted her off him, setting her onto the cold wood of the pier. "It's not a crime. It's sort of surprising, and it's not something I...I think you should..."

He closed his mouth. Then he swallowed. She could see quite clearly he had no clue what to say. It should have been sweet, endearing even, but it just pissed her off. It's not like she hadn't tried all this before. She had. But it hadn't worked.

"What? I should save it for someone special? Is that what you were going to say? My future husband maybe?"

He blinked.

"Well, it's not special. It's a burden. You don't need to know the particulars, but I'm not a freak. I couldn't date for many years because of stuff going on in my life, and when I could date again, well, things never progressed. For heaven's sake, I'm a twenty-seven-year-old, decent-looking woman. I should be able to get laid."

She shoved herself up, rising more like a winged harpy than a fairy princess. Frustration made her dangerously angry.

Abram sat there looking like a fish that had landed on the pier. If he had started flopping and gasping, she wouldn't have been surprised.

"Louise," he said, climbing to his knees. "I didn't mean it that way. I don't think anything. I just don't—"

"Don't trouble yourself to screw me. It's no big deal. I can go another three years without a date. By then I'll be thirty. Hey, maybe I could hire someone. A gigolo to service me. Won't that be novel?"

He stood and grabbed her arms, giving her a shake. His charming grin was gone, as was likely his erection. He looked annoyed. "If you really want me to get the job done, let's go. I'll stop by the gas station, grab a box of condoms, and we'll head to my motel room in Ville Platte. I'll screw you until your head bangs against the headboard. Maybe we can keep the other motel guests awake all night. Then I'll leave in the morning after I shower. Sound romantic enough for you?"

She wanted to hit him. Tears formed in her eyes, and that pissed her off even more. She looked around at their magic, romantic spot that wasn't even remotely beautiful anymore. Dead plants floated on the surface and spiderwebs clung to the railing. A mosquito bit her on the neck. She slapped at it.

He shook his head before lifting a finger and wiping away a tear that must have escaped. "You don't deserve that, Louise. Some stranger, some crappy-ass hotel room. I'm not saying you need champagne and strawberries, but don't give it up to me, baby. You're worth more than that. Give yourself to someone who cares about you. A guy who's not a random stranger."

She brushed his hand away. "Don't worry. I won't force you."

And then she slid past him, feeling like crap. Feeling worse than crap. She'd let him in on her most embarrassing secret. He'd seen her desperation and longing, and though he hadn't flung it in her face, he hadn't done anything to help her with it.

"Louise," he called after her. "Stop. I don't want to leave it this way."

She didn't stop. Kept going. She couldn't have

stopped if she tried. The liquor she'd gulped down to
give her boldness, churned in her stomach along with
what was left of her pride. She reached the end of the
pier and grabbed her shoes, not bothering to put them
on even though the damp grass made her toes numb
with cold.

She would get someone to give her a ride.

If she had to, she'd call Waylon and have him come
get her.

She stomped up the hill, hearing Abram coming behind her. But she didn't turn around. Kept moving toward the light of Rendezvous, toward the merriment.
The loud music. The normalcy of the real world.

Abram grabbed her elbow. "Hey, wait a minute."

She turned. "Look. I want to forget about this.
Okay?"

He didn't say anything.

"I don't know you. You don't know me. We were
two strangers who became nothing more to each other
than…strangers."

"I hurt you."

"You don't have enough power to hurt me because
you don't mean anything to me. All you are is a missed
opportunity to get this monkey off my back."

"Damn," he breathed, shaking his head. "You don't
hold back."

"I'm being truthful. You're a nice guy, doing a nice
thing for a desperate chick. Saving me from myself and
all that. Don't feel guilty and don't lose sleep over me."

He shook his head again. "Come on, Louise, I didn't
want things to end like this. Tonight was good. I enjoyed meeting you."

She inclined her head and gave him a sad smile. "I
guess it wouldn't have been so bad being your honky-

tonk Cinderella if I hadn't gone and made a fool of myself."

He lightly touched her cheek. "You didn't make a fool of yourself. Let me take you home."

"No, I can get a ride. I'm sort of embarrassed and feeling emotional right now. It would be too uncomfortable for us both. Enjoy your stay in Ville Platte. It was nice meeting you."

She didn't wait any longer.

She turned and walked out of his life, thinking she was doubly glad he was a stranger. After all, what girl would want to live out the embarrassment of seeing a guy who didn't want to sleep with her, or rather couldn't, around town all the time?

It would be brutal.

She climbed the porch swinging her shoes and trying to come up with a plan for getting home. Her pride hurt too much to slip the vampy come-hither shoes on, so she set them near the railing and pulled her cell phone out of her pocket. She'd call Waylon. He was likely up playing war games on the computer anyway.

"Louise, stop being stubborn and let me drive you home."

She looked at the time on her phone. 12:00 a.m. "Too late. The fairy tale is over."

CHAPTER FOUR

ABRAM HAD WOKEN with a headache that had nothing to do with the 1.5 beers he'd drunk last night, and everything to do with the mildew present in the damp carpet around the air conditioner in the motel room.

The motel hadn't been the worst he'd stayed in, but it wasn't a night at the Four Seasons. Not that he frequented the Four Seasons often. Holiday Inns and Courtyard Marriotts were his home away from home when out on the road.

This one had no continental breakfast. He wasn't a fan of rubber eggs anyhow, so he'd found a Waffle House with a smart-aleck waitress, decent coffee and a small-town crowd, then tried not to think about the woman he'd hurt the night before.

He hadn't been wrong in redirecting Louise's intent on shedding her virginity, but it still felt like a bad deal. He'd dinged her pride and there was no telling the ramifications of his nonaction.

But he couldn't dwell on it. Louise would be a faded memory in little over a week, even if her innocence and beauty had struck a chord in him. She'd fall in love someday and find the right guy to hold her and love her.

Something jerked in his gut at the thought of her in another man's arms, but he ignored it. It was like missing the numbers on the lottery by two numbers. Regret. But what could a guy do?

Move on.

Today he started his recruitment of the top prospect on the athletic department's tight end list. The Panthers needed Waylon Boyd, and Abram aimed to land the boy—starting with his high school coach.

The diner moved around him, blue-collar sorts with white utility trucks parked outside along with older women and men reading the newspaper. Clinking forks, clattering dishes, and the low hum of conversation. This place suited him fine. Real people. Real jobs.

He caught an older gentleman reading the sports section of the Opelousas paper glancing at him. Finally, on the fourth or fifth glance, Abram nodded.

The man narrowed his eyes. "You by any chance with the ULBR program?"

Abram wore an ULBR windbreaker, but that meant little. Almost everyone in Louisiana had something ULBR in his or her closet. "Yep, I'm with the program."

The man cracked a smile, stood and offered a hand. "I'm Tom Forcet. Forcet Construction. I'm godfather to one of your prospects—Waylon Boyd."

Abram stood and took the man's hand. "Pleasure to meet you, Mr. Forcet."

"Tom, please."

"I'm actually here to meet with Coach Landry about Waylon. Always good to run into a friend of his."

"Good kid. That's the most important thing. Raised right. His late father was my college roommate. Wish he could have seen what Waylon's become. Of course, Lou's done a fine job with him."

Abram hadn't had much time to look over Sam Moreland's notes on Waylon. He knew the kid's parents had been killed in a plane crash about nine years ago. Rather than place the kids in foster care, an older sibling had stepped up to care for them. "Character counts. His talent is evident on the field, but we pay close attention to kids with good values who will reflect well on our program."

"Dang right," the man said, wiping his mouth with a napkin from an adjoining table. "Waylon's the complete package. Does odd jobs around the construction site for me from time to time. Course Lou works for me so makes it easy to keep an eye on the boy. I'll let you get back to your breakfast. Eggs aren't good cold. Good to meet you."

Abram nodded and reciprocated the acknowledgment. Then he sat down to his breakfast, pulling the folder on Waylon Jennings Boyd and spreading it in front of him. Most of the information had been purchased from a reputable recruiting service but also contained comments from the Bonnet Creek coach—height, weight, times in the 40, bench weight, etc. There was a small section noting his personal information—basically address, contact information and name of guardian.

Louise Boyd.

Huh.

Surely, it wasn't the same person he'd danced with last night? The same woman he'd kissed and held in his arms. And nearly had sex with.

The disturbing feeling sliding into the pit of his stomach had nothing to do with the eggs and waffle he'd gulped down. Louise. Not a common name, was it?

He thought hard. She'd said she'd remained a virgin because of circumstances. Or something like that. Raising a younger brother and sister would definitely squash dating. Not to mention working full-time to support a family.

He glanced back at the file. No age given for the guardian.

Tom Forcet had told him Lou worked at the construction company, but he couldn't imagine the beautiful woman he'd met the night before working something as difficult as construction. And being called Lou. Maybe she did the books or something?

Either way, if Lou Boyd was his honky-tonk Cinderella, he'd unknowingly committed a recruiting violation—and not just the slap on the wrist kind. This was the kind that could blow up into a scandal. Opposing fan bases and the press that catered to their neuroses were hungry for dirty tidbits like a coach messing around with a recruit's sister, mother or cousin. If someone found out he and Louise Boyd had nearly done the dirty deed on a dock on Lake Chicot, there'd be shit hitting a fan. Really messy.

But maybe he worried for no good reason.

He took a sip of cold coffee. It tasted oddly of ashes. Or maybe it tasted like unemployment.

"Check, please."

"LORI, I CANNOT LEAVE work to bring you the essay. If I don't move this dirt, they can't frame up for the concrete, and Manuel will be all over my butt. We've finally had enough dry days to make progress. Sorry. You'll have to take a lower letter grade."

"Lou, please. You don't understand. Mrs. Rupple will not knock it down one letter grade, but two. Please. Just on your break." Lori's voice had dropped to a plaintive low whine. It was one she used often. Too often.

Lou pushed her gloved hand against the gear of the front-end loader, knocking the loose knob back and forth. "You're a big girl, Lori. You say you're old enough for a license or working at Forcet, but want me to bring your forgotten—"

"Pleeeease! I barely have an A in her class. I'll wash dishes for a whole week."

"No."

"Lou, I'm begging you. Begging."

Lou pulled off her heavy gloves and tossed them on the dashboard of the large piece of equipment. "Fine, but you have to wash the dishes and do the laundry."

"Thank you, Lou. I mean it. You're the best."

Lou pressed the button on her cell phone and sighed. "Sure I am."

So much for sticking to her guns this go-around. It was the seventh time this year Lou had taken her lunch by running home, grabbing something Lori had forgotten, and then speeding back to the school to deliver her sister from the horrible repercussion of leaving behind her practice uniform or the flash drive holding her PowerPoint presentation. Lori was a lovable, absent-minded goofball with an angel's face. And a pretty big heart. What else was Lou to do?

"Manuel," she called across the worksite.

The project manager jerked his head up. "Yo?"

"Taking my lunch early."

"Lori again?"

She gave him the same look she'd given him the other six times that year. "I won't be long. Then I'll get that dirt moved and in place so you can start the framing after lunch."

"Go."

She walked toward the vehicle that had once been her father's shining joy, a 2003 Tundra pickup. The silver truck now held a dent in the bumper, courtesy of Waylon's first attempt at parallel parking, and a huge scrape along one side from a hit-and-run when she'd gone to the Opelousas Home Depot. But it ran well thanks to her second cousin Reeves who owned Taylor Auto and insisted on giving the truck a free tune-up every year. Reeves took care of what little he could for her, but Lou did her own oil changes. She had to draw the line somewhere.

After banging her work boots against the front tire and taking off the bandana she wore to keep the baby-fine hair that escaped her braid out of her eyes, she climbed inside the cab. She saw one of the guys frown at her, and resisted the urge to give him a specific finger wave. That guy didn't like her much anyway. He was old school. Women belonged at home, folding underwear and stirring peas on the stove. Didn't matter that Lou could handle her heavy equipment like the finest surgeon. Some men were just shortsighted.

Forcet Construction mostly worked the region north of Opelousas, but they built all over Evangeline Parish, even dipping down to Acadia Parish at times. Today they were working the foundation for yet another credit union in Ville Platte, so her hometown of Bonnet Creek lay twelve miles away. Just far enough so that Lou would have to eat on the way back and also far enough to give her plenty of time to think.

Exactly what she needed. More time to think about what a colossal idiot she was.

No.

Lou refused to let her thoughts travel back to the night before. To the embarrassment of throwing herself at a perfect stranger. What had she been thinking? Or better phrased—what had she been drinking? Because her stupid actions had to be blamed on the strong mojitos. She wasn't a drinker. Couldn't handle the woozy, giggly euphoria that had wrapped her up and made her think naughty impossible thoughts. Yes. Blame it on the booze.

Stop it, Lou. Stop thinking about Abram. The moonlight. The fact you can't get a guy to do the deed.

As she turned into the drive of the house she'd been raised in, she made the same promise she'd made five times earlier that morning. No more thinking about last night.

She grabbed the paper, hidden beneath a yearbook on Lori's unmade bed, and hightailed it to Bonnet Creek High School, which sat only a mile away. She pulled into the visitor spot and killed the engine.

She didn't want to run into Coach Landry.

The man was driving her crazy about hiring someone to make a professional highlight reel of Waylon's best plays. Like she had the money for that.

Waylon was an incredibly talented athlete, and if college coaches couldn't see that on the amateur reel she'd pieced together with her own two hands for Coach Landry, then they were stupid. She wasn't hiring a professional service to film him next year. It was an enormous waste of money.

But David Landry was a force to be reckoned with, and with a four-star, blue-chip recruit on his team, he'd taken too personal of an interest.

"Hey, Lou. Lori forgot something again, didn't she?" Helen Barham ran Bonnet Creek High School from the sleek modern desk of the front office. Helen had once been in the garden club with Lou's mother and she was exceedingly competent, if unyielding. The woman had never married nor had children, so she tsked every time Lou brought in her sister's forgotten homework. She was a little hypocritical and gossipy, but many in the small town were. "You know she's—"

"—never going to learn?" Lou finished for her with a wry smile. "I know. I suck at parenting."

Helen wagged a finger. "I've seen worse, Lou-Lou."

"I think she's in Mr. Smith's English class right now," Lou said, darting a glance out the door of the office and pretending she didn't hear her father's old nickname for her trickle so casually out of Helen's mouth. Hearing it made her sad. "Coach Landry's not around, is he?"

The man was notorious for prowling the school hallways, and Lou really didn't want to deal with him today. Really didn't.

"He has some college coach in with him." Helen pointed to her in-basket. "Just leave Lori's assignment with me and I'll page her to the office."

Lou handed the paper off and slipped back out the door. She waved at Mr. Edwards, the custodian whose son played on the football team with Waylon, and nodded at a couple of students who hurried by clutching papers in hand.

She'd just pushed the front door of the school open when she caught sight of the stranger she was never supposed to see again down the hall to her left.

What the hell?

The door came back and nearly nailed her in the nose. She stepped back and watched Abram shake Coach Landry's hand. He wore khaki pants and a purple windbreaker. She was nearly certain ULBR Athletics was appliquéd on the breast even though she was too far away to read the actual letters.

He was a coach.

For ULBR.

His reason for being in Bonnet Creek was her brother.

Hot shame coursed through her body, followed quickly by the desire to flatten the man's nose. He knew who she was—that's why he'd stopped last night. He led her down the merry primrose path, using his charm, his extraordinary good looks to put her at disadvantage, possibly even as leverage, to land her brother, but reining himself in before committing the ultimate in douche-baggery.

What a slimy bastard.

Her boots turned toward the coaches before she could think better of it.

"Hey," she called out, her voice echoing in the hallway.

Both men turned—David with a wide crocodile smile; Abram Whatever His Last Name Was with an "oh shit" lift of his eyebrows.

"Lou, glad you're here. This is—"

She spun toward Abram. "What the hell do you think you're doing?"

"Well, hello to you, too, Louise."

"Lou, now let's watch the language here," Coach Landry said, waving his hand as if he were stroking the back of a horse. "This here's an informal visit—"

She blocked Coach Landry's voice out. Rage choked her. "You—you—ought to be ashamed of yourself. You knew who I was."

"Not until this morning when I ran into Mr. Forcet and then looked at Waylon's file. I inherited this recruiting area from Coach Moreland several weeks ago when he left for the offensive coordinating job with Ohio State. I had no clue who you were."

"Bullsh—" She swallowed the curse even though she wanted to nail him to the brick wall with a volley of creative language. She worked at a construction company. She knew combinations a sailor didn't. "I've heard about how you recruiting guys work. Crawling all over the place, popping up in grocery stores or churches looking to sway recruits or their families. It's despicable. And to try to use me? I can't—"

"Use you? You watch too much TV or something?" Abram interrupted, his green eyes turning a cold emerald. "This isn't a conspiracy. Get real."

Coach Landry ping-ponged his head between the two of them, before broadening his gaze to the area around them. "Maybe we better hold this conversation in my office. For, you know, privacy."

"Sis?" She heard Waylon's voice then and noticed several other students in the hall. Classes were about to change.

She spun toward her brother who was flanked by his girlfriend, Morgan, and his friend Mason. He looked like Goliath next to two Davids. "Go to class, Way. This doesn't involve you."

"Coach?"

Lou pointed a finger at her brother. "You do what I say, Waylon Boyd."

"Chill, Lou. You're acting crazy, making me look like a punk in front of the school." Both his friends looked off, obviously uncomfortable with the situation.

Abram's voice was low, but made of steel. "This is your sister, and she doesn't deserve disrespect."

Waylon's eyes clouded and he looked at Lou. Then back at Abram, before allowing his eyes to dip down to the logo on the shirt. She saw the dawning in his eyes. "Sorry, Lou. Sir."

Abram nodded. She did nothing. Her brother shifted on his size-13 feet. "What's going on?"

Coach Landry stepped in front of her and Abram.

"Your sister's right, Way. Go on to class. I'll talk to you this afternoon after conditioning."

"Let's let the kids move on. Coach Dufrene? Lou?" Landry stepped back and motioned towards his office.

Lou didn't want to have this discussion right now, but she also didn't want to have it out in the hall.

The bell rang, making the decision for her. She walked into Landry's office. Abram followed.

Coach Landry closed the door. "What in the Sam Hill is going on?"

For a moment she and Abram stared at one another. She didn't know how to feel. Never thought she'd see him again. Never thought he could have been using her to get close to her brother. He caved first and turned his gaze on Coach Landry.

"It's not complicated. Last night I stopped at a local bar, mostly to use the john, but then I grabbed a beer. Ended up running into Waylon's sister, but I had no idea Louise was even related to him. We danced and had a beer together. Nothing more."

She looked at the stapler sitting on David's desk, avoiding Abram's eyes. Refusing to show how much more their meeting could have meant.

"It was an unintentional off-campus contact. I think Miss Boyd thinks it was intentional, but that's as far from the truth as it gets. I didn't even know his guardian's name until this morning when I talked to her employer at the Waffle House."

David sank into his worn desk chair. "Ah, hell."

She licked her lips. "I don't like to feel manipulated."

"How in the hell is this manipulation, Louise? What? You think I found out your schedule and stalked you? That's really not how recruiting works regardless of what you may have heard." Abram's voice held anger.

"This is my career, and I wouldn't risk that for a random stranger. You think that's the way we operate at ULBR?"

She gave him a blank stare. She didn't know what to believe but it all seemed too much of a fluke to sit right with her. The man she'd tried to give her virginity to the night before was the coach sent to recruit her brother. It seemed too pat. She knew the lengths schools went to in going after prospects. She read the papers. Watched ESPN. Those bastards manipulated everyone surrounding the prospect, using Facebook, Twitter, casual meet-ups as ways to sway a kid toward their school. So why not seduction? "I'm not sure what your intent was, but I'm going to report this incident to the NCAA."

Coach Landry held up a hand. "Now wait a minute, Lou. Take a few moments to calm down before you decide anything. This is very important. Division I schools are under a lot of scrutiny these days, and we don't want to do anything to jeopardize Waylon. We also don't want to falsely accuse Coach Dufrene of misconduct."

The anger rampaging inside her abated a bit. David was right. This incident could affect Waylon. Not her. No need to smudge anything. Yet. "Fine. I don't have time for this today anyhow. I have a job to get back to, and I'm already late."

Abram stared at her. "Louise, I didn't know you were Waylon's guardian. If you think about it, you'll see I was merely in the wrong place at the wrong time."

"Don't tell me what to think."

Abram shrugged his big, delicious shoulders, and for a moment hot regret flooded her, a sort of longing for what might have been if it had been the right place and the right time.

Waylon's high school coach spread his hands. "We need to keep Waylon out in front of this. The incidental contact can be reported. It's not something that needs to be swept under the rug. Hell, it's a small state. I run into people unexpectedly all the time, so these things happen."

"It's policy at ULBR not to sweep anything under the rug, Coach," Abram said, propping his hands on his hips. With that simple action, Lou felt the balance shift in the room. "As soon as I leave, I'll report the incident to Coach Holt and the compliance department. I don't think anything further will be required, Miss Boyd. If compliance or the NCAA get in touch with you, tell the truth."

But not the whole truth, she thought. No way would she reveal how well they got to know each other. She didn't think Abram would be willing to do so, either. They met, they danced once and they shared a drink. Period. End of story.

"Fine," she said, turning the doorknob. "I've got to go. That dirt won't move itself."

"Later, Lou," David said.

"Louise?"

She hesitated, the door only slightly ajar.

"Had I known, I would never have continued the contact. I'll likely be the coach recruiting Waylon, and I hope you won't hold this incident against me. I truly have the best interests of your brother and the reputation of my institution in the forefront here. Don't doubt that."

She nodded and walked out.

What else could she do?

Both she and the too-delicious-to-have-even-contemplated-in-the-first-place coach had screwed up—and the innocent might end up suffering because she wanted to play Cinderella.

Something ached in her chest, a sort of regret for

what would not be. Not that she'd entertained ideas about the man who'd made her feel enchanting as they danced beneath the moonlight. She'd known he was passing through, but the regret was for having the moment in the first place.

Did she think anything could have been different?

She was who she was, and she'd figured out many years ago her situation wouldn't change until Waylon and Lori claimed lives of their own. Since their parents had died, she'd tried to keep Waylon and Lori's interests above hers. Not because she was a crazed martyr, but because they were all she had left. All she had to ensure something good would result from her temporarily giving up her dreams. She needed them to be safe and happy. Needed them to succeed. Because if they could get out of Bonnet Creek and reach their goals, then so could she.

Maybe it was selfish.

But she needed Waylon to go to college, to get a full ride. She needed Lori to do well on her SAT, to get her own free ride. She needed to see her sacrifice pay off. Really needed to know all those nights she baked cookies for snack day, turned down dates to attend school plays and called out spelling words had been worthwhile.

Okay, yeah. It was definitely selfish.

But it didn't change the fact her future lay in Lori and Waylon succeeding.

And not in pursuing crazy romantic fantasies like a twelve-year-old, starstruck girl.

CHAPTER FIVE

PICOU DUFRENE BLEW out the candles and everyone seated around the gleaming dining room table gave an obligatory clap.

"Happy 65th birthday, Mom," Abram said from his place at the end of the table. He'd intentionally sat away from his sister because trying to carry on a conversation with Sally was more uncomfortable than hemorrhoids.

Not that he'd ever had hemorrhoids. But he could imagine.

Sally had come back into their lives only five months before and the transition hadn't been easy. They all walked around each other like mines were planted beneath Beau Soleil's polished floors and body parts might fly at any moment.

"Thank you," Picou said, plucking a candle from the cake Lucille had made from scratch and sucking the frosting off. "Delicious, Lucille, as always."

Lucille sat next to his mother, like a round, black cherub, smiling at the compliment. She'd been at Beau Soleil for as long as Abram could remember, and she was the best friend Picou had. Scratch that, Lucille was family.

"I know what you like, Picou. Real buttercream frosting just like my Aunt Lula Mae used to make for the governor, and that man wasn't half the person you are. You more deservin' than that ol' rat."

His mother laughed, and everyone else smiled. Abram's brother Nate and his wife Annie took the cake to the antique sideboard and started slicing generous pieces onto Picou's Royal Doulton wedding china, adding the sterling forks to each plate. The sterling had belonged to Picou's mother. All things at Beau Soleil were useful and priceless—the Old South way.

Sally sat quietly, her big eyes taking in the atypical family dinner. His younger sister wasn't accustomed to their ways since she'd been taken when she was three years old by the family gardener. Sal Comeaux and his partner, who was due for parole in a few months, had concocted a kidnapping scheme that went afoul. They'd taken Della, now known as Sally, and left a ransom note in the Dufrene sugar mill. Sal was supposed to kill Della, but somehow couldn't bring himself to do so. He'd taken the child to his grandmother, a tough old Bayou woman, and passed her off as family before he himself disappeared. The Dufrenes had spent twenty-four years believing Della to be dead.

She might have stayed unknown to them if the woman who'd raised her, Enola Cheramie, hadn't fallen ill. Failing kidneys led to Sally being tested, a careless remark about blood markers had led to questions, and an inquiry at the Lafourche Sheriff's office had led to a file being placed on his brother Nate's desk.

Nate had worked with the St. Martin Parish detective unit for over ten years, and when he'd received the file on Sally Cheramie, he had known they'd finally gotten a lead on Della's disappearance. It had almost been too much to hope for, but Nate said when he saw Sally Cheramie for the first time, he knew he'd found his sister.

Sally had her twin brother Darby's eyes—uniquely violet-blue—and mirrored the young Picou in her wedding portraits. But physical similarities only went so far. Sally wouldn't open up to them and the gulf between her and the family never seemed to shrink.

"I certainly wish Darby could be here," Picou sighed, patting Sally's hand. Sally swallowed and Abram could see she wanted to move her hand. The girl they'd once called Della was like a cat in a room of rockers when she was among the Dufrenes. "He'll be home before too long, and he can't wait to see you."

Nate turned from the sideboard and glanced at his sister.

Sally tried to smile. "It'll be nice to meet him finally. Well, I suppose it's more like see him again. When does he resign his commission?"

She spoke with a heavy accent—a distinct dialect spoken by the people inhabiting the bayou south of Cutoff, Louisiana. With a slender frame, long dark hair and bright blue eyes, Sally drew people to her with quiet, unassuming beauty. The woman who raised her had pushed her to excel in school so she might leave the bayou and spread her wings. Sally had used the education she'd gained at ULL to become a teacher, and currently taught second grade in the school she'd once attended in Galliano. She hadn't stretched her wings very wide, and instead clung to the community and the still-ill Enola Cheramie.

He wondered if she would ever accept being the long-lost Della Dufrene.

"Do you not remember Darby at all, Sally?" Annie asked, setting a dessert plate in front of Abram. He looked at the huge piece of cake. He'd be doing an extra mile tomorrow morning for this indulgence. He picked up the fork.

Sally frowned. "Not really, though I must have

missed him when I was little. I called my blankie Dobby."

Abram listened with half an ear after that. What lay ahead for him had his stomach twisting. He couldn't put to bed all that had passed earlier that week—not with an early morning meeting with compliance and the director of recruiting on Monday. Afterward, he'd face Coach Holt before the man headed out to Bristol to film a commercial for ESPN. Abram didn't want to see the disappointment in his mentor's eyes.

After having a brush with the NCAA over the use of a shady recruiting service and allegations of "pay for players," the powers-that-be at ULBR were gun-shy about any other incidents popping up within the program. Small things could be dealt with. They happened. But a newsworthy splash like a sex scandal would do lasting damage and jeopardize the reputation of a program, not to mention cost things like scholarships and bowl games. And all Abram had intended for himself, all his dreams of one day becoming a head coach of a Division I team, would come crashing down around him.

Abram wished it would all go away. Wished he could undo missing the damn exit and stopping for a beer. Wished he'd told Mary Belle an emphatic no when she'd asked him to pretend to be Louise's date.

But if wishes were horses, beggars would ride.

Or at least that's what Lucille had always told him when he wished for cookies, something fun to do or better grades on his report card.

Lucille winked at him. He'd always had a special bond with the Dufrene family housekeeper. There was a woman who "got" him. And a woman who'd fed him, counseled him and swatted him on his backside when he got too uppity.

"Abram, you're quiet as a sinner in church tonight. Hellcat run away with your tongue?" Lucille's gap-toothed smile prodded him to enter the fray. Hellcat was the ragged-ear tom that appeared last month yowling for a bowl of scraps and saucer of milk every night. No one seemed to own Hellcat. Couldn't catch him long enough to mark him with ownership.

"Sorry. Lots on my mind. The job."

"Saw the spring game. Matt Vincent has some work to do. Missed more receivers than he hit." Nate slapped another piece of cake on his own plate. "Damn, this is better than sex, Lucille."

Lucille looked at Annie. "You must be doing something wrong, child."

Annie nearly choked on her coffee.

Picou laughed, Lucille cackled and even Sally looked mildly amused.

"Behave, Lucille. She hasn't married me yet and I don't want you scaring her off with your uncouth ways." Nate grinned, sliding his eyes to his fiancée. She lifted an eyebrow and Abram felt the love between the two of them. Nice to see Nate happy.

Nate looked back at Abram, refusing to let him fade into the background. When it came to his family Abram had always liked the background. If he stayed quiet long enough, sometimes they forgot about him. Suited a lone wolf like him just fine. Or at least most of the time. "So, what's up with Vincent?"

Abram shrugged. "Ask Monty. He's the quarterback coach."

"Yeah, I'll get him on the horn. I have him on speed

dial," Nate drawled as Annie elbowed him. "Aren't you an offensive coach? Shouldn't you know?"

"You didn't hear? I'm the water boy."

"Come on, boys, let's not start," Picou warned, her fork clattering on the china.

Abram snapped his mouth closed and tried to figure some way to get out of there early. His mother was to open gifts after dinner. Abram never knew what to give her, so he'd purchased a gift certificate from a Baton Rouge salon. Standard son gift—not creative, but useful.

"When are we opening gifts?" Annie asked, nudging Nate again. His soon-to-be sister-in-law was perky, fit and pretty with brown curly hair and clear gray eyes. She was a former FBI agent and had met Nate while on an assignment in Bayou Bridge. Five months ago, after finding Della, they'd formed a partnership in a private investigations firm specializing in unsolved murders. Using grants and Nate's savings, they'd hit the ground running, solving a case in Alexandria that had put them in the spotlight and brought more business their way.

Annie had been good for his brother if the smiles were any indication. Before Annie, Nate had rarely smiled. After Annie, he sometimes resembled a blooming idiot.

"Let's go into Picou's sitting room," Lucille suggested, scooting her chair back and grunting as she rose. "You come on with me, Miss Sally girl. I found something of yours the other day when I was cleaning out the cabinets in there."

Lucille didn't wait on Sally. She waddled out and expected everyone to follow. Like sheep they moved their chairs back.

"Hold on," Nate mumbled, shoving the last bite into his mouth.

The sitting room was like every room in the house, filled with posh antiques that had been well used. The fabrics on the chairs and window had been expensive and well maintained, if not out of style by fifteen or twenty years. Family pictures squatted between costly oils and original sculptures. The carpet on the floor was a threadbare Aubusson.

Sally perched on the end of the couch, holding a worn-out-looking pacifier, presumably Lucille's great find. She picked up a gift wrapped in floral paper with a large fluffy-looking bow. "This is from me."

Picou sat in her normal overstuffed armchair and took the gift. Love shone in her eyes when she looked at Sally. "It's wrapped so pretty."

Sally rubbed the material of her skirt between her fingers and gave up a smile.

Picou opened the gift while everyone found a comfortable spot. His mother lifted the lid. "Oh, my."

"What is it?" Lucille craned her head, and Abram noticed her wig was on crooked.

"Look." Picou picked up a small painted canvas and held it aloft. It portrayed a sunset on the swamps and was rather well done. His mother looked at Sally. "Did you do this?"

Sally nodded. "I dabble around with painting every once and while. I thought it suited you."

Picou wiped tears from her cheeks with hands that bore more rings than necessary. His mother liked drama, wearing caftans, crazy feathers and ribbons in her soft gray hair and ornamenting herself like a palm reader at the state fair. She should have looked ridiculous. Okay, sometimes she did look a bit kooky, but it suited her. "Thank you, dear. I shall always treasure it."

Sally kept fiddling with her hem but managed another smile.

Annie handed Picou another small gift. "From us."

Abram could tell it was a gift certificate. He hoped they hadn't bought one to a spa. Rain on his parade, and all that. Nate constantly one-upped him on gift-giving.

Picou pulled the red ribbon from the polka-dotted box. "This will make a good hair bow." She tucked it beneath her thigh.

Abram felt excitement radiating off Nate and Annie as Picou lifted the lid. Maybe they'd gotten her a trip? If they did, he'd be pissed. He'd once mentioned sending her on a cruise, and Nate had freaked over the expense. If Nate went and trumped everyone with a trip somewhere, he'd—

"A grandmother's brag book?" His mother's eyebrows knitted together as she lifted the pink-and-blue photo book from the tissue paper. She flipped the book open and stared at a grainy-looking black picture. Two or three seconds tripped by.

"Oh, my God!" Picou reared back against the chair, her eyes wide, her mouth open. "Is that—is that—"

Annie started giggling and Nate just smiled.

His mother stared with wonder at the picture in front of the book. "Are you telling me I'm going to be a grandmother?"

Nate nodded.

Annie collapsed in laughter.

Picou shrieked.

Lucille clapped.

Annie and Nate had given his mother the gift she'd always wanted. Progeny. A stupid manicure and pedicure seemed like a booby prize compared to a baby.

Like winning a five-dollar raffle ticket after winning a jackpot of over a million.

He looked at his sister, who for once wore a genuine smile. "I think we lost on the gifts."

Sally laughed. "I think you're right."

LOU STARED AT the flashing lights in the driveway refusing to believe what she was seeing.

Officer Harvey Coe climbed from the driver's side and then opened the back door of the car. Waylon, head down, emerged.

"Evening, Lou," Harvey said, walking toward where she stood on the porch. "Hated to be bringing Waylon home this way, but I thought it might be best. He and a few boys were drinking beer down at the Sav-A-Lot parking lot, busting bottles, and such. One of the windows of the store got broke. Thought about arresting them, but being this is boys being boys, I gave 'em a warning and called Mr. Davenport about the window."

Waylon refused to look at her. He seemed to be studying the ragged pansies she'd planted that fall, and since she knew he had very little interest in botany, she knew he was afraid of her. He should be. Fury chomped away inside her. How dare he do something so infantile? So stupid?

"Well, this is such a nice surprise," Lou drawled, swatting away the moths dancing around the porch light before crossing her arms, mostly to keep from knocking her stupid brother in the head. "And here I was thinking my younger brother was at a friend's house working on his research paper. Silly me."

She looked at Harvey who looked at Waylon who kept his gaze on the pansies. Silence lay on them like January snow.

"Well, the boys are gonna have to pay for that window. Davenport said he'd get a bill to all the parents, and you, too. Sorry about this, Lou."

"Thanks, Harvey. Waylon will be calling Mr. Davenport to apologize, and he'll take care of that bill." Or she'd ride Waylon's ass until the middle of next summer. Or until he stopped his irresponsible behavior.

Harvey turned to Waylon. "Look at me, son."

Waylon lifted his head and stuck out his chin. Lou had seen that posturing before—scared little boy trying to be a man. Waylon's brown hair gleamed almost red in the low porch light and she noticed he needed a haircut.

The policeman pointed a sausage finger at him. "You need to keep your nose clean. I better not hear about you messin' around with that Holland boy again. He's trouble, you hear?"

"Yes, sir," Waylon said, shifting in his new Nike workout shoes. He sounded respectful, but Lou saw the rebellion in his eyes. She knew he'd been hanging out with Willie Holland's boy for the last two weeks and couldn't understand the fascination with the high school dropout. This was not good. Cy Holland worked at his father's garage and rode Harleys on the weekend to biker bars all over the state. Cy was eighteen, tough and often in trouble with the Bonnet Creek and Ville Platte police departments.

"Go in the house, Way," Lou said, her voice quiet but firm. Inside she still shook with rage, but she wasn't going to show it to either of the two males crowding her driveway.

Her brother surged past, his unused backpack sliding off his shoulder as he pushed into the house.

"Thanks again, Harv."

Harvey turned to her. "I know things have been

tough on you, Lou, but you're gonna have to keep a tight leash on that boy. He's at an age where he's gonna test you and everybody he comes up against. He's got a lot riding on his shoulders. Better talk some sense into him. Maybe talk to Coach, too."

Lou bristled. Waylon was a good kid, no matter what Harvey implied. Sure, he'd been ill-tempered and difficult lately, but it wasn't something she couldn't handle, and she didn't need David Landry inserting himself even more into Waylon's life. As it was, he spent too much time hanging around the coach's office and sometimes at the Landry house. "Again, I appreciate your doing this. I'll take care of it from here."

"Night," Harvey nodded and walked toward the cruiser still flashing its lights. She winced as her neighbor popped her gray head out the kitchen door and stared at the departing police car. The nosy old woman would have something to gossip about over coffee the next morning.

Lou walked into the house and shut the door.

It was 10:15 p.m. Nearly forty-five minutes past Waylon's school-night curfew.

Lori appeared in the hallway, clad in an old T-shirt and pajama pants. "What's going on?"

Lou shook her head, swallowing her aggravation. "Nothing to worry about. You finish that geometry assignment?"

"Yeah, but I had to call someone for help on that last problem. Hey, is Way okay?" Lori's curls bobbed as she glanced at the closed bedroom door behind her. Her sister had light brown hair, blue eyes and a sweet disposition, and though Lori often sniped with her older brother, she worshipped him.

Lou shook her head, locked the front door and set the security system. "Not if I kill him for being stupid."

"What happened?" Her sister sank onto the worn sofa and grabbed a quilted throw pillow. "You need to talk about it, Lou? Can I help you with anything?"

"No, but will you double-check you have all your homework packed up so I don't have to bring anything to you tomorrow?" Lori had turned fifteen last month, and since then, had tried to maintain a very adult-like demeanor. She asked to set up the bills online, used her babysitting money for a few groceries and jockeyed to become Lou's sounding board on everything from work to dealing with their wayward brother. In one way it was amusing, in another almost a relief to have another person to lean on, even if it was an absentminded fifteen-year-old. "He's under a lot of pressure and looking for a way to blow off steam. No need to worry. Everything's fine."

Lori picked at the stitches on the pillow. "Things are going to change. I heard about that ULBR coach being at school this morning. Waylon's a good player and everyone's going to want him to go to their school. I don't want him to leave, Lou."

"Well," Lou said, picking up a throw blanket, folding it and tucking it away in the hollow ottoman. She also picked up a few soda cans and gum wrappers, tidying the house as was her habit every night before she went to bed. "I can understand not wanting things to change, but that's how life is. It moves whether we want it to or not. But we have to remember, these programs wanting your brother is a good thing. Most guys only dream about what Waylon has."

"What if I don't want it anymore?"

Lou turned around to see her brother standing in

the hall doorway, both hands braced against the door frame. He looked big...and sort of sad. "You no longer want to play football?"

He shrugged. "Maybe I'm tired of it. Maybe I'm sick of being the school's hero—everybody watching me, examining my grades, timing my runs. Maybe I want to be normal."

Lou tossed the matching throw pillow onto the couch next to her sister—maybe a little harder than necessary. "Well, normal isn't going out drinking and destroying other people's property. It's not lying to your family. Or failing American history tests. None of those things you're doing are normal, Way."

"Whatever," he said, walking past her toward the kitchen.

So he was going to give her attitude after coming home in a cop car? No freaking way was he getting away with acting like a shit. Lou followed him into the kitchen. "What is your problem, Waylon? You're close to getting everything you wanted and you're trying to throw it away."

He opened the refrigerator, pulled out the milk and took a swig straight from the carton because he knew it ticked her off. "Nothing's wrong, and you don't know what I want. No one ever asked me what I want. Maybe I don't want to play football in college. I may not even go to college."

"The hell you aren't." Lou walked over and plucked the carton from his hand. "And stop drinking from the carton. It's gross."

"You can't make me go to college, and you can't make me play football. I spend day and night lifting weights, doing cardio and running drills. That doesn't leave me time for anything else except homework and bed. Think I want to live that way? With no fun in my life?"

Lou tilted her head. "Oh, so you want to have fun?"

"Uh, yeah."

"Well, then, let's have fun." She spun toward the purse she'd set on the kitchen desk and yanked it up. "Here, I'll give you a twenty and you run to the Handimart for beer. Hey, Lori, put on music and call some friends. I'll score the pot so we can all get high and drunk and trash the house Mom and Dad worked so hard to build. I'll probably lose my job, but you two can drop out of school to work at a fast-food joint. We'll just party until we lose the house and have to live in Dad's truck. Come on, guys, it'll be fun. Waylon needs fun."

"I don't like beer," Lori said, appearing in the doorway, looking nervous. "I personally think fun is overrated."

Waylon wiped his mouth with the back of his hand. "Sounds good to me."

"It would. You don't have the sense God gave a goat." Lou jerked the fridge open and shoved the milk carton back on its shelf. She actually thought about grabbing a wooden spoon from kitchen tool canister and spanking Waylon's butt for being such a turd. How dare he casually toss away the gift he'd been given? How dare he try to ruin everything they'd been working toward?

What gave him the freakin' right to rip away all their dreams just because he felt a little pressure? The kid had no idea what pressure was.

Taking a deep breath, she stepped back, bumping up against the cabinets she and Lori had painted last summer. *Okay, Lou. Stay calm. Don't lose your temper. This is what parents everywhere do every day. Be the adult.*

"You don't need the sense God gave a goat to man

the fries at the Pit Stop." Waylon leaned against the fridge and gave her a long stare. She wished she could decipher his intent like she once could. Maybe he was being contrary, pressing her buttons for the hell of it. He crossed his arms, mimicking her, and she noted he'd grown nearly as big as the refrigerator he cleaned out daily, but his eyes looked scared.

"In all seriousness, Waylon, I understand. It's spring, you'll be seventeen next month and life hasn't been easy for any of us since you starting getting all this attention." She paused and tried to summon the calm demeanor her father had always maintained with her when she flipped out as a teenager. She needed to make Waylon feel she was on his side. "But you have to use that spongy matter between your ears when it comes to your future."

"Things feel too heavy. I can't handle all this shit, Lou."

She started to correct his language, but the anguish in his voice had her figuratively biting her tongue. "You do have a say-so in your life, Way. If you don't want to play football in college, fine. I can live with you never picking up a football again…but can you?"

His hazel eyes shifted away from her as the impact of her words crashed into him. "No, I love when I'm on the field, just me and the guy I gotta beat. But this whole recruiting thing has me feeling out of control already."

She nodded. It had her feeling the same way, especially after the incident with Abram Dufrene and the realization the process was only going to get more intense. College recruiting was a science and her brother was on several programs' radars. That meant soon there would not be just letters in the mailbox and invitations to specialty camps, but there would be visits, evaluations, weekly phone calls and immense emotional warfare waged on them all. Several years ago, the thought of Waylon being courted by the largest football programs in the nation sounded exciting. Now it felt like another layer, heavy on them, one more thing to yank their chains and deliver conflict in their lives. "I know. It's going to be wonderful, and it's going to be horrible, but that doesn't take away the fact you are something special and have an opportunity to become something spectacular."

He just looked at her. "That doesn't really help."

"Well, how about one night a week, we make a point to sit down and have dinner together? No phones, no friends, no last-minute activities. Lately we've all been going in different directions and need time to regroup. Mom and Dad used to make sure we sat down and talked at least once a week over dinner, so maybe we should start that tradition again."

"Can we order pizza?" Lori asked.

"You don't like my special spaghetti sauce?"

"No offense, Lou, but your talents don't lie in the kitchen." Waylon finally cracked a smile, revealing the boy he'd always been—a charming, easygoing prankster. Here was the brother she'd been looking for over the last few weeks.

Thank God, because Waylon was really starting to scare her. If he didn't want to play football, he wouldn't get a scholarship. Lou hadn't thought of a contingency plan, but she'd be damned if she had to put off college for herself any longer than she had to. It was going to be bad enough being a twenty-nine-year-old freshman.

She banked her fear and rolled her eyes. "Fine. I'll spring for pizza once a week, starting tomorrow night."

Waylon disappeared, and she heard Lori call out a good-night. Lou wiped crumbs off the counter and loaded the dishwasher, hoping her plan worked. Years ago, the complication of raising her siblings lay in last-minute runs to get posterboard or wanting a certain kind of cool shirt. Now her brother and sister were at the stage where their actions affected the rest of their lives.

Not easy being a pseudo parent when you hadn't signed up for it in the first place.

As Lou flicked the fluorescent light off above the sink, it hit her that she hadn't even addressed the broken window and drinking problem. Nor had she talked about Cy Holland and his less-than-savory influence.

Well, she knew the first item of business on the agenda for dinner tomorrow night.

CHAPTER SIX

THREE NIGHTS LATER, Waylon tossed the beer bottle onto the floorboard and shifted Morgan on his lap. She squealed when he grabbed her ass. He smiled because he not only loved Morgan when she squealed, but he loved to grab her ass.

He'd tried to stay away from Cy and his crew after having dinner with Lori and Lou, but after a tough practice and four calls from head coaches of top college programs, his gut had started cramping. All he could think about was escaping that world and doing nothing but drinking and hanging with someone who didn't give a damn about anything. Cy topped that list.

"You got to see the way that dude plays the bass. It's the shit," Cy Holland said, weaving his Avalanche around the washed-out ravines at the edge of the pasture. The headlights showed stupid cows dotting the field before them. "Next weekend we're gonna drive over to Lafayette. Shank's playing at Hooligan's. Two-for-one beer makes it even better. You got an ID you can use?"

No. But maybe one of the guys at Forcet Construction would let him borrow one. "Sure. I got one."

Morgan slid her hand down his chest toward the fly of his jeans. She was drunk and that always made her horny, but he wasn't getting anything on in the backseat of Cy's ride. Not with creepy Leesa Jardine watching them. He didn't know why Cy let Leesa hang with him. She had a nasty temper, ghostlike skin and a horrible acne problem she covered with too much makeup. Every other word out of her mouth was the "f" word, which Waylon never dropped himself. He'd been a counselor at church camp and wasn't trashy enough to use it often. Lou had raised him better than that.

Besides, he didn't smoke the weed Leesa scored from her older brother, a total loser pothead who lived in a room over her parents' garage. He guessed that was the main reason Cy hung out with her. For free pot. Or maybe she just put out when Cy needed quick action or something.

"Stop," he whispered in Morgan's ear as she made contact with her goal. He didn't want to sport a boner in front of Leesa. Too weird.

His girlfriend of three months pulled her head off his shoulder. "What?"

He smiled. "You know what."

She laughed and he realized he probably loved her. Maybe. Her long brown hair and big blue eyes had him wrapped around her little finger, and he liked being there. Not just because she was the first girl he'd had sex with, but because she didn't really care if he played football or not. She wasn't the kind of girl he'd dated before. Morgan wasn't a cheerleader or a captain on the dance line. She wasn't on student council or in any club. Morgan was Morgan. She liked heavy metal music, had a tattoo of a mermaid on her back and smoked Virginia Slims because that's what her grandmother smoked.

And she'd never been to church camp.

Which had been evident from the first time they'd hooked up. She'd kind of blown his mind.

"You sure you want to do this?" Cy looked over his

shoulder. Cy's friend Rory sat in the passenger's seat, where he always sat when Cy's girlfriend Lucy Chong, who lived in Alexandria, wasn't beside him. Rory was a punk and pretty jealous of Waylon. He constantly made fun of Waylon, dropping smart-ass comments about jocks and Christians every time he addressed him.

Waylon felt sorry for Rory 'cause he was nothing but a wannabe and an asshat. Always hating on everyone else, but not bothering to do anything with the person he was. He was like dust mites. Just sort of disgustingly there, but not anything anyone really bothered with.

"Hell, yeah, we're doing this. I've always wanted to try it and I didn't wear my boots for nothing," Leesa said, popping the lock on the SUV and swinging the door open. "Nothing better than dumbass redneck activities. Bet you've done it, Way-way."

He didn't like her even calling his real name, much less the moronic one she insisted on tossing at him.

"Sure," he said, tilting Morgan back so her hair spilled across the leather seat. He deliberately looked at Leesa before he kissed Morgan's neck. "I was cow tipping champ of 2010."

Leesa watched him like a freaky gargoyle. Something pinged in her dark gaze and he knew his little show had bothered her. He just wasn't sure if it was because she wanted to devour him—or Morgan. "Bet you were, stud muffin. Another trophy to put on your shelf, huh? Gotta love a jock whose great claim to fame is pushing dumbass cows down when they're asleep."

"That's not my claim to fame. Just a side talent. One of many. And cows don't sleep standing up."

Leesa snorted and slammed the door.

Morgan looked up with glassy blue eyes. "I think she'd totally do you if I weren't here."

Waylon grinned down. "But you're here, baby. I ain't doing nobody but you."

He laid Morgan on the seat because she was too drunk to try and push cows over. She moaned in protest and reached up and hooked him round the neck for a kiss. He made out with her a little, until she gave up and started snoring, then he stepped from the SUV. Rory and Cy were propped up against the hood, and the truck lights spilled across the pasture, highlighting large clumps of clover and an old wooden fence.

Cy took a swig of beer. "Look at that stupid ass. She thinks she's going to push a cow over by herself."

Rory laughed. Unpleasantly.

"We need to help her, I guess," Waylon said, watching Leesa climb through the fence.

"Ain't you just the team player," Rory drawled, giving another nasty laugh. At that moment, Waylon wondered why in the hell he'd lied to his sister and snuck out with Cy and his two loser pals. Not only that, but he'd dragged his girlfriend out with him. Maybe he had lost his marbles. Or maybe he was tired of who he was. Maybe he didn't care anymore.

"Yeah, I am." Waylon grabbed one of the beers Cy had set against the bug guard, popped the top and gulped down half. Then he set it on the hood, climbed over the fence and walked over sixty yards or so to where crazy Leesa crept toward a still cow. It was obvious she didn't know anything about cow tipping.

He started running full speed at the huge bovine. He and Leesa hit it together. Of course, he hit it a lot harder. The cow didn't stand a chance. It stumbled, legs buckling as it struggled to gain its footing. Hitting the cow felt like crashing into a defensive end in his quest for the end zone.

"Oh, my God!" Leesa screamed. "Did we kill it?"

A loud moo split the night air and other cows started moving around them. The cow they'd tried to tip hadn't gone down.

"I don't know, but she looks mad. Run!" he yelled.

He took off toward the headlights of the truck, realizing there was another wire fence they hadn't seen separating the pasture into two parts. Leesa shrieked and he heard her behind him, so he didn't feel like he was a total jerk for hauling ass out of the pasture. If she'd have fallen, he would have gone back for her. Maybe.

"Oh, God. It's chasing us!" Leesa screamed, sounding like she was about to pass him up, which was impossible. He ran a 4.6 in the 40-yard dash. In fact, a cow couldn't run that fast.

But sure enough, hoofs pounded behind them. He wasn't about to stop and contemplate being chased by a cow. He just hoped like hell they hadn't tried to knock over a bull. In the beams of the truck he saw Rory and Cy laughing like lunatics before scrambling into the cab of the Avalanche.

"No," he shouted as they fired the engine and put the truck into Reverse.

He and Leesa were about ten yards from the fence when he felt something come toward him. It was big and fast and it had horns.

He reached back and grabbed Leesa's arm, jerking her out of the path of the bull. She screamed and doubled her efforts to clear the field. He also fired his jets because he could feel the animal's anger, hear the heavy breath of the beast, feel the thunder of hooves.

It charged toward them as they reached the fence.

"Shit!" he yelled, shoving Leesa between two wooden rails before jumping over the top rail. His boots hit the ground right before his ass did. He fell partly on Leesa as the bull crashed into the fence. Its large head slammed into the wood, making a loud crack. The yellowed horns shone wickedly despite the waning taillights of Cy's truck.

Waylon shuffled back, crabbing himself over Leesa.

"Oh, my God," she cried, scrambling back as the beast launched himself at the wooden barrier a second time. He heard a crack and prayed the wood would hold. His asshole buddies had thought it cute to drive off and leave them to face a deadly animal, so if the bull got out, he and Leesa were in trouble.

The bull snorted and bucked at the fence.

"It's so pissed," Leesa breathed, clutching at his arm.

"Let's back up and see if he will calm down." He tugged her several feet away from the place they'd landed, and thankfully heard the truck heading back toward them. The headlights hit them and then the fence. Finally, the beams found the huge, black bull pacing along the rails. The animal tossed its head and pawed the ground.

"You saved my life," Leesa said, staring at the bull. "You seriously saved my life."

The truck pulled alongside them and raucous laughter spilled out into the night as Cy rolled the windows down. "You dipshits tried to tip a bull. A flippin' bull!"

Rory had tears leaking from his eyes and somehow his laughter pissed Waylon off more than anything. More than his girlfriend passed out in Cy's truck. More than Cy doing something so douchebag as driving off when he realized they were in danger. Something about pathetic Rory Strickland laughing at him made him snap.

He ran around to the passenger side and tried to open the door.

"Hey, man. What's your problem? It was a joke," Rory cried as Waylon reached through the open window and grabbed him by the shirt collar.

"Hey, what the hell?" Cy called, yanking at Waylon's hands. "We were just messin' with you, dude. We weren't really leaving."

Rory gasped as Waylon pulled at him. At that moment, Waylon wanted to beat the ever-lovin' shit out of the skinny loser who'd spent the past four weeks making fun of him at every turn. He was going to wipe the damn pasture with the asshole.

"Stop," Leesa said, gripping his arm. "Waylon, stop!"

He let Rory go.

"Jesus, man. What's your problem? You're freaking crazy." Rory clutched his throat, trying to draw a good breath.

Waylon stepped back, panting. He turned and took several steps away from the truck.

Dear Lord, what had happened to him? He looked up at the stars glittering above him and took a deep breath. Exhaling, he leaned over and found he shook with adrenaline. Or maybe it was anger.

He heard the truck door open and slam shut. Leesa had likely climbed inside.

"Dude, you coming or not?" Cy called out at him.

Waylon shook his head. "I need a minute."

"Just get in the truck. I know you're pissed, but we weren't leaving you. Just messin' around. Chill already." Waylon didn't like Cy telling him what to do. He wasn't getting in the damn truck.

Waylon turned. "I'm not getting in your goddamn truck. I'm done with this shit. We could have been killed or maimed by that bull, so I can't deal with climbing inside, cracking open a beer and acting like it was no big deal. Let Morgan out."

"Like she can walk. She's passed out, dude," Cy said.

"She's going to my house anyway," Leesa said. "But you should come with us, Way."

"No. I'm good."

He knew he should see Morgan home. His girlfriend was drunker than a sailor on shore leave and he'd let her get that way. Of course, Morgan wouldn't have any repercussions because she never got punished. Her mother worked a night shift at a sugar refinery and slept most of the day. But Leesa would take care of her.

Cy didn't bother asking again and pulled away, leaving him alone in the middle of a cow pasture.

Speaking of cows, Lou would have one when he got home two hours past curfew. She'd probably punish him for a month—or try.

He looked back at the bull pacing beside the fence. Maybe he'd rather face off against that bull again than tangle with his sister.

Regardless of the assload of trouble he was in, he started walking toward the house that lay a little over two miles away. He could jog it easily if he weren't wearing cowboy boots.

Shit.

He had too much pressure in his life and it showed. He used to never lose his temper, but with the thoughts of the ACT, the combines, the classroom and summer-long camps, he couldn't stop wanting to punch his way out of life.

Cy, Leesa and even that assclown Rory didn't put pressure on him for anything. They wanted to drink, smoke pot and party. And sometimes play *Warcraft*. That was it.

No homework. No workouts. No talk of college, eligibility or vertical jumps. No football.

He walked up an embankment and found the parish road that would take him home.

Each footstep took him closer to the trouble he'd be in.

Each footstep took him closer to his future.

And closer to an emptiness he didn't know how to fill.

CHAPTER SEVEN

ABRAM WATCHED THE hulking college players pump iron as he leaned against the painted wall outside the strength coach's office. Jordan Curtis nursed a Red Bull and a head cold, but it didn't stop him from barking at the starting center over the deafening music.

"Effort, Wilson, effort. I want your damn eyeballs bulging, son."

The enormous center rolled those eyes and tossed the bar onto the floor with a clank. "I think I perforated my abdominal wall and my intestines are coming out my nose, Coach."

"You know what an abdominal wall is?" Coach Curtis yelled.

"I'm majoring in biology. I have a 3.50 GPA and I've been accepted into medical school. So, yeah," the kid called back.

Abram snickered. "He's smarter than you, Jordan."

His friend took another swig. "I heard about your little tête-à-tête with the Boyd kid's sister."

Abram sobered. Yeah, the whole coaching staff knew about his screwup after he reported to compliance. "You know what tête-à-tête means?"

"I was an English major with a minor in political science, so I know you screwed the pooch."

"There was no screwing."

Jordan grinned. "She a looker?"

"Hotter than shit on shingle," Abram said, running a hand through his hair. It was getting warm in the weight room. Soon the gym would smell like feet and funk. "But that doesn't matter. She's off bounds. Wish I would have done better research on the kid before I took off to Ville Platte. I've learned a valuable lesson."

"Not to stop for a piss?"

"No, to read the file before I get to the town I'm recruiting in."

Abram had spent the last few days meeting with recruiting director Sam Donaldson and the entire compliance department. The incident would be reported to the NCAA, but the compliance department would hold their own internal investigation. College athletics had evolved into big-time business, and any sanctions against a program meant a loss in revenue, a loss in reputation and a résumé on Monster.com for the coach involved. ULBR was careful in keeping track of recruits, recruiters and any rogue boosters who got the idea to help the program by supplying money or other benefits to college athletes.

"They still letting you recruit him?"

"Yeah, why not? It was incidental contact. Neither she nor I knew anything about each other."

Jordan slid his gaze to meet his. "Is that a good idea considering the hotter than shit on a shingle comment?"

He'd had this conversation with himself when Coach Holt had called him on the carpet after he made the initial report. After thinking about the incident, Louise's obvious embarrassment, and the risk to Waylon if something more happened with his sister, he'd concluded he could restrain his emotions where Louise was concerned.

He had to ignore the unnatural attraction for the blond construction worker. This was his career in the palm of his hand. No way would he toss it away for a piece of ass—even one as fine as Lou Boyd's.

"I'm good. Other than a few brief conversations with the guardian, my relationship will be with Waylon. Besides, we need him. Oliver declared for the draft and Briggs isn't where we need him to be. We're looking shallow on the depth chart and coaching can't fix what's not there," Waylon said.

Jordan nodded, his face looking far too heavy for a forty-year-old man in the prime of his life. The divorce he was going through was starting to show. "Filling the pantry's important, and don't worry, I'll work on Briggs. You have good rapport with the guys, just be extra careful with this kid and his fine-ass sister. We don't need the NCAA sniffin' our jocks."

"They do that regardless, but there won't be any slip-ups. I can promise you that."

Abram pushed himself away from the wall and walked over to a group of players. He maintained a good relationship with most of the guys, but he had to be careful that his youth didn't mislead them into thinking they could get away with things on his watch. Always walking the line, striving for balance in all things, but especially in his professional life.

But his personal life pretty much sucked.

He had no love interest.

His friends were all busy with wives, children and keeping the grass trimmed up to standards in their gated communities. Or divorce.

At times, he was lonely, and maybe that was his own fault. He always held back, cautiously content to watch life.

He had to remember there were sacrifices when living a dream. Ever since he'd stepped on the field in

Thunder Valley on Senior Day eleven years ago, he
knew his new dream was to coach on the sidelines of
Panther Stadium. It hadn't been easy. He'd worked his
ass off, first as a graduate assistant at Tulane, preparing film, fetching coffee and compiling scouting reports. Then he'd landed a job as the quarterback's coach
at a Division II school in Nevada. After success there
with a kid who drafted third round, he moved on to
coach tight ends at Georgia Tech. Finally, when Coach
Holt took over for the Panthers three years ago, he'd
cleaned house and chosen a homegrown Louisiana boy
and ULBR alum for his tight ends coach. Didn't hurt
that Abram had worked under him in Nevada. He ten-
dered his resignation at GT, and came home, never hap-
pier to be working eighteen-hour days with little time
for himself for the school that had given him the best
memories of his life.

But sometimes in those waning hours, when he
bunked on the couch in his office, he wondered if there
couldn't be a bit more in his life than eating, breathing
and sleeping football.

For a few magical hours on a rickety bridge on Lake
Chicot, he'd tasted something as good as a go-ahead
touchdown in the fourth quarter. It had struck something in him, a longing for someone to share his life
with, for someone to dance barefoot with beneath the
light of the moon.

But that had been for one moment only.

And it was one that could not occur again. At least
not with Louise Boyd. No matter how much the thought
of her tugged at him.

He glanced back at the boys who were learning how
to become men in front of his eyes. He had to be their
example.

"Move over, Jenkins. Let me show you what you need to be doing here."

"Oh, you gonna show me, huh, Coach?" The huge fullback laughed, jabbing Porter Collins, the starting safety, in the gut. "He can't lift that— Whoa, you're stronger than you look, Coach."

Abram panted under the weight. "Let's hope I can bear it out, Jenkins."

His words held double intent—his job was on the line and he couldn't think with the other brain: the one in his khaki coaching shorts. He had to use the one between his ears.

LOU HAD TO USE THE HEART in her chest this go-around with Waylon. The past couple of months had felt like a tug-of-war with her brother, but now that school was out and summer came at them full-blast, she hoped they'd all get a reprieve.

She looked down at the envelope in her hand.

Be gentle, be supportive. Channel Mom.

Her brother shuffled along the border of the construction site, wheeling a barrel toward where another worker mixed mortar for the stacked stone that would surround the columns in front of the credit union. Lou hadn't been to the site in over three weeks; she'd been working on the construction of a dollar store in Mamou. It was amazing what could be accomplished when the weather was cooperative.

Waylon had spent the last several weeks of May doing odd jobs around the various Forcet Construction sites. It was decent money for a seventeen-year-old and kept him in peak condition for football, which was good considering he'd be heading to several football camps, including one in Baton Rouge on Monday.

Her stomach jolted at the thought.

Abram Dufrene.

She'd talked to him only once since that night almost two months before. He'd been very businesslike, introducing himself as if he hadn't seen her boobs on that pier out by Rendezvous. She played along, putting on her best guardian of the athlete voice, pretending the man didn't haunt her thoughts at odd times. Like at night when she lay alone in her bed reading historical romances, wishing the only broad shoulders or manly parts being bandied about the drawing room were Abram's. Or when she scooped dirt mindlessly at the job, wondering what could have been if she'd not been the sister of a recruit.

Or if Abram had had a condom that night.

Of course, she might as well get the thought of Abram as anything other than a coach who wanted her brother's signature on a letter of intent come February out of her mind. Because that's all he would be to her and to Waylon. She would see him again when she drove Waylon to the campus for the four-day camp. Would she still feel as jumpy about him, or would the strange attraction, the need for his lips brushing hers, the want for his hands caressing her naked skin, have faded away?

She tossed the thought out. There could be nothing between them but a common goal for Waylon. And even that was in doubt at present. Her brother still held reservations about the year he was about to face, despite her encouraging, and perhaps self-serving, pep talks.

"Hey, Way," she called through the truck window.

Her brother turned, indicated he'd be there shortly. He parked the barrow next to the stonemason and headed her way.

"What's up?"

She held up the envelope. "Got your ACT scores today."

"Thanks for ruining my day."

She smiled. "I bet they're not as bad as you think. The work you did with Mrs. Garms will pay off."

"Let me see." He swiped at the envelope she held in her hand. She pulled it back just in time. He growled.

"Let's open them tonight when we have pizza."

"Give it to me," he demanded, wiping the sweat from his hair with a sodden bandana. At that moment, he didn't sound like Way. He sounded like a man.

She held it out and allowed him to take it. She'd planned to hand them over anyhow, but couldn't resist teasing him. After all, even though she had to play mom, she was his sister. "Fine. But you have to eat with us tonight. You're going away for four days and we need to talk about how you need to handle yourself at camp."

He didn't open the envelope, and instead glared at her. "Why do you treat me like I'm a moron? I know how to act."

"I just wanted to spend time together, okay?" she said, backpedaling a little. Maybe Lori wasn't the only one who didn't want to let go. Lou needed to give Waylon some space to make his own decisions, but she was too scared of what that might lead to. Too scared he might quit the team and chuck his future football scholarship away. She kept having visions of him at twenty-three, still living at home, staining the furniture with the grease from the French fry vat. "I'll try to stop bossing you around."

He ripped open the envelope. "Yeah. Right."

She drummed her fingers on the wheel. Waylon didn't say anything for a long moment. "Well?"

He looked up and grinned. "Guess we can start the

paperwork for the clearinghouse. I got a 28 this time on the ACT."

"A 28!" Lou clapped her hands, before issuing a *whoop!* that had half the men at the site looking over at them.

Her brother's smile was sheepish and proud, and once again she found herself thinking about her mother and father and how they should have been sharing this moment with their son.

"I'm proud of you. You worked so hard."

"But you paid for the tutor. Can't wait to text Mrs. Garms. She's gonna be so pumped. This pretty much seals it. I'm going to qualify. Long as I maintain a C average next year, and I know I can do that."

Lou grabbed his arm and squeezed. "So?"

"I want to go tell Coach Landry right now. Or as soon as I finish for the day." He looked over his shoulder at the foreman and called, "Okay if I head out?"

Manuel held up a hand and nodded.

"I'll be home for supper tonight, but can we have it early? Morgan and I are going to catch a movie in Opelousas then hang with some friends."

"Sure. I'll give you a ride over to the school."

She'd finished early at the other site and her entire Saturday night lay in front of her, vacant as the house across the street—the one that had been for sale for over a year. Yeah, she had dust bunnies and spiderwebs on her social calendar. Her nonexistent social calendar. Even Lori had plans for the night—a sleepover at a friend's house.

Maybe she could call Mary Belle? She hadn't been out with any friends since the night she'd met Abram because she felt like things weren't stable enough with Waylon. But now since he seemed to be excited about his scores and ready to take the next step, she should be, too.

She pulled up to the high school, knowing Coach Landry would be there. He seemed to always be at the school. His social calendar might actually resemble her own—and he had a wife and two young children.

"See you later," she called to her brother as he climbed from the truck.

Waylon tossed a wave with the hand holding the test scores. "I'll get a ride home."

And that was that.

Lou backed out of the lot, empty save for Coach Landry's truck and a small economy parked in the Custodian parking spot, and headed toward home. As she drove, she passed streets she'd traveled as a child. Mailboxes of people she knew. Driveways of best friends' parents, teachers and people from church, and all she could think about was getting out of Bonnet Creek.

And Waylon had made the first step toward helping her make that dream a reality. For ten years she'd waited. Only two more to go and she could finally start living again.

Two more years.

But, in the meantime, maybe she could take some baby steps.

She dialed Mary Belle's number.

WAYLON STOOD AT the threshold of his head coach's office, but he didn't knock. Coach had company and it wasn't the kind Waylon needed to interrupt. He could hear the woman moaning through the closed door, and he figured she wasn't Coach's wife.

Made him feel sick.

He dropped the hand he'd raised and stepped back, shaking his head.

What the hell?

Coach had a seven-year-old son and a four-year-old daughter at home, and his wife, Amy, was the nicest lady ever. She always baked the team cookies for the first game of the season and let her kids man a lemonade stand during two-a-days. Why would Coach Landry do something so…so…stupid to his family? All for a piece of ass?

Didn't the man know what he had?

Waylon stepped away and leaned against the polished brick of the hallway. He could go and not let Coach know he'd caught him, but part of him wanted to call the man out. Because it was not only betrayal of the man's family, but betrayal of Waylon. Betrayal of everything Coach had preached in the locker room about hard work, character and morality. About putting the team first. About making good decisions on and off the field.

So Waylon didn't slink out. No. He stayed and waited for Coach and whoever it was to finish their little afternoon delight. Didn't take long. Ten minutes at most and the lock on the door clicked.

Morgan's mom stepped out, buttoning her shirt.

"Oh!" She stepped back, banging into Coach Landry. "Waylon! What are you doing here?"

He didn't respond. Just stood a moment watching Coach flounder and Morgan's mom look like a mouse trapped in a corner. She twitched and pawed at her purse hanging at her shoulder.

"Boyd," Coach Landry said, opening the door wide and trying to act like he'd not been caught cheating on his wife. "Didn't know you were stopping by today. I'm just finishing up a meeting with Mrs. Oliver."

"Yeah, I heard." He rose from where he'd slumped against the wall, but didn't stop making eye contact with his coach. *I know what you were doing, you son of a bitch.*

"Well, um, Coach Landry, nice meeting with you. I'll take all you said into consideration. See you later, Waylon," Carla Oliver said, slipping from between the two of them and clacking her way down the empty hallway toward the parking lot. Waylon hadn't seen the woman's car. She'd probably parked in the strip mall next to the high school.

Coach Landry straightened. Waylon could see the man knew he'd been caught, but he wasn't going to out-and-out admit it. "What are you doing here?"

"Got my ACT scores. You'd been bugging me about them, so I had Lou drop me off. Thought you'd want to see them ASAP." Waylon couldn't keep the coolness from his voice. He felt like he'd caught his dad screwing some bimbo. That's how much the man meant to him. His insides felt cold and empty, like a cavern he'd seen once when Lou had taken him and Lori to Arkansas. Now he wanted to leave. Wished he'd waited until the next day to meet with Coach Landry. Wished Morgan's mom wasn't such a whore.

His coach nodded. "Sure. Yeah. Let's see them."

Waylon didn't move. "I should come back later. I interrupted—"

"You didn't interrupt anything, you hear?"

He heard the warning in Coach Landry's words. "That's not what it looked like, Coach. I don't feel real comfortable right now."

"Come in here."

It was a command. Part of Waylon wanted to obey, but another part wanted to get the hell out of there. He deferred to his upbringing and stepped in the office. No sense in avoiding the talk he and Coach would inevitably have.

The door clicked shut.

"Have a seat, Way."

Waylon sat down in one of the chairs situated in front of the huge desk. It was a place he'd occupied many times. Sometimes they talked about the Saints and their chances of making the playoffs. Other times about leadership. Trust. Faith. Lots of words had been said between him and Coach. But this time, he could find no words or thoughts. He wanted a do-over or a take-back on the whole deal.

Coach Landry settled in his leather office chair and looked sort of sick. "Now, what you just think you saw or heard, Waylon, well, it's not what it seems."

"What do you think I think?"

"I think you think I'm messin' around with Mrs. Oliver."

"You weren't?"

He tented his hands and paused. "I—I—hell, this isn't easy."

Coach Landry fell silent and shook his head before swiping a hand across his broad face. Waylon could see the thoughts flittering through his mind. Deny? Tell the truth? Bribe him? Kill him? Appeal to his mercy?

Waylon decided to help him out. "You're having an affair with my girlfriend's mom."

Coach Landry's head jerked. "No, I'm not having an affair. I'm in love with her."

"But you're married. With kids. With a good job."

"I know all that, but it's different with Carla. I can't help myself. I feel what I feel."

Waylon stared at the man for a good ten seconds,

wanting to punch him for saying something so absolutely idiotic.

Feelings? That's what the man called scratching an itch with the town pass-around? He thought what he had with Carla was special? Yeah, like every other man at the mill where she worked.

"Can I say something here, Coach?"

The man's eyes flickered. "I guess you got the floor."

"No disrespect, but Carla has a dead-end job, a bit of a drinking problem and she's done half the guys at the mill. I get she has a different taste, but you're gonna jeopardize your wife, your kids and your job for a woman who's seen more action than the Sleepy Time Inn? I don't get it."

His coach shook his head. "This isn't about sex. Carla makes me feel like more than a paycheck. My heart's involved."

What an idiot.

Waylon shook his head. "I'm pretty sure you're more than a paycheck to Mrs. Landry, sir. I've seen the way she looks at you, and going by what I heard in here, I'd say it's more about getting laid than your heart."

Coach Landry pushed against the desk. "Watch the way you talk to me, Waylon. You're a kid, and you don't understand these things. And besides this isn't a discussion I should be having with you. I'm going to handle things with my wife myself and would appreciate you not carrying any tales. I don't need this to get out until I talk to Amy."

Waylon stared at the man he'd always respected, always came to for advice. His chest hurt with the betrayal. The man not only lied to everyone around him. He lied to himself. What an asshole.

"Yeah, sure. Fine. I don't run my mouth."

"Good. That's good. Amy's a good woman and doesn't deserve to find out about Carla from the community. She needs to hear it from me."

Waylon stood. "Gotta run, Coach. Lou's ordering pizza and expects me home."

Coach Landry nodded. "So how about those scores?"

Waylon's happiness had fled long ago. Heaviness sat on him like a dark monster, gleefully squashing him, drowning out anything resembling joy. "I'm good. Made a 28."

"Excellent. I'm very proud of you. You knew what had to be done and you achieved it. I'll make sure the schools you're interested in get the word. Have Lou follow up with the NCAA's clearinghouse. We want them kept up to speed so we don't get any delay in your qualification."

"Yeah. I'll do that," Waylon said, reaching for the doorknob. He wanted to get the hell out of there. Suddenly everything had shifted and the man's words felt hollow. Fifteen minutes ago, he would have reveled in the praise of his coach. But not anymore. Something had died inside him. Waylon wasn't sure what it was, but he'd never get it back. "Later."

"We're good?" Coach Landry asked, standing and pulling at the neck of his Bonnet Creek Owls polo shirt.

"Yeah, we're good." But he lied, too. He'd never be good with Coach again.

And he didn't feel like pizza or dealing with Morgan that night. He didn't want to look at his girlfriend because it felt like she was part of the betrayal, like she was tainted. And would Morgan even care her mother helped to ruin a marriage?

Waylon could almost see his girlfriend's reaction.

Lift of shoulder, quirk of lips. "What do I care? She can screw who she wants to as long as she don't screw you."

All he wanted was to be left the hell alone.

CHAPTER EIGHT

IT WAS THE START of camp and Abram didn't have to be standing in the lobby watching people spill out of cars and into the dormitory the prospects used for the ULBR skills camp. But he stood there anyway, telling himself his presence wasn't about catching a glimpse of Louise, but being among the campers he'd work with that week.

But he lied.

He'd spent the past several months trying not to think about his honky-tonk Cinderella, but it hadn't done much good. He kept thinking back to holding her in his arms out on that pier, longing to hear her laugh again, smell the flowery scent in that shiny blond hair, feel her lips beneath his.

Those inappropriate thoughts had nearly driven him crazy, and all he could hope was that he'd built her up in his mind.

She wasn't that pretty.

She couldn't be that sexy.

She wasn't that special.

He had to believe those platitudes because anything else meant he'd gone wacko, off the deep end, a couple sandwiches shy of a picnic...and it meant danger to his plans for his future.

"Hey, Coach Dufrene."

He turned to find Waylon parting the crowd of athletes and parents, heading toward him. Lou was no-where in sight.

"Waylon Boyd. Good to see you." He offered his hand and the kid took it. "Ready to hit the field?"

Waylon grinned, the smile not quite reaching his amber eyes. He'd cut his hair in a buzz and looked about as fit as a seventeen-year-old boy could. "I was born ready, Coach."

"That's what they all say, Boyd."

"Yeah, but it's true for me."

A little cocky but Abram liked a player who had swagger—as long as he could back it up. "Why don't you grab your gear and head over to the registration table? They'll get you checked in."

"Great," Waylon said, craning his head. "Let me find where my sister parked and I'll take care of business."

Abram didn't want to show his interest but couldn't help himself. "Oh, did Louise bring you?"

"Everyone calls her Lou. And yeah. She's kinda pro-tective of me and wouldn't let me catch a ride with Hayden Verdun. She doesn't trust his driving."

Abram smiled. "I have an older brother. I under-stand."

"Yeah, but did he punish you when you spit in your sister's hair?"

No. His older brother Nate had never been old enough to boss him around much, besides it didn't take long for Abram to grow taller and bigger than his older brother. Then, of course, his sister had disappeared. He only wished he could have spit in her hair. "Um, not really. But I bet you're glad to have her around."

Waylon looked thoughtful. "Yeah. Sometimes. I'll be back."

Abram wanted to follow him, but another prospect

interrupted to ask a question. By the time Abram had given instructions about the storage of medicines, Waylon had disappeared.

Just as well.

He didn't need to act like some pervert, trying to accidentally bump into Louise. He may be a little lonely because of his schedule, but he wasn't that damn desperate. Wasn't like he had to hang around a dorm he didn't have to be at with the hope of a chance encounter. Yeah, that would be pathetic.

Then he saw her.

She stood beside her brother, pointing a finger, no doubt delivering some random directive. She wore jeans and a red tank top, and Abram didn't miss several men turning to stare at her. Her long blond hair was gathered in a ponytail low on her neck and small loop earrings winked in her ears. Her skin was a soft bronze and her cheeks looked sun-kissed. She might have come from the beach or from lounging around the pool, but Abram knew she'd gained her tan from working in the dust and heat.

He'd been wrong earlier.

Louise Boyd was special. And that realization unfurled to flash a message in his head: if she's special then maybe she's worth the wait.

He couldn't stop his feet from moving toward her.

"Hey," he said, drawing her attention away from Waylon.

"Oh, Coach Dufrene. Nice to see you again." She stuck her hand out with an uncertain smile. He took it, and though he didn't believe in jolts or electricity pulsing through such minute contact, he felt something. A sort of warmth. A sort of want. She dropped his hand as quickly as she could.

"Good to see you, too, Louise."

"Louise?" The girl standing beside her laughed. "I haven't heard you called that since we were little and you were in trouble."

Louise made a face at the teen before giving a begrudging smile. "Coach Dufrene, this is my sister Lori."

He extended a hand to the girl, who had light brown hair like her brother, big blue eyes like Lou's and a sweet rounded face. "Nice to meet you, Lori. Welcome to ULBR, and I appreciate you loaning us your brother for a few days."

A flush spread across her cheeks. "You can have him longer if you want."

Waylon rolled his eyes.

"Just kidding. He's pumped about being here 'cause we're big fans. Even Louise likes the Panthers." Lori nudged her sister with an elbow.

Abram nodded. "Good. Y'all have any questions I can answer about the camp?"

"No," Louise said, tempering her quick response with a shrug and a smile. "We're good."

Lori looked around the bustling lobby of the dorm. "You need help getting your gear, Way?"

"Yeah, come help me. Give me the keys, Lou."

Louise shook her head. "I'll help you get your stuff up and then help you set up."

"I don't need help making my bed, Lou. Come on, Lori." He snatched the keys from Louise's hand and the two disappeared out the door in a wave of more players streaming inside with luggage.

Abram took Louise's arm as a big lineman barreled through with a huge duffel bag and pulled her aside. "Want to step outside?"

She licked her lips. He felt desire stir. Damn it. "Um, not really. I don't think—"

"Come on." He tugged.

"You sure are bossy," she muttered, following him as he pushed out a side door. He said a quick prayer no one would interrupt him with some inane question about where to put something or if they could bring so forth and so on with them.

They emerged on the side of the dorm sheltered by the plentiful oaks growing on the ULBR campus. It was humid, and the branches dipped low as if bowing, throwing shade on the parking area. He started walking toward a patch of grass anchored within the black soil pushed here long ago by the mighty Mississippi River, which flowed less than a mile away. Louise followed, but he felt her reluctance.

"Should we be doing this?"

He turned. "Doing what?"

"Talking like this. Isn't that a violation or something?"

"I'm talking to the guardian of one of our campers, not passing you money or promising you a Lexus."

She scuffed the ground with a sandal. Her toes were still unpolished, but dainty for a construction worker. He loved the anomaly that was Louise. She meshed practicality with utter delicious femininity. "Yeah, but still, I'm not sure we should be seen together. I talked to the lady at the NCAA and—"

"How did that go?"

A furrow popped up between her gorgeous eyes. "You interrupt a lot."

He shrugged. "I'm a coach. Guess I can be a little too demanding."

"What happened out at Lake Chicot was—"

"—wonderful?"

"See? There you go again." She looked up at him with a frown. "And I'm not sure I view it as wonderful. Maybe parts of it, but anyway, I never should have let the night get away from me. Never should have been so irresponsible. Just a mistake all around, and I'd really like to get past it."

Her words sounded rehearsed—and exactly right. But standing there with her underneath the canopy of the oak made him realize there was no getting past the crackling awareness they had for one another. She could say whatever she wanted, but he knew in his gut she wanted him. "Damn, I wish you weren't Waylon Boyd's sister."

"Why? So we could finish what we started?"

"You're damned right."

"That can't happen."

Reason jabbed him, pacifying the desire threatening to swallow him. "I know. So the interview with the NCAA?"

Louise blinked. "Oh. It went fine. I told the investigator we ran into each other, had a drink and a dance, and didn't introduce ourselves beyond first names. She acted like it wasn't a big deal. I mean, it was an accident, right?"

"Do you still think I bugged your phone or something? My being at that bar was totally incidental. I doubt I would have spoken with you if Mary Jo's boyfriend hadn't drooled all over your red high heels."

"Mary Belle. And I suppose my accusations sounded silly that day at the high school." She averted her eyes.

He knew the reason why she'd jumped his ass—she'd been embarrassed about the intimacy that had almost happened between them. "Not silly."

"I don't usually jump to conclusions, but…"

He chose to ignore the true meaning behind her actions. Anger. Fear. Shame.

"The recruiting process is hard on the whole family." It was something from his standard speech to parents, but somehow it sounded empty when he said it to Louise. "It's okay to ask questions and let the recruiter know if you feel uncomfortable."

She nodded and silence fell between them like the dappled sunlight on the scrubby grass where they stood.

Finally she looked up at him, her blue eyes so guarded, so wary of him, he nearly flinched. "Is that all you needed?"

Desire sucker punched him in the gut. Hell no, that's not all he needed. He needed her, on her back, hair spread out like that night under the moonlight. He needed to kiss her, love her, make her more than a recruit's sister.

He studied her in the afternoon light. The curve of her cheek begged to be stroked. Her blond hair looked soft, silky and all that stuff commercials told women their hair should be. Her neck was delicate and had a place his lips needed to explore. And her eyes, yeah, he could get lost in them. Now he saw why all those dead poets wrote sonnets about a woman's beauty. Now he understood.

He cleared his throat. "Just wanted to make sure our stories meshed because you and I both know it was more than that."

"Forget it, Abram."

"It's not easy though, is it? Bet you've thought about it, too."

"Too?" she echoed, her blue eyes growing soft. She blinked again and straightened. "We have to stop thinking about what could have been. This isn't about us. It's about Waylon. His future. My future."

"Your future?"

"Not with you. I don't mean—" She held up a hand. "What I mean is I have plans for my life outside of driving a front-end loader. When Waylon and Lori graduate, I will be able to move on and pursue my dreams. Understand? It's not just about Waylon. It's about all of us moving forward by making good choices."

He shook his head and pressed his lips together. Damn it. Life wasn't fair, was it? Set a prize before a man and slap his hands for reaching.

Maybe Abram needed to get out more. Go on a date. Call Alison and ask her to dinner. To a movie. To his bed. He had to be feeling all moony-eyed over Louise because he hadn't gotten laid in almost a year. That did things to a guy. Made them obsess about golden beauties. About taking their hair down so it spilled across their shoulders. About unhooking a plain white functional bra and tasting sweet plump flesh. About sliding down no doubt equally functional panties and teaching all about the pleasures of the flesh.

"Stop looking at me like that before someone sees," she said, scanning the area around them.

Abram smiled. Yeah, he needed to pay better attention to his social calendar. He was semierect standing outside a smelly men's dormitory. What the hell was wrong with him? "Guess you shouldn't look so damn sexy, Louise."

"See? That right there. Don't say those things to me."

"It must be the heat or something," he said, more to himself than her. "Sorry."

Her face held a sort of longing and at that moment, he knew she felt the same way. Regretful. Needing more, but knowing it couldn't happen. "I should go help Waylon. He hates when I baby him, but if I don't get the fitted sheet on that bed, he'll settle for sleeping on one of those gross mattresses."

"You're good to him, Lou."

She stopped in the middle of her turn toward the side door. "You called me 'Lou.'"

"Probably better if I think of you that way, huh? But in my mind, you'll always be my honky-tonk Cinderella." He brushed by her, heading back toward the dorm.

She followed him, not meeting his eyes as she stepped through the door he held open. He couldn't help himself, he took a deep breath, inhaling her sweet scent. He'd store it in his mind. Memorize it. Take it with him—

Then she looked up at him with beautiful blue eyes filled with remorse. The regret pricked him like a bramble, tangling and wrapping around him, not letting go. For the second time in the last few months, he acted out of character because maintaining who he'd always been took a backseat to touching Louise one more time.

For some reason, nothing else mattered.

"Ah, hell," he muttered, grabbing her elbow as he twisted the emergency stairwell doorknob behind him.

"Abram," Lou said, tripping over his foot. He didn't let her fall. Instead, he grabbed her around the waist and hauled her against him, capturing her mouth with his as the door clicked shut.

Her protest died as he slid a hand around to cup the back of her head. The feel of her hands wrapping around his shoulders felt like a third and long conversion. She opened her mouth and kissed him in return and it sucked him right back to that night on the dock.

Magical.

And Abram Dufrene was hungry for that particular magic in his life—and he wanted it with Louise Boyd.

She broke the kiss and looked up at him, her lips wet and doubly tempting. "What just happened?"

He tipped his forehead to touch hers and sighed.

She closed her eyes.

"Lou?"

Her eyes opened. They looked as naked as before and he saw all she desired deep inside them. "What?"

"When this is over and if you are not with someone, will you think about the concept of us?"

A storm of emotions marched across her face, and a few seconds ticked off before she pulled his arms from around her waist. She tilted her head and studied the empty stairwell towering above them. "This isn't a wanting-me-because-you-can't-have-me sort of thing, is it?"

He shook his head. "Nah. It's a wanting you because we've got something more between us than your brother. This started before Waylon."

Her eyes met his and he willed her to feel what he felt.

"I know you want more, but it's not mine to give right now."

"I'm not talking now. I'm talking later."

She nodded. "Okay. Maybe when this clears we'll see where we are."

"Yeah?"

She nodded and pushed a stray strand of hair from her eyes with a trembling hand. "But for now, it has to be business only."

"Business only," he repeated, stepping back. Damn it, he shouldn't have kissed her. It was like eating a potato chip. Can't have just one. His mind told him to stop.

But his heart didn't listen, just dragged his intentions behind, kicking and screaming. He'd never understood when people screwed up their lives because they'd acted with something other than their heads.

Now he did.

And it was going to be damn hard to uphold "business only" with Lou.

"Go find Waylon and Lori. I'm walking a flight up where I'll hopefully clear my mind and stop acting so irrationally." He started climbing the stairs.

"Hey, Abram?" Her voice echoed in the corridor.

He glanced down at where she stood with her arms wrapped around herself.

"I really wish you'd had a condom that night," she whispered, keeping her eyes on the fire hose curled near the door.

He closed his eyes and then heard the door slam shut.

LOU TRIED TO DROWN OUT Lori's soft snores as she drove back to Bonnet Creek in the waning light of the day. They'd stopped at the Mall of Louisiana before grabbing some nachos at a local Mexican place. Lori had gorged herself on chips and salsa and now happily clutched a new book about a werewolf or a grim reaper or some other creature haunting the night as she dozed beside Lou in the passenger seat.

Lou didn't know how her sister read about vampires and goblins and still managed to sleep so soundly every night. Lou liked viscounts and fancy carriages. Come to think of it, she'd always secretly been a Cinderella kind of girl.

And to one man, she was a honky-tonk version.

Her heart thumped as she thought of his words. *Think about later. The concept of us.*

She'd wanted to say yes. Wanted to admit she wanted that man more than she wanted chocolate doughnuts when she was PMSing. Oh, heck, not even close. She wanted him more than anything she'd ever wanted. So how was she supposed to proceed from this point on? Pretending there was nothing between them?

It couldn't truly be business only if she wanted to lick his stomach and wrap her legs around his waist, indulging in every naughty fantasy she'd had regarding something she'd never done.

So all she could do was cling to those sweet stolen moments—moments of magic beneath stars, inside stairwells. Okay, kissing in the stairwell of an athletic dorm hadn't been romantic, but dancing on that rickety wood pier under the light of the moon had likely been the most romantic moment of her life.

How sad was that?

And she'd tried to forget about him. Really, really tried. In fact after she'd called Mary Belle last week, she'd actually gone out to a club in Lafayette. And she'd danced with a couple of guys. And she'd let one guy kiss her even though he'd tasted like cigarettes and talked about *Jersey Shore* a lot.

Damn it. She had tried.

But living the single life hadn't been as fun as it had once sounded, and after the third time they played Lady Antebellum, she was ready to go back to her romance books and *Iron Chef*.

The irony struck her because for years she'd yearned for what she'd missed out on in life. Had resented what had happened to her that Thursday afternoon when she'd been a very normal eighteen-year-old.

When the sheriff met her at the door.

She'd just finished hammering out an article for the

last newspaper of the year—the senior edition. As the head cheerleader of the Bonnet Creek Owls, she'd been in charge of the sports pages. The article had been on senior All-District players in all sports offered at the AA school. She'd been wearing cutoffs and a Hooters T-shirt—the favorite joke around her school. She remembered being annoyed as she walked to the door because her mother was supposed to proof the article before Lou sent it to the school newspaper advisor. Then her dad was going to teach her the chords for a Clapton piece she'd been struggling with. They were both late in getting home from their new enterprise—an aerial transport company that also did photography for oil and gas companies. Her parents had bought the plane only six months before, using all their savings to launch the dream company.

But everything had changed when the sheriff met her at the front door.

"Hey, Lou." She saw the flickering emotions in his watery eyes and knew what he was about to say. "I don't really know how to say this, honey, but there's been an accident with your folks."

And with that sentence, Louise Boyd's world had flipped over. Suddenly, she was in charge of her brother and sister, two kids who cried every night for two weeks for their mom and dad. Everything she thought was important faded into the background. No more planning the party after graduation. She couldn't go. No more marking up catalogues for bedding for her dorm room at Ole Miss. She couldn't go. No hanging out with her best friends at the lake on the weekends. She couldn't go. Not without two kids—one of whom couldn't swim—a bottle of sunscreen, floaties and a box of bandages for her accident-prone brother.

Lou went from being a carefree eighteen-year-old with dreams of playing the guitar on stage to being Mrs. Doubtfire, sans the wig, padded bra and hilarity.

Nothing funny about bedwetting, putting the family pet down and holding a funeral for Snowball, while keeping up with vaccinations, dental appointments and PTA activities.

Nothing fun at all.

But it was what had to be done. Neither of her parents had had much family. Her uncle in Colorado was willing to take Waylon and Lori in, but he was a bachelor and it was so far away. They had a few cousins in town, but no one wanted to take two kids in and raise them. She'd had a hard choice to make. Send Lori and Waylon to Colorado and perhaps ruin two lives already shaken by severe grief or keep them in the same house, the same town, the same school and ruin only one person's life.

What other choice could she have made?

So she'd bucked up, sent back her music scholarship and looked for a job. Luckily, her father's best friend Tom Forcet had an idea to help her out. After spending several months in a heavy equipment training program and apprenticing under experienced workers with a few construction companies, Lou went to work handling a backhoe for Forcet Construction. At first, she'd balked at the idea, but the job pulled down a good salary, one she'd never have as a waitress or secretary. And, she was good at scooping dirt. Who would have thought that Miss Bonnet Creek Cotton Princess of 2002 would don a hard hat and steel-toed boots and work in hundred-degree heat?

So she hadn't really ruined her life, merely postponed it.

Once Waylon and Lori were both enrolled in college, standing for the most part on their own two feet, Lou was leaving Bonnet Creek and finding her own dreams again.

And someday…love.

"We almost home yet?" Lori yawned.

"Few more miles. We just passed Opelousas."

"Good. I can't wait to dive into this book. It's the second in the series and I'm dying to find out what happens to the fairy king. He's so yummy."

"A yummy fairy king?"

"Oh, he is. And so was that football coach. He burned my eyes. Is he the guy you yelled at in the hall? The one you met when Mary Belle took you out for your birthday?"

Lou didn't want her sister talking about Abram being hot. It reminded her he was indeed cornea-scalding. "I didn't yell at him—just trying to make sure Waylon is protected."

"You know, Waylon's almost the same age you were when Mom and Dad died. He's going to have to start taking care of himself. Me, too."

"Oh, well, then. Could you start by picking your clothes up off the bathroom floor? I have to wade through them every night to get to the bathtub."

Lori rolled her eyes, or at least Lou thought she did. "That's not what I meant."

"Look, I'm not trying to control Waylon. I thought Coach Dufrene had tried to pull something over on us, that's all."

"He's really cute."

"Stop talking about him like that. He's a coach. And he's way too old for you."

"But not for you, Lou-Lou."

She managed an eye roll of her own. "I can't go there with him. You know that."

"But you want to. I saw it in your eyes when you looked at him." Her sister's voice teased, but there was truth in the words. Obviously Lou had failed to hide her awareness of Abram as a man.

"You didn't see anything. He's an attractive man. Doesn't mean I'm going to jump his bones or anything."

Lori snorted. "I'd jump his bones."

"No, you won't. I'll kill you if you do any jumping."

The exit to Ville Platte appeared and Lou steered toward home, hopeful she could do a better job of hiding her feelings for sexy Abram Dufrene before September hit. Once the season started, he'd become a fixture in their lives along with many other coaches clamoring for Waylon's services as tight end.

Maybe she needed a distraction. Joey Fontenot, the local produce manager at Dixie Foods, had repeatedly asked her for a date, and she had repeatedly turned him down. Maybe it was time to say yes. Joey couldn't be that bad…and she would know if what she felt for Abram wasn't merely her libido kicking into overdrive.

Besides she had to keep taking those baby steps, didn't she?

And then if…

No. She couldn't allow herself to dwell on Abram's last question of her. The concept of us.

Stop it, Lou. Take the date with the perfectly nice grocery store manager with the sweet smile and slightly pudgy middle. Joey's a decent guy.

But he wasn't Abram.

And that was the problem.

WAYLON WATCHED the other players run up and down the indoor practice facility. When his turn came, he effortlessly moved around the obstacles and grinned at the coach clocking his time.

The man lifted his eyebrows.

The extra time he'd spent running stadiums and focusing on lunges had paid off. He felt good doing the drills. He'd gotten faster, and even the head coach, Leonard Holt, had stopped to watch him.

"Get some water," one coach called after blowing the whistle.

Waylon moved to the water station, falling into line. There was some good talent at the camp, but that was to be expected. ULBR wasn't the only camp held in the state, but it was popular because the facilities were awesome and there was a good chance of someone who'd been flying under the radar getting some looks. Waylon wasn't under the radar. He was flying high above it in the limelight, but he tried not to let that affect him.

He wanted to be grounded in this whole process.

But he was scared.

Everything seemed too big and was coming at him too fast.

He hadn't expected this level of interest, but as he got bigger, faster and stronger, he'd mowed down the competition on the field. Coach Landry had started talking, promoting, putting his name out there, and before he knew it, scouts had shown up to Podunk Bonnet Creek to watch him practice. Then they came to his games. Recruiting services called. And suddenly, he was this blue-chip recruit with colleges chomping at the bit to get him on their incoming 2012 roster.

Flattering.

But overwhelming.

"Yo, Boyd, you shave time off the shuttle?"

He inclined his head toward Hayden Verdun, who

played for the Owls' archrivals, the Ville Platte Bull-dogs. They'd played against each other their whole lives. "Been working out every night doing stadiums and crap. Probably going to train with Cody for the rest of the summer."

"Cody? You never worked with him before. Thought your coach has always been your guy."

What was he going to say? He caught Coach Landry screwing around and now he didn't want to be around the man? But it was the truth. He'd decided to start working with Cody Craven, a popular personal trainer at Body by Cody in Ville Platte. He just couldn't be around Coach right now. "Trying something new is all."

"Cool. That stuff with your sister and Coach Du-frene blow over?"

Shit. Waylon turned around, tossed the paper cup in the trash and jerked his head indicating Hayden needed to step out of line to have this talk.

Hayden got water and walked over to where Waylon stood near a collapsible bench.

"What makes you think there was anything between Lou and Coach Dufrene? Everyone knows what hap-pened was a mixup. Why bring it up in front of those guys?"

Hayden made a face. "I'm not outing your sister, dude. Just asking. I saw her and Coach Dufrene at the dorm. Looked intense, you know?"

Hayden had never been a good friend. They'd done some 7-on-7 tournaments together before, and the defen-sive end was the only other prospect from his area being looked at by college scouts. But Hayden wasn't get-ting the serious looks his father wanted, which seemed to stick in the craw of both father and son. Waylon smelled trouble brewing and didn't like where Hayden was headed. "Well, any time the NCAA is involved, things are tense. Nothing happened between them, so it's no big deal."

"Not what my dad heard, but whatever. See you around," Hayden said, strolling back toward the tables holding water where many of the other campers had gathered. Hayden high-fived a strong safety out of O. Perry Walker in New Orleans and then punched a wide receiver from Georgia on the arm.

Waylon felt like punching something himself—or maybe someone. Hayden would do. The dude was jealous because Waylon was getting more press, more looks and more letters of interest. Hayden wasn't a bad end but he wasn't particularly as big or as fast as he needed to be. His words told Waylon what he needed to know. Hayden was not a friend and would look to make trouble for Waylon if he could…or if his father could.

And they both would use whatever necessary.

Even the stupid accidental incident between Coach Dufrene and Lou. Anyone who knew Lou knew nothing happened. His sister wasn't the type to mess around with any guy, even if she'd been drinking. That's what made her so tough to deal with sometimes. She never messed up, always figuring the checkbook down to the last cent, always remembering to put the trash out on trash day, put on sunscreen and send birthday cards a week ahead of time. She'd never do something as inappropriate as hooking up with some random guy at a bar. She didn't even hook up with guys she'd dated for weeks or months. Not that she'd done much dating at all.

Hayden was barking up the wrong tree if he was looking to find something going on between Dufrene and Lou.

CHAPTER NINE

ABRAM OPENED HIS office door to find his mother and sister standing in the hall of the Football Operations building.

"Surprise!" Picou said, with a smile the size of Dallas. His sister, Sally, didn't look as excited about the ambush. In fact her blue eyes seemed to apologize. "Your sister wanted to see where you work, and since she was in town when I was in town, I told her I'd show her the posh digs the Panthers operate in."

"Mom," he managed to say, stepping forward and closing the office door behind him. "Uh, I'm finishing up camp and I'm late. I should be at the practice facility by now."

Sally smiled. "Sorry, Abram. We should have called. Picou thought you might get away for lunch."

"Oh, well, I can't do lunch, but if you want, you can go with me. I've been intending to have you up for a while anyway." He wanted to step carefully around Sally because at times she seemed so lost within their family. Enola Cheramie was in hospice care and not doing well, and Sally clung to the past she knew rather than confronting the uncertain, and sometimes uncomfortable, present. He didn't understand why it was taking her so long to come around and accept who she was—a Dufrene.

"See? I told you he wouldn't mind. Now you'll get

to see some of those strapping young men gallivanting around in those tight shirts that show their muscles." Picou nodded as if ogling football players was a national pastime.

"Mom, that's disturbing."

Picou laughed. "For your sister, dear. She's only twenty-seven. And there are some handsome coaches around here. I've seen them with my own two eyes."

Sally shook her head. "I'm good."

Picou patted her daughter's shoulder. "Dear, you have to want to get over that accountant."

"He wasn't an accountant. He taught fifth grade."

"Well, he looked like an accountant." Picou waggled her fingers at Sue Ann, the receptionist he shared with two other coaches. His mother wore a flouncy skirt that brushed her bright orange toenails, which peeked out from Birkenstocks, and she wore a pink flower behind one ear. She was unequivocally Picou.

On the other hand, his sister was subtle in her beauty. Long-limbed and browned by the Louisiana sun, Sally wore a printed sundress and tasteful silver sandals that matched the hoop earrings in her ears. Her long straight brown hair framed violet eyes that seemed to stay wary no matter what the situation. He supposed being kidnapped as a child did that to a person.

"Come on," he said, ushering them down the hall past the coaches' offices and meeting rooms. "We're heading to the indoor practice facility. Let's take the stairs so you can see all the trophies."

After spending more minutes than he could afford looking at the exhibits in the grand foyer of the Football Operations building, they finally emerged in the colossal practice facility where Head Coach Holt addressed the prospects along with their families. He hoped like hell his mother didn't interrupt the man because though Picou had good Southern manners sometimes she elected not to use them.

His eyes sought his guys, the ones he'd be calling come the first of September, balancing their recruitment with a very demanding football season. He had four present in this early camp. Three more expected in the one in July. His eyes naturally landed on Waylon, his top must-get prospect. Who was he kidding? His gaze skipped by the big tight end and landed on Lou.

She sat with her chin cupped in her hand, and like a magnet, her gaze found him. He felt a little pulse jumpstart inside him, and he wondered if the longing he felt was like a flare going off in the cavernous space. Could everyone see how badly he wanted her?

But no one paid attention to his hunger.

Or Lou's.

Because even though many yards separated them, he could see she felt the same way. She turned her head, breaking the bead they had on one another.

"Who are all these people?" his mother whispered loudly. Several coaches turned toward them. Picou smiled and did the finger waggle at them. She even winked at Jordan Curtis who'd been to Beau Soleil for dinner before.

"They're high school kids attending a summer camp. Several are serious prospects for the Panthers for our next recruiting class." He whispered his response softly, so his mother would get the hint.

"Oh, so you're trying to impress them."

"No, they are trying to impress us. We're ULBR."

A smattering of applause told him camp was officially over, but he still needed to make final contact with the four he'd being calling upon in the next school year. Might be nice to use his mother and sister to portray a more intimate, family-like vibe. "Come meet the guys I'll be recruiting this year."

"Ooh, that would be so nice. I can help you get them to come to ULBR."

"You don't need to do that, Mom. Just be yourself. Kind of." He must have looked alarmed because Sally stifled a smile. Though Sally had only been reconciled with his mother for less than a year, she'd learned the power of Picou. He jerked his head, and Sally followed him and their mother across the turf toward where parents and campers stood in clumps. Some campers didn't have parents present; others seemed to have brought the whole family. Either way, a personal send-off was always a good idea.

He pinned Lou, Lori and Waylon down, and started working his way toward them, allowing Picou to be charming and his sister to lend sensibility to the conversations with the prospects.

Finally, he reached Waylon. He lightly touched Lou on the elbow and felt her reaction—immediate awareness.

"Waylon, you looked good throughout the whole camp," he said.

The boy smiled, and Abram noticed his grin was similar to his sister's—when she managed a smile. "I feel good. I've got a better idea of what I need to work on, and I'm going to take that one blocking drill back to Coach Landry. Also, I appreciate the time you took with me."

"Seeing a guy want to get better motivates me to be a better coach, so you don't have to thank me." He stepped back and placed a hand on his mother's back. "I'd like you to meet my mother, Picou, and my sister, Sally. This is the Boyd family—Waylon, Lori and Lou."

Picou smiled warmly and extended her hand, first to Lou then to Waylon. She actually reached out and pinched Lori on the cheek. The girl made a startled face, shifting wary eyes to her older sister, but smiled regardless.

Lou shifted her gaze around, not uncomfortable, but definitely not at ease. Guess she hadn't expected him to throw his mother at her. Not that there was any reason for her to feel weird about it. They weren't in any sort of relationship. Yet. In fact, he had to spend the next few months forgetting about how delicious the blond construction worker tasted.

Lou licked her lips.

Damn it.

"Nice to meet you both. Waylon has enjoyed getting to know your son. He's been—"

"—the best coach a boy could have. Yes, I know. He was like that from the very beginning. I remember once when Della was learning to crawl… Um, Della is Sally, but that's a long story. Anyway, Abram was about seven years old, and he'd get down on his belly and scoot, trying to show her how to crawl. The boy was born to coach."

Great. His mother sounded like she was trying to sell a used car to the Boyds, and like she might launch into telling them every wonderful thing he'd ever done. "Okay, Mom, the Boyds are probably ready to get on the road. Let's not hold them up."

Waylon caught his eye and within the boy's gaze Abram saw a mixture of bemusement and, perhaps, a longing. This family had no parents to chatter on and on about accomplishments. Waylon had missed out on a crazy mother laundry-listing his accomplishments. Had missed out on an overbearing, but well-intentioned father looking out for his son's best interests. Waylon and Lori had been cheated, yet also blessed with a person who'd sacrificed in likely more ways than could be seen.

That person looked at him. "You're not holding us up, and I enjoyed meeting your family and appreciate the staff here at the camp. Waylon just mentioned how much he learned."

Sally smiled. "As a teacher, I love hearing the impact I make on my students. I bet Abram feels the same."

His sister looked at him as if she'd imparted something brilliant. He bobbed his head.

"It's wonderful to be able to make an impact in someone's life." Lou's words were simple, but the emotions that moved through them, along with the way her blue eyes met his sent a zing of something more than awareness between them.

Could everyone see the invisible ties that linked them?

Or was it merely wishful thinking on his behalf?

"You should come to Beau Soleil for dinner sometime," his mother said.

Okay. Yep. Others could see it.

He looked at his mom. Her violet eyes assessed Lou. It was as if Picou had morphed into the bionic woman and calculations were ongoing inside her head. If he listened closely enough, he could hear the *baw wah wah wah* sound of the matchmaking scan in process.

Lou lifted her eyebrows. "Uh, well, that—"

"—can't happen, Mom. Waylon is a prospect and

there are rules regarding contact," Abram said, lifting his gaze from the two families assembled around him. Most people were leaving the facility and with the initial hurdle in Waylon's recruiting process, he didn't need the extra scrutiny of the staff. He also didn't need his mother trying to interfere in any way, especially in his love life. He and Lou were a non-issue at this juncture and they both needed to tread carefully, which meant he could not do something as stupid as he did a few days before. Eyes would be watching, followed by tongues wagging.

"What would be the harm, Nate?" Picou shrugged one shoulder.

"Abram," Sally said.

"What, dear?" Picou turned to her daughter.

"That's Abram. You called him Nate."

"I know who he is. I gave birth to him, and this one nearly killed me he was so big. Anyhow—" Picou swiveled her head. "Coach Holt, come over here a minute."

Oh. No.

Leonard Holt's head lifted at the sound of Picou's voice, periscoping until his gaze fell upon Abram's mother. He ended his conversation and like an obedient spaniel, headed their way. His mother smiled the smile she reserved for helpless men. "Leo, darling, tell Abram I can have Lou and Lori Boyd over to Beau Soleil for dinner. How in the devil could that be seen as anything other than Southern hospitality? I have no stake in football."

She said "football" as if it were a dirty word.

Coach Holt, recently divorced and not easily swayed by anyone, gave his mother an uncharacteristic smile. "Why, Picou, I doubt the NCAA could withstand any assault you'd launch upon them. As long as this is not an attempt to recruit Waylon nor sway him or his family in any way toward ULBR, you can have friendships."

"Exactly." Picou smiled, placing a hand on the coach's forearm. "I certainly support Abram in his endeavors, but I've never done anything outside the rules…much."

Leonard raised one of his bushy eyebrows. "Picou Dufrene, you are something else, woman."

Abram thought he might vomit. On the other hand, his mother preened. "And what about you? When can I expect you to come to Beau Soleil for dinner?"

Sally glanced at him with wide eyes, and Abram tried not to make a face. His mother and Coach Leonard Holt were flirting. Ugh. Talk about a weird situation all around. He turned to Waylon. "Let me walk you guys out."

Lou's face was absolutely straight, but amusement shone in her eyes. Waylon tapped on his phone. "Sure."

"I'm coming with y'all," Sally said, almost too quickly.

They walked toward the open door, leading toward the outdoor practice fields. Sally made conversation with Lou while Waylon messed with Lori in true older brother fashion, aiming to embarrass her in front of the other prospects making their way to their cars. It was obvious Waylon and Lori had a healthy relationship—and also obvious Lori had gone to great pains to fix herself up for the trip to pick up Waylon. She wore a lipstick too dark for her and shorts a little too short—all deemed to attract the other boys in camp.

Abram took in the early summer afternoon as Lou told Sally about their parents' infatuation with country music and thus the reason their names were so odd.

"So I get Waylon's name obviously and Lori being short for Loretta Lynn. But Louise? I don't remember a country music legend with that name," Sally remarked as they neared the parking lot.

"Well, there used to be a show on TV hosted by Barbara Mandrell, and my daddy had a thing for Louise, one of the Mandrell sisters. My momma told him he could never have that Louise, but he could have me. I hated the name because I sound like an old blue-haired lady, but at least he didn't like Irlene best. Can you imagine?"

Sally laughed, and Abram realized it was the first time he'd heard his sister do so. He glanced at Lou and Sally, two women alike in age, disposition and beauty, not to mention, each of them carried her vulnerability far below the surface, cautiously guarding herself against any and all who might crack them.

"Well, that's a silver lining. Plus, I like the name Lou. It's got character," Sally said.

Waylon snorted. "Sounds like a sweaty old fat guy who eats bologna and feeds stray cats."

"Nah, more like a construction worker," Lori said, nearly tripping over one of the ever-present roots of the live oaks dotting the campus.

"Real funny, Lori," Lou said, explaining to Sally she worked for a construction company.

They neared an older truck badly in need of washing. Lou pulled out the keys and tossed them to Waylon. "You drive."

"But I want to drive. You said I could practice." Lori folded her arms across her chest and made a standard teenager face. One that looked both threatening and whiny.

"Not in Baton Rouge."

"He's only a year and a half older, and you said once I got my permit I could drive every now and then. I need to practice."

Waylon slid in and fired up the truck. "Too late, shrimp."

"This sucks!" Lori said, opening the passenger door and slapping her brother on the back of the head.

"Yay. Fun," Lou said under her breath, lifting the duffel Waylon had dropped when he caught the keys. "Thanks so much for all your help, Coach Dufrene."

"Sure," he said, wanting so badly to say more. To tell her how awful it was that things had to be this way. "I'll be in touch in September, and we'll arrange for Waylon to take an official visit later in the fall."

"Nice to meet you," Sally said with a wave.

"Wait!"

Abram turned, along with both women, to see his mother hoofing it across the campus toward the parking lot where they stood. She blazed a trail in her flouncy skirt and jangling bracelets, waving a car to stop so she could cross in front of it.

"Lou, I wanted to get your telephone number and address so I might send you a proper invitation to Beau Soleil. It's a wonderful house. They filmed a movie there just this past year, can you believe? A horror film, but no matter, the house was in many of the shots. You will come for a visit, won't you?"

"Um, I guess. Of course."

Picou beamed at her, and then propped an overly-dramatic finger upon her cheek. "And maybe one or two of my children could happen to stop by."

"Oh, Mrs. Dufrene, I'm afraid you have the wrong idea. I don't have—"

"What she's trying to say, Mom, is that if you're thinking—"

"I'm not thinking anything other than making some new friends in Bonnet Creek," his mother said, with a shrug practiced by a professional ingénue. "That's okay, right?"

Lou's cheeks were pink. She nodded her head. "Sure."

"After all, I would never interfere in the lives of my children. They are all grown and can choose their friends for themselves. No one needs his or her mother arranging things, right?"

"Mom," he warned.

"No, I'm sure they don't." Lou averted her eyes and dug in her purse for a pen before scratching contact info on an extra envelope. Picou met Abram's gaze over her bowed head. And winked.

Oh. God.

His mother's mission in life was to see all of her children in healthy relationships, with lots and lots of grandchildren galloping under the oaks of Beau Soleil. She could claim whatever she wanted, but she had plans for Lou.

And if he were wise, he'd stay far away from his mother—and the lovely blonde. One day he might have a shot at something with Lou, but until then he had to forget he wanted her a little more than he did her brother.

It stunned him to realize how true his last thought was, and it scared him. He was on a professional track moving full-steam ahead toward his goals in coaching. He didn't want to jump track over a woman. So he needed to focus on Waylon and try to bury the agreement he had with Lou. He had many months before him where she could be nothing to him but the sister of a recruit.

He only wished he could make himself believe it.

WAYLON FOUND LOU washing dishes in the kitchen. Lou was always washing, waxing or fixing something as if the ghost of their parents sat on her shoulder with looks of disapproval. That was Lou's problem. She didn't know how to let things slide.

"You're not really going to go to Coach Dufrene's mother's house, are you?" he asked, wiping milk from his upper lip. Like he needed her to bitch about him drinking out of the carton again.

Her eyes zeroed in on the milk carton on the counter behind him. Busted.

"What was I supposed to say? I couldn't be rude."

"She thinks you're into Coach." He ignored the fact Lou kept looking at the half-gallon and leaned against the fridge.

Lou pulled the plug on the sink, allowing the dirty dishwater to drain away. "Can't stop what other people think."

"You aren't, are you?" Some little bubble of fear surfaced when he thought about Hayden and his words of portent. *Portent* was a word he'd learned for the college entrance test, and warnings were popping all over the place. Even he saw that.

"What?"

"Into Coach."

"Of course not. He's nice-looking and probably the catch of the year, but I'm not really in the market. Besides, it would be a colossal conflict of interest."

"Because of me?" He didn't have to ask the question. Of course, he knew the answer. Lou always did the right thing, and that's why sometimes she was so hard to talk to. Besides, she wouldn't jeopardize his recruitment. Sure, she acted like it was all about him, but he knew she couldn't wait to get rid of him and Lori.

"I don't really want to discuss this, Way. It's non sequitur."

"What does that mean?" That word hadn't been on his list.

"It's not relative to what can happen. Coach Dufrene is recruiting you to play for his university. All contact must be documented. The same goes for me because I'm your guardian. Dating would be a little too much contact regardless of whether we wanted it or not."

Longing tinged her words, and even though she wouldn't admit it, he could tell Lou wished things were different. For a moment he almost felt sorry for her. Had to suck to be Lou sometimes. "So if I weren't a recruit, you wouldn't be interested?"

"I'm not looking for a relationship right now. You've got a big year coming up, and Lori's got the SATs this year. I'm busier than ever at work, there isn't time for—"

"—a life for you?"

She jerked back. "I have a life."

"No, I mean someone for you. You don't do anything for yourself. I hadn't really thought about it until today when I saw how you were around Coach, but you don't have much of a life. Don't you think you should get out more?"

Lou tossed the towel onto the chipped ceramic counter. "What do you mean how I acted around the coach?"

"You know, like a girl," he said, feeling like a scientist poking a specimen to see what might happen. He'd never thought about Lou as a woman. Hell, she'd practically dried up and withered in the best years of life, but it wasn't too late. If she started wearing girl clothes and hanging out more with Mary Belle and Brittney.

"I didn't act any particular way around Abram. I acted like Lou."

"You just called him Abram."

Busted.

And she knew it. Lou snapped her mouth closed. "Put the milk back in the fridge and stop drinking out of it."

Waylon couldn't stop the grin that twitched at his lips. God, he loved the upper hand. "I know girls, Lou. I'm around them all the time, and I know when a girl is into me. So I'm not stupid."

"Well, you can know this. Nothing is going to happen between me and Abram Dufrene while he's recruiting you. No matter what I feel toward him. Right now my goal is simple. Get you into college, self-sufficient and out of this frickin' town so I can get out, too." She slammed the cutlery drawer and pushed by Waylon.

"Hey," he called following her. "Why are you so pissed?"

She stopped in front of where Lori sat watching a rerun of *Gilmore Girls*. "I'm not pissed. And you should watch your language."

"Wait a sec, you're leaving Bonnet Creek?" Lori sat up.

"Yeah. Go figure. I never wanted to live here, not that you two would ever know that." Lou jabbed a finger at him then his sister. He swore he saw tears swimming in her eyes, but it could have been the flickering light of the TV. "It's always about you. About lunch money or clean socks. About new cleats or selling cookies for the Girl Scouts. You ever think I might not want to do any of this? Ever strike you that I'm a twenty-seven-year-old dried-up spinster?"

He thought about hugging Lou, but she looked mad enough to hit him. "We didn't sign up for any of this, either."

Lori's mouth got that crying look, all narrow and trembly, but she didn't say anything. Just looked at their older sister with scared eyes that seemed to deflate Lou.

"You know, now is not the time to talk about my future. What I do after you both reach a legal age isn't anyone's concern but mine." Lou stalked to the TV and punched a button. "And you're watching too much TV, Lori. You're frying your brain."

Lou stomped out of the living room, leaving them looking at each other.

"I can't believe Lou wants to leave Bonnet Creek," Lori said, pulling a throw pillow into her lap and twisting the fringe.

"Can't you? Who the hell wants to stay in this crappy town?"

"I would," Lori said, looking back at the blank screen.

"Grow up, Lori," he said, grabbing the truck keys and opening the front door.

"Way—" Lori said, jumping up from the couch.

"I'm going out," he yelled loud enough for Lou to hear. He ignored his other sister, standing there looking lost.

Life felt too intricate right now, like the pieces of that model tank Aunt Ora had bought him once. Million pieces spread out everywhere that couldn't possibly come together to make anything that would work. He'd thrown that damn thing in the garbage after a few days.

He'd tried to do the right things, but they turned out feeling wrong. The same town, the same friends, the same house full of rules had him feeling like he was choking. Feeling like he wanted to say the hell with it and throw it all in the garbage.

Something was wrong with him.

And that something scared him.

He didn't know how he'd keep himself together for the upcoming year.

CHAPTER TEN

October 2011

IN A WHIRL OF meetings and camps, Abram's summer
flew by. Before he blinked the football players were re-
porting to camp, and two-a-days had him intense and
focused on the development of his tight ends, along
with the offense in general. Carl Domaigne, the offensive coordinator, had the coaches in daily meetings focusing on getting the new scheme perfected. Abram
barely had time to think about clean underwear, much
less the empty spot in the bed he never slept in anyway. His couch had been his bed for more nights than
not. The opener against Oregon State came and went
with a win and some smaller out of conference schools
quickly dealt with. Now the first SEC game loomed that
weekend, and Mississippi State was no slouch under
Coach Dan Wheeler. The Bulldogs' defense was stout
and came at the offense like dogs possessed.

It had been a hard week of practice, but he looked
forward to tonight and another chance to talk to Lou—
after he spoke with Waylon, of course.

Once he packed his bags for the weekend and made
a few calls to other recruits in his area, he collapsed on
the leather couch, placed a cold Abita beer on the coffee
table, and turned the volume on the TV down.

The phone rang three times before Lou answered. "Hey."

"Hey, how're things in Bonnet Creek?"

Her voice was low and slightly husky. He'd never heard her sing, but somehow he knew she'd have that smoky Adele tone. "Okay. The Owls have a big game against Mamou tomorrow night and Way's been practicing hard which is good because it's keeping him focused. Let me hand the phone to him."

He took a draw on his beer, smiling as he heard Lou calling for Waylon and the phone scrabbling around on something. Maybe a table or the couch. Either way he liked to imagine her in her nightgown, hair down, maybe a cup of tea or even a glass of wine in hand.

"'Lo?" Waylon's voice jerked him from his tame fantasy. The kid sounded tired. Whether it was as a result of the incessant phone calls from the many Division I schools across the country or from the practice he'd finished several hours ago, Abram could only guess.

"How are things going, Waylon?"

"Fine. I guess."

Yes, these high school athletes were whizzes when it came to the art of conversation. "Good. Good to hear. Y'all ready for tomorrow night? I hear the Demons run the spread. They got a good sophomore receiver."

"Yeah, but our D can handle them."

More silence. Usually Abram had little trouble building a relationship with his recruits. Most were happy to talk about themselves, spouting new clean jerk records and shuttle times. Some even talked about movies, girls and, gasp, football. But not Waylon. Abram felt like every response was forced. The only upside of the conversation resulted when Waylon turned the phone over to Lou.

And that shouldn't be happening.

Abram needed to reach Waylon on some level.

"Spoke with Coach Landry last week when he came to campus for a workshop. He said you'd stopped coming by his office this year. He seems worried about you."

"He don't need to worry about me. He's got a full plate on his own."

He didn't miss the edge to the words. Waylon's performance on the field and in the classroom were satisfactory, but his attitude had steadily devolved into surliness. Seemed to have something to do with David Landry. Abram should drop it. A kid's relationship with his high school coach wasn't any of his concern. His concern was to get Waylon Boyd's signature on that letter of intent come the first of February, but for some reason he dived in anyway. "You having a problem with Coach Landry?"

"No. Not really."

"Just something you don't want to talk about?"

"I got no problem with him. I do what he tells me."

"Listen, Waylon, I know your coach is worried, and I sense your sister is, too. You need to talk to someone if you are having problems. Being recruited is stressful."

"You volunteering to be my shrink?"

"No, but I can lend an ear and help you find someone to talk to if it comes to that."

"I don't need a shrink. I need to have everyone get off my case. That's what I need." Waylon's voice carried anger and fear. Abram had heard the same tone in his younger brother Darby's voice years ago. When fear makes a home in a teenage boy, it always finds an outlet. Usually, it's not a pleasant one. Darby ended up in military school, a gift from Martin Dufrene, who would not tolerate watching his youngest son self-destruct.

Abram's father was a hard taskmaster, but he knew what was right for Darby. Hadn't Darby straightened up, gone on to the Naval Academy and then law school?

Abram liked to think he balanced his father's discipline with levelheaded guidance and the end result was a good coach. It bothered him Waylon didn't have another man to help him through this stressful period. Lou was his sister and guardian, and though he could see how much she loved her brother, he knew the boy would never open up to her. His relationship with David Landry had seemed solid when he'd first met Waylon, but something wasn't right there, either.

"Fine. But outside of recruiting you, Waylon, I've grown to care for your family. I don't want to see you struggle on your own with this. You need someone you can depend on to talk things out with you."

"Lou does that. Look, I'm good. Seriously."

But the words were a mere platitude by a teen not wanting to address the things that were hard in life. He needed a guide, someone who had no stake and could bring some levity to his situation. It wasn't up to Abram to provide that because he definitely had a stake in what Waylon decided to do regarding his college football career. "Okay, let's talk a little bit about how we can fit you in our scheme, about what the Panthers can do for you and about what you can do for us."

Abram launched into a pretty much one-sided conversation about Waylon's talents combined with the possibilities ULBR could give him. Abram followed his usual song and dance, tailoring the offer to the boy, after having gauged what was important to him from the prior discussions they'd had.

Finally, Waylon said, "Wanna talk to Lou now?"

Abram gave an inner sigh of relief. "Sure."

Waylon fumbled the phone for a moment before he heard Lou's voice. "Hey."

"You know I like to talk about you rather than your brother usually, but something's up with Waylon."

She breathed heavily into the phone. "I know. He's not been himself for a while. I get several weeks of easygoing, but then it's back to this sullen, weird Waylon. I don't really know what to do."

"I think it involves Landry somehow. Waylon told me he's been working out with a new guy, and every time I mention his coach, he acts strangely."

"I can't imagine what's wrong. David has always been a steady influence on Waylon, and I know he's the closest to a father figure Waylon's had since Dad died." He heard the worry in her voice and felt powerless.

"Maybe you should talk to Landry and see if you can figure this out. Trying to make this decision carries a lot of stress for a young guy. He's handling calls, letters, pressure from all sorts of directions, and he needs all the support he can get." He wished he were there to push the blond strands from her eyes, to cup her cheek, murmur in her ear all would be well.

But he couldn't, so he stuck to what he'd been over the last few weeks—strictly professional with a side helping of friend, even if attraction lurked around the corner of his mind. His emotions were more tangled than the vines growing along the bank of the Bayou Teche behind Beau Soleil. And like the sucking mud of the bank, he was helpless to fight against it.

But he was giving it the old college try.

In a few weeks, he'd be in Bonnet Creek to attend the Owls' game against Ville Platte. He'd sit in the stands, watching Waylon, trying not to watch Lou.

He'd see her…and want to touch her. Kiss her. Claim her as his own.

Shit.

"How are things looking for Mississippi State this weekend? Y'all ready for the Bulldogs?" Her question was soft and he heard the click of a door shutting. Maybe she'd gone to her room. He liked to think she wanted to talk to him in private.

"Always," he said. He didn't want to talk about football. Weird. "What about you? What will you play tonight? Last time you said you were practicing Zeppelin."

"I don't know. I might be too tired to drag my guitar out tonight."

"What kind of guitar do you have?"

"You're interested in my guitar?" He could hear amusement in her voice and it warmed him. Football, Bulldogs and Waylon faded to the background as a sort of contentment settled around him. He wanted to imagine Lou strumming the guitar, her hair around her face, her eyes narrowed in concentration as she sang and played.

"I play my daddy's Taylor. It's an acoustic that was his pride and joy, and I love fullness of the sound. Reminds me of all the times I sat with him and learned chords on my old Epiphone."

"What songs did he teach you?"

"Well, all kinds. My dad liked country music best, but he also liked some of the singer-songwriters of the '70s, like Carole King, Gordon Lightfoot and James Taylor. I play those a lot because they remind me of him and life when it was simple. What music do you like?"

And so it went, Lou talking about music, baking cookies for the pep rally bake sale and Lori's grades for the first nine weeks, him watching the minutes tick down on the time limit he was allowed to talk with a recruit or his parents.

"I've got to go, Lou."

"I know."

"As always, it's been good talking with you. Tell Waylon I wish him luck tomorrow night."

"Okay. Bye."

The phone clicked and the line went dead. For some reason he wanted to throw it across the room. What kind of life was this for a thirtysomething man? No life outside work and when he did get a few minutes, he salivated over talking to a woman he couldn't have. But maybe come March…if she still wanted him…if he still wanted her.

If…if…if—his life revolved around ifs.

Hard to live with uncertainty.

LOU STUDIED Joey Fontenot as he flagged down a waitress to complain about how his steak was cooked. A man had a right to have his steak cooked as he wished, but Joey had already sent it back once.

He turned to her. "I work in a store around meat every day. I know a good cut, and this is not one."

"Mmm-hmm," she said, chasing her chicken around with a cranberry. Her salad was pretty good, but her appetite was nil.

Ironically, after she'd hung up with Abram on Thursday, Joey had phoned. At first she thought it was Abram calling back, and had even teased him about wanting her to sing him to sleep. Poor Joey had been plenty confused.

And because her heart had felt bloody rare after her conversation with the sexy ULBR football coach, she agreed to have dinner with Joey on Saturday night.

She'd convinced herself it was best to move on, and going out with Joey had seemed like a step in the right direction.

But it had been a misfire. She should have never trusted a knee-jerk reaction.

"So Waylon played good last night. I figure the Owls might make the playoffs." Joey waved emphatically at the waitress who seemed determined to ignore him.

Lou didn't want to talk about her brother, football or playoffs, but it was better than talking about herself. "Yeah, they might make it this year."

"He's good. Getting lots of looks, I hear. Heard ULBR, Bama and Texas are all treating him like a bone." He swiveled his head, and Lou wondered if he might flag the woman down with his napkin.

Yep. Like a flagman for NASCAR.

The waitress made a face and headed their way, parking her hip against the table, lifting a painted-on eyebrow. "Yeah?"

"Now the steak is overcooked. I specifically asked for medium. I know what medium is, and this—" he pointed at the steak "—is not it. Get me a new steak."

"You said you wanted it cooked more. We cooked it more." Her chin jutted out and her eyes dared him.

"I'm sending this back." Joey crossed his arms and gave her a condescending look for a guy who spent most his time feeling melons and rearranging squashes.

The waitress whipped his plate up and threw daggers at him with her eyes. Lou smiled and gave one of those "what you gonna do?" looks, glad she already had her salad because whatever Joey got back would likely have a special sauce.

Her date leaned back with a self-satisfied smirk. He probably deserved special sauce.

"So, what school is Waylon leaning toward?"

Suddenly it struck her. This date wasn't about her—it was about her brother, about being in the know with his recruitment. "Did you ask me out because you wanted to go out with me? Or did you really want to go out with my brother?"

"Huh?"

"Is this about Waylon?"

"No. About you. Look, I'm nervous. I figured it was a safe topic." He shifted in his chair and looked contrite. "Truly."

"Okay." She and Joey Fontenot were going nowhere past this date, but she didn't want the rest of the evening to suck. They still had to drive back to Bonnet Creek. Plus, Joey always saved her the best watermelons. "I wasn't trying to jump to conclusions. I've been assaulted by recruiting all week, so I was hoping this would be a nice break from debating the best cleats for turf or what college has the best athletic facilities."

The waitress set a new steak in front of Joey and took off without filling the iced tea glasses. He made a face. This steak definitely wasn't a good cut, but she'd be willing to bet it would be cooked medium. She studied the surface and didn't see any evident spit. Maybe Joey had gotten lucky.

"I understand. Well, not really. But I can see how tough it would be to have that sort of attention on you. I talked to Hayden Verdun's dad yesterday. They're dealing with the same sort of thing. Maybe you could talk to him or Helen and see how they're handling it."

"That's a thought," she murmured, redirecting her attention to hunting for another piece of chicken in her salad. The Verdun kid was decent, but he was not on the same level as Waylon. The Verduns had pushed and promoted their son from the moment he'd started walking, making sure he had the best equipment, the best camps, private coaches and opportunity. They controlled the program at Ville Platte with money and influence, even hiring a recruiting service to promote Hayden and shop him around to college programs.

Lou doubted they'd be much help.

"So how long are you planning to do construction? Can't be easy on a woman." Joey cut into his steak and grunted with approval. He chewed and looked at her with perfectly nice brown eyes.

Wonder how he'd take it if she slapped him silly?

Who was he to suggest she couldn't be happy in a construction job? Of course, she had no plans to hang around Forcet Construction any longer than she had to, but she did a hell of a good job behind the switches of her Caterpillar. "You know, I'm not sure. I doubt it will stay my chosen profession forever."

"How do you feel about working in the grocery business? You could start at checkout, but with assets like yours, I'm betting you could move up quickly."

Really? Did he really just say that?

"Wow, what an opportunity. Do I have to sleep with the produce manager to get the job?" She smiled sweetly, perhaps even dumbly.

He nearly dropped his fork. "Uh, no. That's not what I meant."

She arched an eyebrow.

"Seriously. Look, Lou, I've been interested in you for a while now. We'd make a good team, both at the grocery store and in our personal lives. Sorry if I offended you."

She broke eye contact with him because as uncomfortable as she felt when he pitched a fit about how his steak was cooked, this was ten times more uncomfortable. "Guess I jumped to conclusions again. I'm a little defensive about being the only woman in town wearing a hard hat and moving earth."

He zeroed in on his steak, and silence fell.

Why had she tried going on a date?

Oh, yeah. Testing to see if what she felt for Abram was a fluke.

She'd hung out in produce waiting for Joey to ask her again, and it had taken three months and a buttload of fruit before he'd gotten up the courage. But what a disaster. She'd be more comfortable sitting on thistle than sitting here poking through a salad with Attila the Diner.

Yep, this little experiment had cured her. No more dates with Joey.

"Dessert?" the surly waitress asked, clutching the bill and looking as if she'd sell her soul to the devil to get them to leave.

Joey looked at Lou questioningly.

"No, thank you." She placed her napkin beside the salad bowl and tried on a smile.

"Guess that will do it." Joey reached for the bill, shoved a couple of notes inside and then slid it to Lou.

She stared at the folded leather.

"Do you have enough to cover it?" she asked as the waitress frowned at Joey and busied herself with picking up their dishes.

Surely, he didn't expect her to go dutch? It was a first date. Gentlemen always paid on the first date, right? She didn't know. She hadn't been out on a date in a long time.

"I figured a woman like you wouldn't want me to pay for the whole thing."

What the hell did that mean?

She lifted the bill jacket and grabbed her wallet from the purse hanging on her chair. Great. She wasn't worth buying dinner. Something about that smarted and the only thought in her mind at that moment was Abram Dufrene would have never treated a lady this way.

Joey hadn't pulled her away from Abram.

He'd shoved her toward him.

She rose and walked toward the door, not bothering to wait on the cheap produce manager. He followed because she heard the blip unlocking the car doors. She wondered if he'd ask her to chip in for gas, too.

The ride home was painfully silent. Joey fiddled with the radio, flipping it from country to rap back to country again. The night sky looked suitably velvety and date-like. Too bad. Such a waste.

They pulled into her driveway and Joey killed the engine.

"This didn't go so well, I guess. I'm sorry about that," he said.

She shrugged. "It was worth a try."

He leaned forward.

No, he wasn't.

Yes, he was.

His lips met hers. She pulled back not because it was totally inappropriate for him to assume she'd let him kiss her, but because there was nothing to stay there for. No fireworks. No sweet desire throbbing. No anything.

"Do you want to try a do-over sometime?" he asked, draping his hands across the steering wheel. Lou could see a glare on his thinning hair from the light of the moon and hated herself for unfairly comparing Joey to someone else through the filter of moonlight.

"As in another date?"

"Yeah."

She shook her head. "I don't think this is meant to be, but thanks for—" she paused because he hadn't bought her dinner "—driving."

She opened the door and climbed out without a backward glance because Joey, though nice and clueless, wasn't worth risking neck strain. She pushed the door shut and walked to the front door.

Inside she could hear Waylon and some of his buddies yelling at the television and it made her smile. Something about going for it on 4th down.

She walked in to four guys yelling at the TV.

"What's up?" she shouted toward her brother.

"Hey," he said, his eyes not leaving the screen. She peered over the shoulder of his friend and fellow Owl teammate Brian Meeks, who was not meek at all. In fact, Lou was certain he ate metal for the fun of it.

On the screen ULBR was midfield with thirteen seconds left on the clock. They were behind by three points. Players ran on, then off. The chains moved and the refs airplaned their arms.

If Lou had had a knife, she could have whittled the tension into small bite-sized pieces.

Waylon's eyes were beaded in on the action as he leaned in, forearms on his knees.

She returned her gaze to the television.

And there was Abram talking to a huge kid, nodding and making motions.

And that's all she needed to know that whatever they had between them was absolutely real. After that horrible date, seeing Abram, even if it was from such a huge distance, sewed it up for her.

She wanted not just any man, but him.

The players jogged back on the field, the whistle blew and the offense became a blur. The quarterback dropped back and faked a handoff. The defensive end bit, freeing the quarterback to roll out. It felt like slow motion as he drew the ball back and launched it a good sixty yards. The cameras followed the perfect, tight spiral as it zoomed toward the end zone.

The receiver leaped, hands open as the ball fell right into his breadbasket…and then hit the ground.

"No!" Waylon yelled as the other guys groaned and collectively fell back in despair.

"I can't believe that shit," Brian said.

"Ahem." Lou cleared her throat.

"Oh, sorry, Lou," he amended.

Another friend pointed toward Waylon. "That's why they need you, dude. Briggs has no hands. I swear even my grandma could've caught that."

"Could have just as easily happened to me."

"No way." Brian shook his head. "ULBR needs you."

Lou searched the screen looking for a glimpse of Abram during the replay and then panned the deflated ULBR sideline. She didn't see him, but she knew that as much as ULBR needed her brother, she needed Abram.

Because Abram might very well have sent his steak back, but with a gentlemanly smile. He'd have paid the bill, held open the door and talked about anything other than football—well, maybe football would have been okay for a while—but he'd have listened to her. Just as he'd been doing the last few weeks each Thursday night.

She'd waited over ten years to start her life again. Surely, she could wait four months, six days and eleven hours more until Waylon signed his letter of intent.

CHAPTER ELEVEN

WAYLON TOOK ANOTHER draw on his beer and watched his teammates screw around in the headlights of the truck. They reminded him of clumsy puppies, fighting over a chew toy. Lou had let him take the old wreck out tonight, which was odd because she didn't give the keys up easily. He guessed she felt crappy about the ULBR loss. Either that or her date must have really sucked.

But what had she expected with Joey Fontenot? The dude was such a tool. She really needed to expand her horizons. Maybe she should try a dating website or something because there wasn't much available in the way of decent guys in Bonnet Creek. Maybe Cory from the gym would work for her, even if he was kinda stupid. He had a good body at least—but the thought of Lou doing the kind of things he liked to do with girls who had good bodies made his skin crawl.

Ugh. No need to go there.

"Hey, here come some ass wipes from Ville Platte," Brian said, releasing the Owls' left guard from a headlock and snatching up his Texas Rangers cap from where it lay in the dirt. "What the hell they doin' out here? They never hang at the pit."

The pit was an abandoned dirt pit on the outskirts of Bonnet Creek but close enough to Ville Platte that some of the kids from surrounding schools showed up occasionally to drink and hang out with other kids in the parish. For the most part the Evangeline Sheriff's Department left the place alone because many of the deputies could still remember their days of hanging at the pit, drinking borrowed alcohol and raising what little hell a kid could in a small town. It was the go-to place for screwing, drinking and wasting time.

Waylon tossed the beer can in the back of the truck. He'd already had two and knew he couldn't risk another since he'd driven. The last thing he needed was a DUI, and Lou on his ass even more than she already was. If it wasn't his grades, it was picking up his socks or knocking the dirt from his cleats. He knew she wasn't being unreasonable, but it didn't make him feel any better. For some reason he felt so itchy in his skin he wanted to scream at Lou, at Lori, at everyone who expected something from him.

And that included the teammates he hung out with tonight.

Half of him had wanted to blow them off after the Mississippi State/ULBR game; half of him wanted to cling to what he'd once had with the guys he'd grown up with playing Pop Warner and PlayStation.

His eyes narrowed when he saw who drove the Jeep bouncing toward them. Hayden Verdun.

"What the hell does he think he's doing?" Waylon asked no one in particular. There were a few other cars parked out in the pit, some other teammates, some guys who had no stake in what was about to go down.

Because something would go down.

He tasted that in the night air.

Waylon's blood already heated when he thought about Hayden and the last words they'd spoken to each other. In the past few weeks, he'd woken to Hayden staring at him from the pages of the *Villa Platte Ga-*

zette. He didn't know who Hayden's dad had dirt on, but he'd done a good job getting his son some press in the local papers. Hayden had even been featured in the *Alexandria Chronicle* and *The Opelousas Journal.* For some reason, it stuck in Waylon's craw to see the smug smile of the dude he'd once lined up next to and called teammate. He wanted to plant his fist in Hayden's face.

"Yo, what's up?" Hayden called through the window. "You numb nuts thinking about how bad you're gonna get beat next Friday?"

"Thinking about what you're gonna look like with a toe tag. Your momma's gonna cry, but I'll be there to give her my shoulder." Brian patted his slab of a shoulder.

"Screw you," Hayden said, slamming the Jeep into Park.

"That's what I was thinking. Your momma's pretty."

Waylon shook his head at his friend. "Enough, Brian. We don't need any talk of mamas. We can handle our business well enough without stooping to pettiness."

Brian grinned. "I like pettiness."

"You guys are losers." Hayden grinned at the guys stacked in his Jeep. "Which we'll be glad to prove in six days' time. All it'll take is 48 minutes."

"Yeah. Whatever." Waylon turned away from Hayden and his idiot friends. They tempted him too much. Something deep inside, a primal need, hummed for satisfaction. As if by throwing a few punches, he could satisfy the anger. But he knew it would only complicate his life. Nothing good would come of kicking Hayden's ass. Nothing. Except maybe momentary release from all the crap weighing him down. Better to heed the small kernel of sense planted in his brain and cancel the expectation of something going down.

He slid into his truck and cranked the music up. He'd found an old Foo Fighters CD in Lou's room and borrowed it so he could hear some of their early stuff. She'd probably had it since high school, yet it still sounded fresh and cool. Not his standard fare, but he liked it.

"Where you going, Boyd? You afraid what I'm preachin's the truth? Or maybe you got some recruiting calls to answer."

Waylon looked at Hayden. What a tool.

Hayden's door swung open and he climbed out. "That's what I thought. Golden boy's too afraid to do anything to get himself in trouble. Oh, yeah. Never mind. His sister's already done it for him. Screwing the coach has advantages, doesn't it? She get you a scholarship, Boyd? Your sister open her legs to get your ride, dude?"

Waylon turned the music down. "Are you as stupid as you look?"

Hayden's eyes narrowed. "Stupid?"

"Yeah. Stupid." Waylon draped an arm over the steering wheel trying for nonchalance—another word he'd learned for the ACTs—but he was anything but indifferent. In fact, he could hardly keep his hand from forming a fist. "I could beat the ever-loving shit out of you with one hand tied around my back…and I don't need Lou to sleep with anyone to get me my ride. But how's your daddy like holding his ankles?"

Hayden advanced. "Holding his ankles?"

"Yeah, so he can take it up the ass to get you yours… 'cause everyone in the parish knows your daddy's bought your way from the time you were in diapers."

"You son of a bitch!" Hayden pulled at the truck door, reaching in toward Waylon.

Waylon laughed and pushed Hayden in his chest.

The boy stumbled before gaining his footing and coming back for more. "You're just jealous 'cause you ain't got no mom and dad. You wish every day you had what I have."

That was it. He didn't know if it was the way his words rang true, or if he just wanted to beat the hell out of something, but Hayden would do.

He waited for his rival to get close enough and slammed the truck door open, knocking him back. Quick as a cockroach, Waylon slid out. "I'm not jealous of you, Hayden. You'll be playing in Lafayette while I'm breaking records in the SEC or the Big Ten. I may not have parents, but I have one thing you don't—more stars behind my name."

His words were mean, but he didn't care. Hayden had something he wanted, but Waylon would never admit to missing his dad or wishing his momma waited for him when he came home. He couldn't form the words *I'm depressed. I'm scared. I'm alone.* But he could kick Hayden Verdun's ass.

One of Newton's laws bounced in his mind. For every action there is an equal and opposite reaction.

Hayden was about get some reaction.

He barely had time to draw back as Hayden's fist flew toward him. Instead of hitting Waylon on the jaw as intended, it crashed to his shoulder. Wasn't a bad shot, but it wasn't a good one.

Waylon took a good one, delivering a strong right and connecting with Hayden's nose. He felt a crack and it satisfied.

"Hey, hey," guys yelled around them. He felt arms grab at him, saw others reaching for Hayden. Hayden shrugged them off and landed an uppercut to Waylon's solar plexus. He felt air whoosh out of his lungs, but was able to cock back his fist and hit Hayden firmly on the left cheekbone. There was no crack this time, but Hayden dropped to his knees.

Waylon allowed his friends to pull him back.

Hayden struggled to his feet, wrestling himself from his friends. He launched one more punch Waylon's way, managing to draw blood. Waylon felt his lip split and tasted copper pennies.

Hayden went back for a second helping, but Brian blocked it and shoved him back. He fell into the arms of his friends.

A siren split the night air.

Waylon wiped a trickle of blood from the corner of his mouth and turned his head. Why were the cops here?

"Shit," Brian breathed. "Who called the po-po?"

Waylon broke free from his friends' hold and straightened. Hayden also stood and turned toward the deputy striding their way. Waylon didn't know this guy though he wore the familiar brown and khaki uniform.

As the deputy moved toward them, he shouted, "Okay, bust this up. Bust it up!"

They had busted it up.

The deputy stopped, hand on his piece as if he might draw down on someone. He looked at Waylon who'd stepped back in line with his friends, and then he glanced over at Hayden, who really did look as if he'd come out on the short end of the stick. His lip swelled, his nose bled and even in the dim light afforded by head-lights and a full moon, Waylon could tell he'd likely have a black eye.

"Someone called in a fight. What's this about, gentlemen?"

The radio at the hip of the deputy squawked but those gathered around said nothing.

"Oh, I see. It's gonna be that way." The man reached for the radio.

"Naw, just a misunderstanding," Brian said, waving a hand the size of Texas in a call-off motion. "We stopped."

"A misunderstanding?" the deputy repeated, raising the radio.

"Ain't no damn misunderstanding," Hayden said, ripping himself from the arms of one of his teammates, pointing at Waylon. "That son of a bitch attacked me."

"The hell he did," Mason Vidrine said, emerging from around the truck. Mason didn't play football, but he was the vice president of the student council and son of the mayor of Bonnet Creek. "Hayden started it, riding in here like he owned the place and ragging on Waylon."

Waylon didn't say anything. He merely stood akimbo, refusing to apologize for smacking Hayden around. He should have remembered everything his Sunday school teacher had told him about turning the other cheek, but he didn't feel so holy lately. In fact, he felt so far from the boy he'd once been he was afraid he wouldn't be able to remember him. Plus, he refused to answer to the snot-nosed asshat's accusations.

"That true?" The deputy studied Hayden, wagging his head like he studied horseflesh or a tricked-out sportscar.

"No. We came here like anyone else. We weren't looking for trouble." Hayden crossed his arms and spoke in his best "my daddy is rich" voice.

Brian faked a sneeze. "Bullshit."

A few guys laughed, but the deputy didn't seem to find it funny. "Enough."

Everyone shut up.

"Okay, this little party is over. Some of you have

been drinking and, in case you hadn't figured it out yet, you're underage and it's illegal. I want the drivers of the vehicles to line up so I can ascertain whether you'll be allowed to drive home. You're all getting a verbal warning, but next time, I'm gonna haul your asses in."

A few people groaned. Waylon saw a couple of kids slink off, afraid to be seen out partying and participating in things that would make their mommas cry...or put them under lock and key until they turned eighteen. He'd do the same if he could.

"And you two." The deputy, whose name tag might have said Soileau, pointed at him and Hayden. "I'm calling your parents to come and get you, or I can take you in for public drunkenness and resisting arrest. Your choice."

"But we didn't—" The deputy silenced Hayden with his eyes.

Then he lifted the radio to his mouth and called for backup.

Yeah. This was a complete bust-up and Lou was about to come down hard on him. Just what he needed.

LOU PULLED OUT OF Coach David Landry's driveway and headed toward the pit. Inside, she was a mass of anger, disappointment and fear. Outside, she was as she always was—calm and collected. "Thank you for coming with me. I don't know what to do with him, but I'm hoping you can help."

David stroked his upper lip. "I might make it worse. Things haven't been tight between me and Waylon in a while, and I'm not sure there's much I can do about it."

She heard the resignation in his voice. "Why won't he talk with you any longer? You've always been the guy he's gone to for advice. I just don't get it."

She glanced at the coach, but he refused to look at her. He seemed almost aloof, not particularly pleased to be pulled from his bed at 11:48 p.m. to go talk some sense into her blockhead brother, but could she blame him? "I'm really sorry I had to ask, but a few of the college coaches recruiting him have suggested I talk to you. Waylon's not handling this year well."

"Nope, but I'm not sure I can help."

"Yeah, you keep saying that," Lou said, swinging the car onto the blacktop and pressing the accelerator. She'd lucked out, Mary Belle had been home with a cold and let her borrow her car. Lou needed to get another car soon since the truck had seen better days and Waylon would eventually need something to take to college. Hopefully, the construction business stayed strong and gave her plenty of overtime so she could get something smaller and more fuel-efficient.

Miles disappeared beneath the little green Corolla, and if it had been another night, the drive would have been nice. The full moon lit pastures now yellowed with anticipation of winter and showcased the swaying trees rustling with the first true cold front of the year. Something heavy and hot burned in her stomach as she neared the pit, and she said a little prayer Landry could do what she could not—break through the barriers her brother had stacked around himself.

"Well, here we go," breathed David as they bumped toward the cars and trucks clustered in the raw dirt.

Lou climbed out, not bothering to wait on the coach. His attitude told her she was likely on her own.

The crowd parted and she saw Waylon leaning up against the truck across from a fuming Hayden Verdun. They both looked rough, and she figured they'd done some waling on each other.

"Who are you?" a deputy she didn't know asked.

"I'm Lou Boyd, Waylon's sister and guardian."

"Okay, wait over there by your brother, please. Officer Sloan and I will be with you after we make sure these kids aren't too impaired to get their sorry butts home."

"Hey, Matt," Lou said, nodding to Matt Sloan, a guy she'd dated before he went to the police academy, married the academy director's daughter and then came back home to work for Sheriff Guidry.

Matt gave her a wry smile. "Sorry about this, Lou. Glen Soileau's been after these kids for a while and your brother gave him the reason he's been looking for."

Lou nodded. Waylon refused to look at her. Instead he studied his boots.

She leaned next to him on the truck for a few minutes, both of them silent—until her brother registered Coach Landry had come with her.

"What the hell's he doing here?" His brown eyes met hers and she could see something dark flicker to the surface.

"You need someone besides me to talk to."

"Not him." Waylon's reply sounded like glass ground underfoot.

"What's wrong with you?" she hissed under her breath. David stood near a few of his other football players, thumping a few on the head and giving some choice words.

"Nothing."

"Yeah, this is exactly what nothing looks like." She crossed her arms and tried not to yell at him. "Way, you got in a fight and I got a call from the sheriff. Something is wrong with you."

"I defended myself. I tried to walk away, but Hayden

wouldn't let me. And, so you know, some of it was about you."

"Me?"

"Yeah, someone told him you hooked up with Coach Dufrene and he's trying to use that to start something."

"I haven't hooked up with Abram," she whispered heatedly. Okay, she wanted to get down and dirty with the sexy tight ends coach, but that opportunity had skipped by her and she wouldn't give in again until... well, she wasn't thinking about that right now.

"I know, but people like to smear the truth around to suit themselves, Lou. Hayden doesn't like me 'cause I'm getting more offers than he is, and his dad is just as bad. That makes them both dangerous."

Lou felt her heart gallop at the thought of someone making a mountain out of a molehill. Part of her realized the hooking up bit could easily have been true. If Abram hadn't had the good sense to set her aside that night, there might have been a seedy motel, tangled sheets and a hollow feeling of disappointment in her past to solidify claims of misbehavior. Surely a few kisses couldn't count against them? Surely. "You still shouldn't have hit him. That's going to make it worse."

Waylon looked down at her, his dark eyes hard. "He's an asshole, Lou, and sometimes you have to bust assholes in their mouth to shut them up."

Okay, point made. She wasn't certain she agreed with her brother's logic but she could respect his need to do something.

"Waylon." David's voice left no doubt. He expected Waylon to come to him, but her brother crossed his arms and pretended as if he hadn't heard the order.

"Go." She nudged him.

He adjusted his gaze on a dark horizon and didn't budge.

"Get over here, son." Waylon's coach pointed a finger to where he stood. The other kids being screened by the deputies fell silent and watched the battle of wills.

At that moment, a beautiful white Cadillac SUV pulled into the circle of the parked cars and Don Verdun emerged. The deputy she didn't know moved to intercept him, murmuring low words toward a seemingly very angry man. Don glowered at his son, before turning a venomous glare toward Waylon. He shrugged off the deputy and stalked toward her and her brother.

Lou felt her stomach tighten as she stepped in front of Waylon.

"You." The man pointed a stubby finger over her shoulder at Waylon. "I should have known you'd be causing problems. We're going to file assault charges, you little bastard."

Lou stepped forward so her eyes met Don's and he understood he'd have to go through her to get to the seventeen-year-old behind her. "I don't think so, Don. Your son started this by throwing the first punch. There are more than enough witnesses to back that up."

Don leaned in close, so close she could smell toothpaste and bourbon. Maybe the deputies needed to check his ability to drive. If she lit a match, they'd all go up in smoke.

"No way my son went after your brother. Everyone knows Waylon's fallen into the wrong crowd. He's been busted before."

Coach Landry placed a hand on the man's shoulder. "Come on, Mr. Verdun. No need for this. Take your son and go home."

Don spun. "Who are you to tell me what to do?"

"*I'm* telling you," Matt said, drawing the man back forcefully. "Take your son and go home before I haul him in. This was a tussle between boys who have a beef. Let them settle it on the field Friday night. Or we can make this official and you can see your son in the paper in something other than the sports section."

Don shrugged out of the deputy's hold and Lou could almost see the man's thoughts. He'd had too much to drink and he didn't need trouble for his son. Don was a hothead, but he wasn't stupid.

"Fine," he growled, jerking his head toward Hayden, who'd been clutching his swelling nose with a napkin someone had found. Hayden slunk behind his father, not even bothering to turn around and glance their way again.

"Now, you." Coach Landry pointed to Waylon. "Come with me."

"I'm going home with Lou," Waylon said.

"You'll go home, but not before you talk to me."

Matt tapped Waylon's arm. "Go with your coach or get in the back of my car."

Waylon's mouth thinned, but he shrugged. "Fine."

Normally, Coach Landry would have wound an arm around Way's shoulders, but he didn't touch him. He moved into the dark shadows away from the others standing around the gathered trucks and cruisers still flashing red and blue light across the empty pit.

Lou watched her brother, reading his rigid body language as his coach crossed his arms and started reading him the riot act—or some version of get your act together.

A parent or two pulled up, kids disappeared and the deputies cornered her with the ol' this-better-not-happen-again speech before climbing into their perspective cruisers and bumping down the road. With the sound of the cars fading, Lou could hear every word spoken between Waylon and his coach.

"This isn't about me, Waylon. It's about you and your behavior. What are you doing, son? Seriously, character is important. These college scouts are looking for talent, which you have in spades, but they don't want some hotheaded troublemaker who can't make smart decisions on their team."

"You're one to talk." Waylon's voice grew belligerent, swelling in the empty night. Lou straightened, but remained at the truck.

"This. Is. Not. About. Me."

"Yeah, it is. How can you come out here and talk to me about character, huh?"

"Come on, Way."

"No, you said you'd handle it, but nothing has changed. Mrs. Landry still doesn't know, and we both know you're still dipping your stick in the wrong engine."

Lou swallowed. David was cheating on Amy? How did Waylon know about it?

"Listen, my personal life doesn't concern you."

"And mine doesn't concern you."

"The hell it doesn't. Everything about you concerns me. You're giving Lou grief, pulling away from the guys who block for you, who line up next to you, and doing your damnedest to wreck your chances to get the hell out of here and claim a position on one of the best college football teams in the country. So, yeah, it is my business."

"Why don't you stop?"

"Stop pushing you? Stop expecting the best in you?"

Waylon took a menacing step toward his coach. "No, stop screwing around on your family."

Coach Landry squared up on Waylon. "That is not your place, Waylon Boyd."

Waylon's face contorted. "Why would you throw your family away? Don't you know what this will do to your kids? You're nothing but a piece of garbage. You're nothing but a—"

Lou rushed toward Waylon and Landry because it sounded like either Waylon was going to start crying or punch his coach. She didn't know what in the hell was going on, but knew she'd been wrong to bring Waylon's coach into the fracas. She hadn't known things were so broken between them.

"Hey," she said, pushing Waylon back, wedging herself between the two big bodies. "That's enough."

David's eyes snapped to hers and she saw the fear in them, the utter loss of control. The moment was pregnant with bitterness tinged with regret laced with frustration.

"Step back, David," she said, giving him a small push.

He fell back. She turned to her brother. "Get in the truck and go home. We'll talk there."

Waylon's breath came in jagged bursts. He looked near to a breakdown.

"Way, go," she said, laying a hand on his shoulder.

Finally, her brother nodded and walked toward the truck, his strides long and angry. She'd not seen him this emotional since her parents had died. Grief wasn't as complex as some thought—quite simply it was utter, desolate hurt, embedding itself in the heart for weeks, months and years until the pain was a mere echo in the soul, always present but only a shadow of itself. But this resentment, this fear inside her brother, scared her more because it was like a cornered beast—unpredictable.

She didn't do well with beasts.

David straightened. "Look, Lou—"

"No, I don't want to know what you're doing in your marriage or your personal life. It sickens me for Amy's sake, and God help your poor kids if you're throwing them aside for another woman. I don't care about you. I care about Waylon." She felt her legs tremble with indignation at this man Waylon had once trusted. This coach had been his North Star, steadily guiding him, giving him the advice Waylon needed to be successful. But now...

"I understand how you feel, Lou. I get Waylon feels some sort of betrayal, but what I do in my private life has no bearing on my relationship with him. I'm still his coach. That's my job."

"You don't get it, do you? You were more than a coach, David. You were the one guy he could count on. Life's coming at him fast, with this big decision, this huge pressure to perform well on the field every week." She shook her head. "If you aren't accountable to your team then how can they be accountable to you?"

The night cloaked the tears that sprang in her eyes. Not for Landry. No. He didn't deserve even a sniffle. Her tears were for her brother. Landry hadn't intended to take the boy on to raise, but he'd played a role that had come dangerously close. Whether it was wrong or right wasn't the question. It merely was.

"I'm not his father. I don't owe him an explanation. Moral character doesn't define our relationship, Lou. I could kick kittens or steal from the Salvation Army kettle every Christmas. That doesn't change the fact I have a role as his coach...and his coach only."

Lou sighed. "You're pathetic."

She turned on her heel and walked back to the car, sick she had to share the ride back with the man.

Part of her knew his words to be very much true. The other part of her wanted to lash out for allowing Waylon to depend on that relationship so much. She'd always thought David to be a good role model for Waylon. Well, that statue on the pedestal Way had built had just tumbled down, breaking into itty-bitty pieces.

And all the team's players couldn't put that image back together again.

CHAPTER TWELVE

ABRAM FELT ANTICIPATION build in his stomach as he pulled onto a street beside the stadium where the Bonnet Creek Owls were set to play the Ville Platte Bulldogs—and it had nothing to do with the game. The parking lot and side streets of the small community were filled to capacity with trucks and cars parked in front of small wooden houses encircling the well-lit stadium. Some ingenious kid had roped off his mostly dirt yard and sold parking for $5.00 a pop.

He pulled in. "Got room for one more?"

The boy wearing sagging jeans and a Bulldog T-shirt eyed his F250 pickup. "That's a big truck."

"I'll give you a ten spot."

"I guess you can park in the driveway. My momma ain't going out in this mess no way." He held out his palm and Abram greased it before easing onto the broken pavement behind an ancient Pinto.

After locking his truck and tipping the kid an extra five to make sure no one messed with it, he started toward the already rocking stadium. Tubas set a low bass beat as the drums rat-a-tatted in that familiar Friday night cacophony. Coaches' whistles and the hum of the crowd accompanied the football rhapsody. Moths flew around the tall stadium lights, dancing in the night air as the scent of peanuts and popcorn reached his nose.

Nothing better than Friday night football. Except maybe Saturday night. Or Sunday afternoon.

And tonight he'd finally set eyes on the blonde who'd invaded all his free thoughts, which were not as many as one would think, since he mostly dwelled on rival defensive schemes and the offensive efficiency of the ULBR Panthers. But every night before he closed his eyes he thought of her.

Which was damned crazy.

But didn't change the fact she haunted his thoughts and his dreams. Hell, he lived for those one-hour calls on Thursday night, nearly dancing around like a kid on Christmas Eve before he got to Waylon on his list of recruits. Pathetic.

"Wanna program?" a cheerleader asked, jabbing it his way as he approached the gate.

"Sure," he said, digging out more money and doing his part to support the Dog Pound, the booster club for Ville Platte. Hayden Verdun was on the front cover, arching up for a ball in midair. He'd claim it as an expense item since he needed to have a list of numbers and a place to jot comments. He never carried a clipboard. Too telltale for locals who'd want to chew his ear off about their hometown stud. He rolled the program and forced it into his back jeans pocket as he shelled out another seven bucks for admission.

He deliberately avoided the home stands to his right and headed around the track toward the visitor section, which was his normal protocol since the hometown folks usually knew each other and stared at a guy sitting alone at a high school football game. He liked to blend in, and it didn't hurt Lou sat on the visitors' side.

Okay, it was the main reason.

His eyes searched for her as he stayed in one lane,

walking around the end zone. He didn't see her among the throng of people, mostly because blue and white pom-poms shook as the Owls took the field. Forcing his eyes on the players jogging out for the kickoff, Abram spotted Waylon. Easy to do since he was the tallest kid out there.

Many of the kids nervously shifted their feet or jogged in place trying to pump themselves up to head downfield and throw blocks. The kickoff returner squatted and rubbed his gloved hands on shiny white pants. But Waylon stood perfectly still, hands on hips, loose, elegant and prepared. Abram liked the quiet confidence of the boy.

The ref blew the whistle and the football sailed into the air, end over end into the lights before falling just short of the returner. The kid wearing number 87 tried to field it on the bounce, but the ball flew over his shoulder pads and hit the ground behind him. Defenders advanced as the returner scrambled after the rolling ball. It felt as if it were in slow motion, but finally the kid got to the ball, picked it up and pivoted in the direction he was to be running.

Maroon and gold jerseys descended on him as he scrambled to the left. One seemed likely to bring him down, running full steam, setting up for a killer tackle.

But then the defender flew through the air as Waylon launched himself low, connecting with a satisfying crunch, laying the defender out so the returner could turn the ball upfield. Number 87 got to the thirty-five yard line before he was brought down.

Waylon leisurely hopped to his feet, slapped his hands together and then extended a hand toward the Bulldog still lying on the field.

Yeah, Abram liked this kid.

More whistles blew, players jogged on and off the field, and Abram made his way past the big-bellied guys smoking cigars outside the chain-link fence and the somewhat thuggish-looking guys ribbing each other and rehashing the days they galloped under the lights, recovering fumbles, intercepting balls and dancing a touchdown shuffle in the end zone.

He slid into the metal bleachers, eyed a spot up high, and looked for Lou.

Bingo.

Right in the middle next to the woman who'd started all this—Mary Belle Whoever—sat Lou.

Abram had told himself it didn't matter what he wore on this little trip north. But regardless of his affirmation that this was merely another evaluation of a recruit, he'd gotten a haircut that afternoon, squeezing it in after walk-throughs at the Panthers' practice. Then he'd shaved for a second time and pulled on a freshly ironed long-sleeved twill shirt Nate's new wife Annie had bought to match his eyes. He'd buffed his leather boots and used the stupid body spray his mother had put in his stocking. Yeah, Picou still insisted on stockings for her very grown boys.

But when he saw Lou, he knew she'd done the same.

The stadium lights made her lip gloss shine brighter and the blouse she wore was lower cut than anything he'd seen her in since that first night at Rendezvous. The blue was definitely an Owl color, but it wasn't a spirit T-shirt like most of the others surrounding her. It was soft, feminine and he knew she'd worn it for him.

Her eyes moved from the field to search the stands, and her gaze found him.

It shouldn't have felt so good to see her, but it did.

He couldn't stop the twitch of his lips as hers curved in response to catching him coming up the metal steps.

Everyone stood and shouted as a good play took place on the field. Lou stood but she wasn't looking at the game, she looked at him, holding his gaze. Abram slowly climbed the steps, knowing he couldn't sit near her, but refusing to stray too far from sight. He continued walking up the steps, and finally, Lou glanced toward the field.

He slid past a few older gentlemen in ball caps and windbreakers with John Deere logos and settled onto the back row where he could lean against the railing—and where he could study Lou's shining hair when he wasn't actually doing his job of evaluating talent.

He withdrew the program and pulled the roster from where it nestled between advertisements and glossy pictures of the dance team and clicked his pen to take notes.

For a good ten minutes he was able to focus on the game, jotting in his own shorthand notes about the play of the various players. Of course, he was technically there for Waylon, but he already knew they'd offer him, so he concentrated on some of the underclassmen who might have future potential as recruits. He noted only one kid to keep an eye on.

Lou glanced back once, pinpointing him, before turning back and watching the game. He knew she was very much aware he sat behind her by the way she held her head.

"What you been scribbling down over there?" The question came from his left.

Abram unclicked his pen and turned to the older man with thick squared glasses behind which bushy eyebrows arched above dark intelligent eyes. The man had an underbite and a drawl that had good ol' boy written all over it.

"I'm writing up notes on a few players."

"You from Opelousas?"

"No."

"I know you damned high school coaches like to show up to watch and learn our plays—"

"I'm not a high school coach if that sets your mind at ease," Abram said.

The man closed his mouth and stared hard at him. Two other cronies tipped forward, a stalwart front of protection. A few seconds ticked by and Abram wondered if he might be "politely" escorted out by three old farmers.

"I'm a college coach evaluating a few players."

The bushy-browed guy cocked his head like a coonhound.

"With ULBR."

A smile broke. "Ah, hell, why didn't you say in the first place? Now that's a different story."

A hand was extended, and Abram became acquainted with Earl Guidry, Jimbo Carr and someone who called himself Smiley. He chatted a few minutes before nodding toward the field, clicking his pen and scratching a few more unnecessary notes in order to keep from being drawn too far into a conversation about the Owls' need to run the veer and how it would work a whole helluva lot better than what they ran now.

Lou glanced over her shoulder to find him, before taking in his seatmates. Her eyes laughed and she gave a smile that rivaled the halogen lights above them. Obviously, she knew the men next to him.

The clock wound down, the half ended and the Owls jogged off the field with a seven-point lead.

"I'm goin' for coffee. You want any, Coach?" Smiley asked, rising and causing every vertebra in his back to crack. He patted his shirt pocket and withdrew a twenty-dollar bill. "My treat, fellas."

"You can't drink coffee this late. You're gonna be up all night pissin', Smiley."

"Don't you worry about my prostate. I can have a dang cup of coffee if I want it." Smiley hitched up his pants and walked toward the aisle that would take him down to the concession stand. Half the stands cleared out, making their own way down for a snacks or a smoke.

Abram waved a hand. "Nothing for me. I'm going to be heading out before too long."

Smiley grunted and eased down the steps.

Abram saw Lou stand, she did a little jerk of her head and he got the message she wanted him to follow her.

Gladly.

He rose. "On second thought, I'm gonna stretch my legs, fellas."

The older men nodded, already wrapped up in their conversation about the Ville Platte coach and how he recruits kids from the private schools.

After making his way slowly down the crowded aisle of the metal stands, he found Lou standing off in the shadows away from the people crowding around the cinder-block concession stand. Mary Belle stood beside her, looking into a compact, coating her lips with lipstick. She snapped it closed, her eyes zeroing in on him. "Well, I'll be. If it isn't my cousin Abram."

"Cousin Mary Belle, good to see you again," he said, before turning his gaze on Lou.

Her hair was longer and she'd put on a little weight, which looked good on her. She'd been too thin when he'd last seen her in June. Odd, it had been so long. Seemed like it was only yesterday he held her in his arms in that empty stairwell, and the weekly conversations they'd had for the past seven weeks had knit her even tighter to him. Deeper and deeper he fell into Lou.

"Hello, Coach Dufrene," Lou said with a mysterious smile.

Mary Belle raised her eyebrows. "Pretty formal for a man you almost got naked with."

"Oh, my Lord, Mary." Lou looked like she wanted to choke her friend. A dark blush flooded her cheeks. "That's not what happened."

Abram winked at Mary Belle. "Not for lack of trying."

"Don't say that," Lou muttered, looking around.

Mary Belle elbowed her. "No one's listenin' to us, sugar. They're all trying to get nachos before they run out of cheese. And he's just flirtin' with us."

Abram shrugged. "I'd say the statement was false, but that would make me a liar."

Mary Belle twisted her lips. "I know you want me to stand here to give you cover and all, but I can't listen to talk of nakedness. I mean, I can, but it's probably not a good idea. I'm likely to attack the next guy who comes around the corner."

Smiley walked by carrying two coffee cups and chawing on a dip.

"Ugh, never mind." Mary Belle shivered. "I'm going to get some peanuts. Be right back."

Abram didn't bother watching Lou's friend walk away. His eyes were on the beauty in front of him. Pink still stained her cheeks and her pretty blue eyes flitted around nervously. She looked inexperienced, unsure and very tempting.

On one hand, it ruffled him his job kept them from one another. On the other, the fact she respected the rules endeared her to him even more—because she loved her brother, wanted to do the right thing, and didn't know how to juggle wanting to do the right thing with wanting something for herself. No, Lou wasn't a typical twenty-seven-year-old woman worried about what size diamond should grace her hand or what club had the best selection of potential husbands. She didn't get pedicures or wear designer clothes. And she didn't know how to handle a man falling in love with her when it wasn't a man she could have.

But that man couldn't stop himself, could he?

Not when he lay in bed thinking about the sweetness of her smile or the way she'd look in her plain white cotton panties. When had granny panties ever been so sexy? Screw Victoria's Secret. Give him Lou in underwear that came six to a package any day.

Someone brushed against him, drawing him out of his thoughts of unmentionables and into the present moment.

"So how have you been, Lou?"

"You know how I've been. I talked to you last night." Her brow crinkled, drawing her cute nose up a bit. He wanted to drop a kiss on it then gather her into his arms and drop kisses in other strategic places.

"Oh, yeah." He smiled, looking into her eyes, watching them soften.

"It's weird. I've only seen you in person three times, yet…" She yanked her gaze from his, glancing out at the band trotting off the field. He loved how blue her eyes were.

"I know. It's like we know each other too well," he said, wondering if he could touch her in some way with out it looking like he was some pathetic overgrown kid. He reached out and brushed the back of her hand with one finger, hoping no one would see the caress.

Something flared in her eyes. She shoved her hand in her front pockets. "You shouldn't."

He stepped back. Lou was right. He shouldn't touch her because the energy humming between them was enough to make him want to do something crazy—like kiss her again. "Sorry."

"So, you looking at some other kids besides Waylon?"

Football. Yeah, right. The actual reason he was here. "I've got a few notes on some kids. That Hayden Verdun is having a good game."

Lou made a face. "He's good. I guess. But we're going to beat the dog mess out of 'em."

"Spoken like a true fan." He grinned, nestling his own hands in his jacket pockets. It was safer that way.

"Well, doesn't this look cozy," a voice interrupted. He turned to find an older man, a good foot shorter than he, standing behind him. The man wore an expensive leather jacket and ostrich boots. The shirt peeking out of the collar was maroon, designating him a Bulldog fan.

"Don." Lou lowered her chin, like a queen nodding to her subject. A sort of iciness had entered her voice and Abram got right away "Don" wasn't well liked—at least not by Lou. He wondered why. Had the man done something to her? His mind galloped with possibilities of this man hurting this woman standing before him. Abram didn't like him on the very plausibility.

"Lou." The man returned the nod as cold as January before turning to him and sticking out a hand. "Coach Dufrene, I saw you come in the stadium earlier and wanted to introduce myself. Don Verdun. My son is Hayden, number 88 for the Bulldogs."

Abram took the man's outstretched hand. "Good to meet you. Call me Abram, please."

The man's grip was too tight. Overcompensating for his stature.

"Hated I missed you this summer—business trip kept me from the closing day at camp. Hayden said he learned a good deal from you."

Lou shifted in her clogs. How Abram knew they were clogs, he hadn't a clue. "Well, I'm so glad to see you again, Coach Dufrene. Look forward to our visit in a few weeks when we come up to ULBR." She looked Don straight in the eye as she uttered those words. They sounded like a throw-down challenge. Don's dark eyes narrowed.

"Good night, Lou," Abram said, wishing like hell Verdun would beat it and give him a few more precious minutes with the woman who'd kept him on pins and needles since dancing with him on the dock at Lake Chicot.

"Night," she said, sliding past them, waving Mary Belle, who balanced peanuts, popcorn and a soda in her arms, over to the entrance of the stands.

He felt Don watch him watch her.

"I enjoyed getting to know your son, Mr. Verdun. He's a good football player."

"Yes, he is, and he's improving each game. The camps this summer helped him."

Abram didn't want to stand and talk about a kid that likely had no shot at taking a scholarship slot at ULBR. Hayden could play Division I ball, but likely at a smaller program. Abram could tell the father's dreams for his son were much bigger than reality. "That's what the camps are for. They're a win-win. We get to meet some of the best talent in the state and the kids get an opportunity to grow in their positions."

Don parked hands on his hips. "We'd like to take an official visit to ULBR this fall. We've been waiting on ULBR to give us a serious look. Hayden's definitely worth it."

Abram took an inward deep breath. "We may have to do that, Mr. Verdun. I'll talk to Coach Holt and we'll be in touch."

Don nodded. "Good, good. I think you'll be glad you did. Waylon Boyd's not the only kid around here who can play. I hope you'll keep that in the back of your mind. I heard about what happened at Rendezvous and understand you have a special relationship with Lou—"

"Hold on a sec." Abram held up a hand. "The incident between me and Miss Boyd happened before either of us knew who the other was, and it was reported to compliance and the NCAA. We've been very honest about that."

"But I have eyes, Coach. I can see what's going on here."

Abram clenched his fists. "There's nothing going on. I'm recruiting her brother—I've made no bones about that. Waylon's sister is a good person, easy to like, easy to talk to. This isn't some slimy sort of thing, Mr. Verdun. Let's not paint it what it isn't."

Much.

"I'm not implying anything. Just imparting what I've heard, is all. I really hate to see people dragged through the dirt when there's no need." The man inclined his head at a few people walking by before turning toward the field. Air horns blasted into the night mixing with the roar of the crowd as the players took the field. "I'll be looking for that invite for an official visit because I know you want to be fair in all this. Gotta run. My son is always better in the second half and I wouldn't want to miss it."

Abram watched as the man turned on his expensive boot heel and headed for the track skirting the field.

Something in his gut cramped at the veiled threat in the man's last words. He wanted to follow him, spin him around and tell him to do his damnedest, but then there was the whole slight element of truth to the accusation. On the surface, he had nothing going on with Lou. Underneath, somewhere near his heart, and definitely somewhere beneath his belt, he very much had something going on with her.

The past several years had proven without a doubt a person who wants to make trouble or a name for himself can do so. Unproven accusations against college football players or collegiate programs were squeaky wheels—dangerous squeaky wheels because the press loved them.

If a sports reporter sniffed an inappropriate relationship between him and Lou, he'd blast the airways with speculation, resulting in the media parking their asses on stools at Rendezvous to get the real story. They'd haunt the citizens of Bonnet Creek looking for the slightest wrinkle in any accounting of what went down between him and Lou that night. They'd line the streets in front of Lou's house. Yes, the few brief encounters he and Lou had had would be turned into some tawdry story of sex, scandal and recruiting violation. Destroying a kid with talent and dreams wouldn't matter at all if a reporter could get a byline and run with a story, no matter how ridiculous it was.

Abram couldn't allow that to happen for more reasons than he could name on all fingers.

Which meant Hayden Verdun might need a second look.

It wasn't that the kid wasn't a legitimate recruit. He was. It was merely that Abram didn't have a gut feeling about him being able to fit into their schemes. He wasn't tall nor athletic enough, and the dad's interference threw up bigger warning flags. He'd been around football too long not to recognize the type.

"You coming up, Coach?" Smiley yelled across a sea of people all moving toward the stands.

Abram moved along with them, like a salmon upstream. He reached the older gentleman. "Think I'm going to watch the third quarter from down here then head out. We got a game of our own tomorrow."

Watery blue eyes met his. "Ah, hell. It's a blindfold team."

Abram arched a questioning eyebrow.

"You could beat 'em blindfolded."

Laughing, Abram clapped him on the shoulder. "We better not think that way, Smiley. Having our asses handed to us on the field would be easy compared to the fires the fans will be lighting to burn us at the stake. We prepare for every opponent."

Smiley gave him a grin that showcased two silver partials and a couple of pieces of tobacco lodged in his teeth. "I'd be bringing the starter fluid."

"Exactly." Abram started toward the opening leading to the track. "Tell your buddies I enjoyed sharing the bleacher with them."

Abram chanced another glance at Lou, finding her watching him as he moved toward the exit of the stadium. He'd watch a few minutes of the third quarter before heading back to Baton Rouge. To stay longer would be too much temptation. Somehow seeing Lou made it ten times worse. Not necessarily out of sight out of mind, but more like looking at a piece of chocolate cake on the counter and inhaling the wonderful chocolatyness of it, knowing you can't even dip one finger in the frosting for a taste. Better to remove the temptation.

Over the past few weeks, he'd grown to know Lou. Learned the nuances in her laughter, the worry in her voice, and the delight in someone asking about her—what inspired her, what fueled her and what made her who she was. Their conversations had had nothing to do with a pigskin ball and sixty minutes. It had been about Lou. About him. About life.

And he'd starting falling toward love for the first time in his life.

Lou was different than any other woman he'd ever known.

Maybe some would think him silly. Cynics would brand him under her spell only because it was a long-distance, yearning kind of thing, but for centuries people had fallen in love over distance, penning longing letters of passion, of hope for a future. Today people even fell in love online. So was it preposterous to think he could fall in love over the course of a brief telephone call once a week?

Maybe.

He didn't know if it was actual love, but it was something he wanted to explore…if the opportunity ever presented itself.

And somehow he'd have to ensure it did.

He turned back and watched Lou for a few moments, noting the curve of her cheek, the swing of her straight golden hair shining beneath the lights, the smile focused on her friend beside her.

Yeah, she was definitely something.

As he walked to the gate, he felt other eyes on him. He searched the maroon and gold crowd to his right and found Don Verdun watching him. The man arched a knowing eyebrow.

Worry made a home in Abram at that very moment, and he knew what lay ahead would be anything but a walk in the park.

CHAPTER THIRTEEN

WAYLON SHOVED HIS helmet on the shelf and straightened the pads so he could shut the locker door. As always, he was the last person out of the locker room, preferring to grab a shower before heading out to tackle the night. After piling off the bus, his teammates had dumped their stuff in their lockers or laundry and hightailed it out the door before Coach could find them and give them an earful about missing a block or dropping off too early in coverage, but Waylon had never worried about getting his ear chewed before.

And he wouldn't now.

His routine had always been a long shower after the game, and he wasn't changing it because he didn't want to deal with Coach Landry. They'd said their piece to one another last weekend. He played for Landry and that was it. Keepin' it professional. End of story.

Before leaving the stadium in Ville Platte, Lou had tossed him the keys to the truck, electing to stay in town with Mary Belle and a few friends. Lori had skipped the game altogether because her best friend Sara had a birthday weekend planned in Dallas. Lori had given him knucks before heading out the door that afternoon, and she hadn't looked back. Wasn't too often either of his sisters got invited anywhere. Lou was Lou, and Lori's cautious nature and nerdy tendencies held her back from too much trouble.

So Waylon was on his own tonight, which suited him just fine.

His phone buzzed as he shoved his wallet in his back pocket. Morgan. "What's up, babe?"

"Hey. Good game tonight." She sounded distracted, her enthusiasm forced.

He slammed the locker closed. "Always good when we win."

"Yeah. Um, look, I'm gonna hang with Leesa tonight. Sorta a girls' thing, you know?"

"You don't want to go out?" He held the phone in the crook of his neck as he walked toward the double doors of the locker room. Cool air met him as he pushed into the parking lot to find the old wreck the only vehicle left. Even Coach was gone and he was always last man out. Guess the custodian would lock up.

"It's not that I don't wanna hang with you. It's just Leesa's been having some issues, and I told her I'd stay with her tonight."

He rolled his eyes because Leesa always had some sort of problem, and he suspected her main one was she was hung up on Morgan. It wasn't that he minded a little girl-on-girl action, but not with his girlfriend. "Yeah, okay. Whatever."

"You're not mad, are you?"

"Nah. I'll hang with Brian and the guys. They said they were heading out to Vidrine's camp to play poker and drink beer, so we're cool."

"Good. Well, have fun with the guys."

"Later," he said to no one, mostly because Morgan had already hung up. She'd been acting weird lately, blowing him off and refusing to have sex with him. Something was off-kilter, but he wasn't going to over-think it. The victory tonight had him feeling better than he had in a long time. Beating Ville Platte was always a good thing.

And seeing that asshole Verdun sniffling like a bitch had been the icing on the cake.

Lou would say he shouldn't take such pleasure in something so low. Lou would never grind her heel on anyone when he was down. But Waylon wasn't like Lou. Or maybe he was. Hell, he'd offered Hayden his hand after the game. The dude had shrugged it off, but it had made Waylon feel better that he'd tried to make amends, even as he had taken satisfaction in watching his rival fall. Waylon guessed he wasn't as good of a guy as he should be.

Conflicted. Yeah, that was the word to describe him.

He shook his head and cranked the old truck, cringing at the loud rumble as the engine fired into the empty lot. He pulled out and grabbed his phone as he stopped at the first stoplight. Lou expressly forbade him to talk on the phone when he drove, and normally he didn't, but he dialed Vidrine's cell number.

"Yo?"

"I'm coming out. You need any beer? I can stop at Trucker's."

Mason hushed a few guys. "Nah, man. We got you covered. You remember the way?"

"Yeah."

"Need some bro time, huh? I saw the pics."

Something clicked in Waylon's brain. At first, he wasn't intuitive enough to recognize what that click was. Then the click became a smack upside the head. Was it bitter irony? Or some sixth sense? "Yeah. Definitely need some bro time."

He hung up, pulled the truck to the side of the highway and tapped his phone screen. Took him ten seconds to find his profile on Facebook. Ten seconds more to find the pictures of Morgan sitting in Hayden Verdun's lap, poking her tongue down his throat.

"Ah, hell no," he whispered to himself as he scrolled through the pics. Morgan laughing as Hayden chugged a beer. Morgan kissing Hayden while he grabbed her ass. Hayden's face nuzzled between Morgan's breasts.

Bile rose in Waylon's throat.

That son of a bitch.

There had been one picture where Hayden had looked directly into the camera while a very drunk Morgan lay across his lap. His eyes spelled out victory. Waylon knew then and there those pictures posted for everyone to see had been meant for him alone.

Checkmate.

Waylon pressed the button to exit out of Facebook. The pictures had been taken before tonight. Probably last night after the pep rally. Morgan had disappeared after the traditional bonfire saying she was tired and wanted to go to bed early. Waylon had been beat himself and had wanted to hit the sack early, too. He'd turned his lamp off at nine o'clock while Morgan had gone out and probably screwed the guy Waylon had thought he'd beaten on the field that night.

Guess Hayden had the last laugh.

Waylon punched the steering wheel and felt his knuckles bruise. Inside, his stomach churned and he thought he might vomit. Then his heart squeezed so tight it felt like it might burst. He swallowed the betrayal, refusing to allow tears to form.

Why had Morgan done this?

He laid his head on the wheel and tried to grapple with the situation. He thought he and Morgan were okay. Maybe not as goggle-eyed over each other as they'd been back in the spring, but he didn't think she'd cheat on him like this—with that asshat Hayden Verdun. Waylon knew he'd been in a bad mood lately. Things had been tough with Coach, with the recruiting crap and with Lou staring at him with big blue eyes full of expectation. The pressure had built around him, making him feel as if he couldn't breathe. The only place he didn't feel the pressure was on the field—the one place where his mind left and his body did what it was made to do—run, block, hit, veer, explode.

But this? God, it hurt.

Waylon clenched the steering wheel, his throat raw from the unshed tears. He didn't want to feel this way. It made him weak. Made him feel like half a person.

And it pissed him off.

Hayden Verdun. Waylon lifted his head and put the truck in gear, allowing the anger to flood his body mixing with the pain of Morgan's infidelity. Hayden had threaded the needle under his skin long ago, and he had little doubt that this had been absolutely intentional. If the pain ripping through his chest was any indicator, Hayden had succeeded in his mission.

Waylon passed the turn that would take him out to Vidrine's camp and pointed the wheels toward home. He didn't want to be around anyone right now. Didn't think he could handle it without drinking too much and spoiling for a fight. If he encountered Hayden or Morgan right now, no telling what he might do.

He glanced at the phone. He wanted to call Morgan and ask why. He wanted to call her a perfidious bitch, another word he'd learned for the ACT. He wanted to hit someone. He wanted to curl in his bed beneath the quilt his grandmother had made him right before she died. Right before his mom and dad died. Right before his world went to shit.

He tasted the tears before realizing they'd fallen. The steady yellow lines of the highway blurred and he felt a tightness in his chest he hadn't felt since his parents' funeral.

Wasn't being Waylon Boyd, a four-star, blue-chip recruit just peachy?

At that moment, he hated his life.

"WHERE'D YOU PUT my book, Lou?" Lori called, her head stuck in the back of the new crossover SUV Lou had just signed the papers on at Ville Platte Motor the day before. Her sister's butt wiggled as she poked through the three overnight bags sitting in the hatchback of the slightly-used but new to them GMC Acadia.

"In the side pocket of your bag," Lou said, shoving a gear bag with Waylon's workout crap beside the old leather duffel her father had used.

"Oh, yeah. Here it is." Lori withdrew a paperback with a dancer on the cover. Might have been innocuous but for the blood pooled around the dancer's slippers.

"Is that blood?" Lou asked.

"Uh, yeah, she's a vampire."

Well, that explains it. Lou shoved the hatch downward, latching it before glancing over to where Waylon stood away from them talking on his phone, stabbing the air with his finger and likely saying some words that would have gotten him a dose of vinegar five years before. Lou still didn't like those words but nowadays she picked her battles.

Instead of being another adventure, the short trip to Baton Rouge would be about as fun as a tetanus shot. Waylon's pointed anger hadn't necessarily gotten worse over the past few weeks, but it hadn't gotten better. Waylon remained close-lipped about the Coach Landry situation, saying only he didn't want to talk about what had happened between them. When she pressed, he lashed out, stating Landry was his coach, nothing more.

"Way, we need to get on the road if we're going to make it by lunchtime. Mrs. Dufrene is expecting us."

Waylon nodded, said a few more words and then pocketed his phone. They were expected at ULBR for the start of Waylon's official visit by late afternoon, but Picou Dufrene had insisted Lou and the family come to the Dufrene family plantation Beau Soleil for lunch. Somehow she couldn't make Abram's mother see that contact with a coach's family was a bad idea.

Picou kept saying it had nothing to do with Waylon. Nothing to do with football.

And deep down, Lou knew the woman was telling the truth because this didn't have to do with anything other than Lou. Somehow, Picou had gone bloodhound and picked up on the scent…the potential…between Lou and her son.

She sighed as Waylon wordlessly opened the passenger door and dropped into the seat without another word.

"Everything okay, Way?" Lori asked from the backseat.

"Yeah. Fine." Waylon jabbed earbuds into his ears and tapped something on his phone, effectively silencing the women in his life.

Lou sighed then went back to double-check the house was locked. Pleasure bubbled up when she turned and jogged back to the car sitting shiny and as pretty as a daffodil in their driveway. It was under a year old, traded in by an older woman who decided she wanted a sedan after all. It was immaculate, with leather seats that still held a new-car scent. The price had been right and Lou felt almost giddy at the prospect of driving it down to Baton Rouge.

They backed out of the drive, sped through town, and less than an hour later, took the exit off I-10 that would take them to the old plantation outside the small town of Bayou Bridge. The landscape around the exit was flat and just like any other exit off an interstate— gas stations, fast food and economical motels—but after traveling a few more miles, Lou discovered a charming town with antiques stores, bed-and-breakfasts and tiny restaurants hugging the bayou that wound through the town. After crossing the steel bridge and noting another one lining the banks of the Bayou Teche, Lou turned onto the highway that followed the graceful curves of the bayou twisting through St. Martin parish. The periodic glimpse of the water showed off enormous live oaks draped with lacy moss.

Lou slowed after a few miles and searched for the entrance to Beau Soleil, finding it rather easily since it announced itself with huge wrought-iron gates nestled into an oak-lined drive. The drive twisted much like the highway they'd followed to reach the antebellum home.

"Look, a cemetery," Lori said from the backseat.

Sure enough a small, gated graveyard stood to the side, flanked by trimmed rosebushes.

"This was a family estate, and many plantations and older homes have their own cemeteries," Lou said, slowing down almost respectfully as they passed the consecrated ground.

"Thank you, tour guide," Lori said.

Waylon didn't take the earbuds from his ears, but Lou noted he perked up and looked around, which was a little bit of a relief. He'd been in such low spirits over the past week she wondered if she would have to take him to a doctor or something.

"Oh, cool," Lori breathed when the house came into view.

It was a huge rambling pale yellow, white-trimmed building with a wide porch and gleaming windows. There seemed to be no distinct style to the house, but altogether it was impressive and charming.

A horseshoe drive curved around to a walk, but a gravel parking lot sat to the right. Lou pulled in.

Waylon finally tugged the earbuds out of his ears. "Are they rich or something?"

"I don't know," Lou said, turning the car off and looking through her purse for some lipstick. "Does it matter?"

He shrugged, wound the cords of the headphones around his phone and sat it in the cup holder.

"You're leaving your phone in the car?" Lori asked, jabbing her head between the two front seats. "I thought it had become part of your arm."

He gave her a withering look but said nothing. Lori laughed. She was in a good mood as usual, and if anyone could jar Waylon from his doldrums, it was his younger sister.

"Come on, guys. We can't stay long, but I figured if we didn't stop by, Mrs. Dufrene would send the state police after us." Lou swiped her lips with some color and climbed out. She tugged the new blouse she'd bought a few days ago down, smoothing her hands over the jeans Mary Belle had insisted she buy to go with the top. They were faded and sort of hip. Made for looking good—not work.

Picou met them on the porch and clasped Lou's hands. "Welcome, Boyd family, to Beau Soleil."

Lou smiled because the greeting sounded a lot like the greeting the dude on *Fantasy Island* gave to guests. She'd loved catching the reruns of that show on cable when she was younger—and maybe Beau Soleil was like the island. Maybe she'd find something she was looking for here.

Or from here.

"It's so pretty," Lori said, swiveling her head. Lou dropped Picou's hands and did the same, taking in the black rockers on the freshly painted porch along with the swaying baskets of ferns. Beautiful stained glass topped each ceiling-to-floor window and the beveled glass door held the etching of a crane.

"Thank you, honey. Annie—she's my new daughter-in-law—and I just updated the outside of the house. I think it turned out nicely. Now y'all come on in. Lucille and I made my grandmother's recipe for pralines this morning."

The inside of the house was dark and smelled like burnt sugar. Lou's eyes followed the sweeping staircase that rose up to the upper floors. The woodwork was beautiful and the chandelier that hung over the foyer had to be original with ruby crystals strung between the traditional clear drops.

A rotund black lady pushed past a swinging door, her smile as wide as the Mississippi. "Well, here you all are. I've been waitin' to get a look at—"

Picou shook her head and gave the woman a sharp look.

Lucille's brow furrowed. "—this young man who is such a good baseball player."

"Football," Waylon said.

"That's what I meant." Lucille grinned and shot an apologetic look at Picou.

Lou chose to ignore the situation. She could see what was going on as plain as day.

"You've been waiting to meet him?" Lori asked with a funny look.

"Lord knows I do love a good ballplayer," Lucille said, grabbing Waylon by the arm. "Come on in my kitchen. I know what a boy like you likes, and I make a mean cherry pie. You like cherry pie?"

Waylon laughed and Lou felt something warm spread near her heart. She hadn't heard him laugh in so long.

"Who doesn't like cherry pie?"

Lucille cackled. "Wouldn't trust 'em myself."

Waylon disappeared into what Lou presumed to be Lucille's inner sanctum.

"She's always been partial to athletes. Abram was always her favorite. I think it's because they eat a lot." Picou's brow wrinkled and merriment skipped in her odd violet eyes. Today Abram's mother wore a sort of kimono threaded with bright orange silk. It was gaudy but the stitching looked well done—sort of like its wearer.

Lori moved toward the kitchen. "Think I'll have some cherry pie, too. Is that okay, Lou?"

"Or course."

"Hope Lucille lets you in," Picou said.

Lori stopped, turning with widened eyes.

"She's joking, Lori," Lou said, with an aside look at Picou who nodded.

"I knew that," Lori said with a smile before pushing through the still-swinging door.

"She's an adorable girl." Picou waved an arm indicating Lou should pass her and go down past the kitchen door toward an open doorway.

"A little gullible," Lou said, heading past a gleaming dining room replete with crystal chandelier, dark antique sideboards and a huge table set with Haviland Limoges china. Lou's grandmother always drank her tea from that pattern. Of course, she'd only had one cup and saucer she'd bought in a Salvation Army store. The contrast was marked.

"Your home is lovely. How long have you lived here?" Lou asked, stepping into a warm sitting room. Her dad would have called it a den, but there was nothing den-ish about it. Bright with lovely careworn rugs, the room had a bank of windows and one whole side of bookshelves filled with leather-bound masterpieces and dog-eared paperbacks. An overstuffed couch centered the room in front of an ornately carved fireplace over which an oil hung of what Lou presumed to be the Dufrene boys.

"It was built before the war by my great, great, great-grandfather Henry Laborde who won the land in a card game." Picou said "war" in that age-old Southern way that meant the Civil War. "Originally, it belonged to the Chita Mauga Indians and there are still sacred mounds on the acreage surrounding the estate. Been in my family since that time and much of the woodwork and flooring is original. She's much like an old whore, still holding on to her days of grandeur. My own painted lady."

"Beautiful," Lou said, glancing out the window to the back patio with its wrought iron furniture and flowering urns. Trees shaded the large expanse of backyard that extended all the way to the Bayou Teche. From here, Lou couldn't see the narrow water, but she knew where it lay from the way the massive live oaks draped along the horizon.

"Yes, a singular beauty," Picou said, settling into an armchair. "So you tell me about you and your siblings.

Abram's told me something of you, but he's a man. They usually stick to facts."

Lou wondered again why she was here—at Beau Soleil chatting with Abram's mother. She shouldn't have come, but the older woman had spent the past week on the phone insisting she accept the personal invitation to tea that had arrived in the mail several days ago. A flipping invitation with Picou's monogram blazing across the heavy ivory vellum. Tasteful, warm and very adamant.

"Um, I'm just a regular sort of girl," Lou said, perching on one side of the couch. From her vantage, a young Abram stared at her from the painting with quizzical green eyes and overly large hands. He had to have been about thirteen years old, a boy already growing into a man but clinging to wisps of childhood. His expression wasn't fierce as his older brother's nor was it as devilish as the younger. Merely uncomfortable sitting in the ladder-backed chair.

She lifted her eyes from the painting and found Picou watching her. "Come now, Louise. I've never thought of you as regular. You're much more interesting."

Lou shifted on the sofa and flipped through her mind looking for the mental notecards on conducting polite conversation in the middle of awkward social situations. Nothing emerged, so she licked her lips and pointed to the painting. "Are those all your children?"

Picou nodded. "Except for Della."

"Della?"

The older woman waved. "Sally. Sally is Della."

Lou tried not to let her confusion show.

"Della was taken from our family when she was but three years old. The family gardener concocted a kidnapping scheme with a former employee of my husband's company. For over twenty years, most believed her to be dead. Nate found her, or rather she started asking questions about some things that didn't add up. We were reconciled nearly a year ago."

"That's crazy," Lou said, trying to take in the concept of losing a child and then regaining her as an adult.

"It is. It's been very difficult on Sally. Della. I don't even know what to call her at times. The woman who raised her, the woman she still calls family, is grievously ill and in hospice in Houma. Sally teaches in Lafourche Parish and only visits me on occasion."

Lou felt something tug at her heart at the sadness in the older woman's eyes. Both she and Sally had seemed to get on well when Lou had met them, but, of course, that had been only once.

"Actually, it's part of the reason I invited you to come to Beau Soleil," Picou said, picking up a book lying on the side table next to her chair. "You are of the same age, and she needs a friend."

"Excuse me?"

Picou didn't blink. "All the books I've read about reconciling parents with their distant children encourage seeking a third party to help facilitate the relationship between parent and child."

Lou sank back onto the sofa. "I thought you invited me here because of Abram."

"Abram?" Picou's brow furrowed. "I read auras and energies, my dear. The day I met you I sensed a powerful connection between you and my daughter. That night I dreamed about you. You'd found Sally in the woods and brought her out. I knew at that moment you were part of our future. Dreams are powerful indicators of not only the subconscious but of the forthcoming."

Lou didn't know what to say. She'd been blindsided.

Sure, she liked Sally, but she'd no idea Picou had wanted her to come to Beau Soleil for any other reason than Abram. "Oh."

The older woman fiddled with the heavy braid that lay over her shoulder. "Sally laughed when you were around. You're the same age, and I sensed both of you needed a friend. I thought—"

"I like Sally, but I don't think you can force a friendship any more than you can fit a square peg into a round hole."

"No, you can't, but I had this feeling. In fact, that was part of the surprise today. Sally will arrive in an hour or so, and we're going to the game tomorrow night. I asked Abram to get us tickets near you and your sister."

Lou didn't know what to say about this sort of friend matchmaking. She glanced back at the painting above the mantel. At Abram staring at her with an almost empathetic look. With Lori hanging out with her best friend's family this weekend and Waylon hemmed up with recruiting, Lou would be alone, but she didn't want the stress of Picou and Sally. "That sounds—"

"I thought so," Picou finished, not allowing her to disagree.

Silence descended and Lou could hear the tick of the grandfather clock sitting near the open doorway. She said a prayer Waylon and Lori would bumble into the room, distracting Picou from her really weird plan.

Didn't happen.

"Um, Picou, I'm not sure—"

"Piddle," Picou interrupted. "You've got to go to the game anyway. Might as well have some friendly faces with which to share the event. I don't much care for football, but Panther stadium on a Saturday night is more than a football game. Sally has never attended one, so I told her to come on up."

"I should look for Waylon and Lori."

"I make you uncomfortable."

Lou stopped in midaction as she rose off the couch. "No."

"I can tell. It's odd because usually I make people feel comfortable." Picou tapped the book she still held. Her eyes looked misty, perhaps even tear-filled.

"Mrs. Dufrene, you don't make me uncomfortable. I suppose I just found it odd to be invited here, especially since Waylon is being recruited by your son. I'm not sure what sort of role you see me playing in your daughter's life, but I—I—"

She fell silent at the expression on Picou's face.

"She doesn't want to be part of this family." Picou raised eyes that shattered all the misgivings in Lou.

"What?"

"From the beginning it has been very hard for her. For all of us. Sally spent twenty-three years away from us, raised by another family. Her grandmother Enola Cheramie played no part in the kidnapping and had no idea the girl she raised as Sally was Della Dufrene. My daughter loves her grandmother and refuses to even think of leaving the Bayou. I'm not trying to rip her from all she's known, but I still feel misgiving, maybe terror, in her. Feel like the slightest wrinkle will have her pulling back so hard and so fast I will never reach her."

The words tumbling from Picou's lips were deeply personal and they tugged at Lou. Here was a mother who wanted nothing more than to be a part of her daughter's life. What Lou wouldn't give to have her own mother back. What she wouldn't give for all of them—her, Lori and Waylon—to be part of a family again. With a home like Beau Soleil. With a support network to lean on when the chips were down.

But Lou was alone.

Especially with Waylon pulling away, struggling with some demons Lou couldn't hunt down and destroy for him.

Outside her weekly conversations with Abram, she'd felt so isolated. Like Picou. So maybe she should shut up and let the woman and her daughter sit with her. Without protest. "I understand, and I think it'll be nice to have friendly faces beside me at the game. Glad you thought of it."

Picou withdrew a lace handkerchief from her kimono and dabbed her eyes. "I knew my vision was right all along. There's something about you. Something good for this family."

Visions? Good Lord. Lou didn't believe in that nonsense, and the only thing she could deliver to help the Dufrene family was her brother on National Signing Day—and even that was beyond her control. At that moment, she felt as if she'd been dropped into a parallel universe.

The doorbell rang.

Picou leaped from the armchair and slid on some strange-looking slippers as she walked toward the open doorway. "She's always early. Excuse me for a moment and I'll fetch my daughter and refreshments."

Lou didn't have time to answer, for Picou flew out the door. Instead she rose and walked around the room, heading specifically toward the pictures lining the bookcase. There were many—most of them pictures of three little boys. One had been taken at a beach, another at a picnic, several among the oaks hunkering outside the house. In every one of them, a person could pick out the personalities. The oldest brother was serious and domineering, just as his sturdier stature and dark hair suggested. The youngest had golden hair and bright blue eyes with a devil-may-care grin and hungry eyes. Abram had a quiet strength, a sort of bemused expression. His light brown hair and loose-limbed elegance had him awkward during the early teen years but confident in his late teens. His smile held mystery.

There were but three pictures of the Dufrene daughter—one with her twin brother as infants. Another as a toddler with light curls, blue eyes and a drooling grin. And the last presumably taken at Christmas with all four sitting on a red blanket beneath the arm of a bowed live oak. All the boys looked bored and refused to smile, but Della smiled a sweet grin beneath an enormous red-and-green plaid bow.

"Here she is," Picou said, balancing an old-fashioned silver tray with a plate of pralines and a pot of tea.

Sally slipped inside, the wary look she'd worn last time firmly affixed. "Good afternoon, Lou."

Lou set the photograph of the Dufrene children back on the shelf. "Hey, just looking at some family pictures. You were a darling baby."

"Funny how light my hair was. It's so dark now," Sally tugged on a loose lock.

"She was the cutest baby ever. So easygoing, too," Picou said, setting the tray on the coffee table. "Let's have a treat and then we can talk about a plan for the game. I have some friends who tailgate near the basketball—"

"Well, that's one thing I wanted to talk to you about." Sally perched on one of the chairs in the seating area.

"My grandmere is not doing well today, so I might have to duck out on our plans for the game, Picou."

"Oh," Picou said, pouring a cup of tea with an unsteady hand. "I hope she's not too bad."

"Just weaker, but her blood work came back and doesn't look good." Sally accepted the tea before looking around as if she might find an escape hatch. If she did, Lou would go with her. This whole scenario felt like the red shoes she'd worn the night she'd first met Abram. Not meant for her.

"I'm so sorry to hear she's not doing better," Picou murmured, picking up a praline and nibbling. "Abram was looking forward to your going."

Picou looked at Lou expectantly. Like she thought she might help persuade her.

"Um, these pralines look good," Lou said, walking toward the silver tray and picking up the carmelized pecan candy and taking a bite.

All three women averted their eyes to various places around the room.

Lucille appeared at the door with Lori and Waylon behind her, and Lou gave an audible sigh. "Woo, this boy can eat. Picou, we need more boys around here to feed. Been too long."

"Won't be too long till we get us another Dufrene boy. Annie and Nate are at the doctor's office today for a checkup." Picou's face grew soft and her eyes sparkled as she looked at Lou. "My son and his wife are having a baby—little Paxton Laborde Dufrene is due next month."

"That's wonderful. Congratulations," Lou said, rising from the sofa, using her brother and sister as a reason to make a getaway. "Guess we need to get on the road."

Lori groaned. "Do we have to go yet? Lucille said I

should walk along the bayou. I'm going to take pictures on my phone and send them to my friends."

"Yes, let your brother and sister piddle around a bit more. I haven't had company in so long. Finish your tea, Lou," Picou ordered.

Lou suppressed the urge to say, Yes Ma'am.

"You go on, Lori. I'm gonna stay here." Waylon made a beeline for the candy, grabbing two, before sitting in a chair a size too small for him. "I like your house, Mrs. Dufrene."

"You can call me Picou."

He nodded as he chewed the praline. "The food is really good. Can Lucille come stay with us for a week or two? Or a lifetime?"

Lucille shook her head. "I ain't going nowhere, but I'll feed you anytime you be needing it."

Picou nodded. "She's good for something."

Lucille grunted but held on to her smile.

Lou watched Lori and Waylon as they interacted with the Dufrene family. It was odd. Usually teenagers didn't want to hang with older people, but her siblings looked delighted to gobble up sweets and tea, hanging on to stories of the old house and the people who'd walked the floors for over a century. Here's what they'd all missed out on. Grandma's cookies, trifling gossip and the sweet smells of a much-loved home. This is what Lou had failed to give them.

To give herself.

But what choice had she had?

Lately she'd wondered if it wouldn't have been better to have sent her brother and sister to Colorado. She could have gone to college somewhere close to her uncle and allowed them to feel more of a family than what they did. Obviously, she hadn't met her brother's needs and now Lori was scared to death to let go of Bonnet Creek and the past that would never be regained. Would they have fared better under their bachelor uncle? She'd like to think not. Up until this past year, she'd congratulated herself on doing a pretty decent job.

"We really do have to go now." Lou used her best stern voice.

Waylon took two pieces of candy and stood. "Thank you for inviting us to stop by, Picou. Mrs. Dufrene. I hope you didn't go to all this trouble for me."

Picou's brow furrowed. "Of course not, dear. I've no stake in where you decide to play football. I merely wanted to get to know your sisters better. They interested me."

Her brother delivered his own befuddled look. "My sisters?"

"When I find people interesting, I like to get to know them."

"So you don't find me interesting?" Waylon sounded confused.

Picou laughed. "I believe you have too many people interested in you, Waylon."

"Yeah, too many," he said, shoving his hands into the pockets of his jeans. "I'll find Lori. Thank you again for having us."

"You're welcome."

Sally looked at Lucille. "I hear you have pie?"

"Come on. There's one piece left. Might as well finish it off," Lucille said.

They called out their goodbyes and disappeared, leaving Lou alone, once again, with Abram's mother.

Picou walked through the hall toward the foyer, pausing when she reached the front door. She turned and looked thoughtful. "You thought I invited you here because of Abram. Am I missing something?"

"No," Lou said quickly. Maybe too quickly.

"I've been known to misread an aura or an energy. Perhaps I picked up on the wrong current. There were some currents present. Strong ones," Picou mused, almost to herself.

"Mrs. Dufrene, with all due respect—"

"Picou."

"Okay, Picou. There can't be anything between your son and me," Lou said, using a firm voice. Like if maybe she could get Picou to believe the statement, she would, too.

For a moment the woman looked at her hard as if delving into her mind, or more likely her heart. "'Water finds a way' is a saying we use all the time in these easily flooded areas. Have you heard it before?"

"Sure. It means that no matter what one does to prevent water from coming in, often it will go where it wishes."

Picou nodded. "Exactly."

The older woman opened the door and ushered her onto the wide porch, but said nothing else.

"Thank you for having us," Lou said, extending her hand toward Picou, wondering if she always left such cryptic comments floating in the air.

The woman ignored her outstretched hand and instead enfolded her in a hug. "Thank you for coming. Beau Soleil needed you here."

Lou stepped back when Picou released her. "No offense, but you say such strange things."

Picou smiled. "Now, that's a compliment."

CHAPTER FOURTEEN

ABRAM TOOK A moment to breathe deeply and survey the commotion around him. Some players were dressed and sitting in the locker room quietly, earbuds in ears, eyes closed. Others were half-dressed, heading to the trainer to get wrapped, still others were joking around, lacing up cleats, adjusting pants and doing other weird game-day routines. But above all else there was a hum—the sheer electricity, indescribable to those who'd never experienced game day. The hum was so intense it was nearly palpable.

"Yo, Coach D, you want me to see if Doc will give me a little something-something for first half?"

Something-something was a cortisone shot and the receiver's strained ankle likely needed it.

"Go ahead and see what he says." Abram moved toward the meeting room where the offensive coaching staff sat reviewing strategies and the game plan. The work had been done, and the hay was in the barn. And still the coaches needed something to occupy their thoughts as much as the players did.

For a moment, Abram hesitated, standing in the hall, leaning against the Wild Panther board of goals, and recalled last night.

Lou.

Just the thought of her, smiling, unsure, delighted, contemplative as she licked chocolate icing off her fork in Coach Holt's dining room made him ache. Usually, he didn't attend the reception held for prospects' families, though coaches had a standing invitation. Normally he elected to go over scouting reports and fret over last-minute adjustments to the offensive schemes, but last night he'd gone to the dessert reception, dragging an unwilling and somewhat suspicious Jordan with him.

Coach Holt had noticed.

Had the head coach suspected it had to do with Lou?

Abram wouldn't put it past the man to pick up on those pulsing silent signals. Holt was known for his ability to smell bullshit for miles, so why wouldn't he suspect his tight ends coach was head over heels in lust, love, whatever with the top tight end prospect's sister?

Lou's eyes found his several times, and when he'd moseyed over to talk to her, he'd noted how uncomfortable she seemed among the other recruits' parents. She was a beautiful unique painting in a gallery of boring landscapes, and didn't even realize it.

He'd tried not to eat her with his eyes. "How's everything going?"

"Well," she said with a self-conscious shrug. "Everything has been impressive. The academic center was state of the art, and the tutors were 'hot' or at least that's what Waylon said."

He smiled. "Yeah, we find the smart ones who have other attributes, as well. Makes studying easier to schedule."

"He liked the professors who ate lunch with him. Made it more real for him, and it reminded me this is more than about football."

"It's about his total future," Abram remarked, grabbing a powder-sugared cookie and placing it on his plate. "Most of these kids have stars in their eyes, thinking they'll be playing on Sunday. They neglect to realize most of them won't even make an NFL combine."

Lou licked her lips and studied the buffet lamp. "Your home is lovely."

"My home? This is Coach Holt's house."

She blinked and jerked her eyes to meet his gaze. "I meant Beau Soleil. I dropped by on the way, remember?"

"Picou," he said, nibbling on the cookie. He could only imagine what his mother had done to shove Lou his way. No sense in telling the meddling matriarch something between him and Lou wasn't going to happen anytime soon. Lou had said business only and he was trying like hell to uphold her request. "Did she show you her Italian lace wedding gown? Suggest how wonderful it would look on you?"

Lou nearly choked on her punch. "What?"

"She's been parading women in front of me for the last four years. One time I went home and she had three sitting on the couch like it was the damn dating game." He shivered dramatically. "You can't imagine what she's like."

"I think I can." Lou smiled, setting the empty cup on the waiter's tray as he circled through the chatting parents. "But she's not matchmaking me and you, she's matchmaking me and Sally."

He frowned. "Huh?"

"She thinks Sally could use a friend. Oh, and me, too, of course. She wasn't arranging an interrogation for your future spouse, not that I'm saying that's even a possibility, but she was setting up a play date for me and your sister."

"Why isn't it possible?"

Lou blinked. "Stop."

"Stop what?" He leaned closer and tried to make it look like he reached for a chocolate chip cookie. "Stop wanting you? Stop needing to touch you, wrap that pretty hair around my fingers, slide my lips down—"

Lou's plate crashed to the floor. Everyone stopped midconversation and stared. Her face flooded with color. "Oops. Sorry."

She bent at the same time Abram did and their heads bumped.

"Ow," he said, rubbing his forehead.

"Stop doing that," she hissed, scooping up fruit dip with a napkin and retrieving the unbroken glass catering plate that had rolled under the huge buffet.

"I can't help it. This isn't fair."

She plopped a tart on the plate and lifted blue eyes to him. "Don't you know life is unfair?"

The sadness in her voice killed the flirty words on his tongue as he realized she was right. Life wasn't fair. Hadn't she experienced that every day since her parents had been killed? He'd heard the longing in her voice when she talked about music and her hope one day it would once again be more than a hobby, something more than playing a guitar in her bedroom every night? Lou had made sacrifices—more than he'd ever been confronted with.

Not having her was the biggest sacrifice he'd made since he'd let Nate sit shotgun the last time they took Picou to New Orleans for Jazz Fest. Abram didn't make concessions. He got what he wanted. Always had.

He rose, took the plate from her, and motioned his wingman over. "Have you met Jordan Curtis?"

His words were loud enough that everyone could hear and impersonal enough to indicate she was nothing more than the dozen other prospects' parents.

"Oh, no. Hello, Coach Curtis." She held out a hand to Jordan, who shot him the look as he took it. Abram knew what the look asked. *Yeah, she's gorgeous. Yeah, I'm smitten. No, I can't help it.*

So he'd stood there and pretended they were nothing to each other. Even as he wanted to claim her. Have her beside him. Tell the coaches, the program, the NCAA to kiss his ass.

But he wouldn't.

He couldn't.

Doing so would mean tossing his own dreams away—and those of the boy standing next to froufrou-looking curtains talking to a quarterback prospect.

"You coming, Dufrene?" the offensive coordinator asked, shoving a visor on his head and interrupting Abram's thoughts. "I'm sitting in the booth tonight. Need all you guys to be my ears. Dave Wambecker will bring the heat. Always does. We're looking at lots of different blitz packages. On our toes, fellows, on our toes."

And just like that, Lou faded to the back burner where she'd simmer, hotly, in his mind. Right now it was time to handle Alabama.

"We're ready, Coach. Always ready."

WAYLON HAD SPENT the day taking in the sights and sounds of ULBR football. He could smell spicy jambalaya and seductive bourbon in the air along with a sort of buzz of expectation. They'd spent the morning doing some more touring of the campus, culminating in a tailgate with gumbo, sausage sandwiches and pulled pork. He'd looked longingly at the beers in everyone's hands, but knew he'd have to settle for a soda, even if beer went better at a tailgate.

A pass hung around his neck and later after the band

came down the hill, they'd get to go on the field and watch the team warm up.

The sky was clear cerulean, leaves swirling with the cool wind, the sun hot on his shoulders. A good day to watch football. An even better day to play football.

The crowd moved around them, everyone in purple and black with the occasional red-clad fan tossing out good-natured taunts. All in good fun. All in the name of the game of the gods. Football.

"Look at those guys." Lori pointed at the line of students lined up to enter the stadium. Several wore purple-and-black leisure suits and one even wore a purple Batman costume. "That's crazy dedication."

One of the hot girls who'd been escorting them around campus laughed. "We're all crazy. That's the best thing about this place. Doesn't get any weirder or more wonderful than a Saturday night in Panther Stadium."

Her eyes slid to Waylon. At that moment he forgot her name. Rula? Ryan? Something like that. She smiled and gave him that "you better like all this and say so" look.

"Cool," he breathed and grabbed another bottle of water from the tub at his feet. He glanced at her name tag. *Riley.*

"We're about to go to the stadium," she said, flipping her long highlighted hair over one shoulder. He caught the scent in the breeze. She smelled like Morgan and his heart squeezed. Bitch.

He shoved thoughts of his now ex-girlfriend into the back of his mind. They were over. He'd broken up with her before leaving Bonnet Creek. No sense in thinking about her when Riley stood next to him, smiling in her tight ULBR T-shirt and body-hugging jeans. She was smoking hot and seemed willing enough. Well, at least willing to escort him around campus.

He pushed a hand through his hair, which he'd started growing out into a shaggy cool look, and parked his hands on his hips so his shoulders looked broader. "You going out with us tonight?"

She lifted her eyes and her mouth twitched. "I'm not sure, but I'll give you my number so if I do we can meet up."

Sweet.

Lori's mouth opened, but he gave her a laser look that said "shut up." She'd seen it enough to clap her trap shut and look puzzled. He hadn't told either of his sisters he'd broken up with Morgan.

"Cool." He pulled out his phone and tapped in her digits. "I don't really know the guys on the team I'm going with so it will be sweet to have a friend."

Her eyes turned into gray silk. "Then you should call me."

He hoped like hell the Panthers beat Alabama tonight, otherwise the guys assigned to him would be in crappy moods. He wanted to feel good tonight. To forget about Coach Landry, Morgan and all the shitty stuff in his life.

He wanted to toss off the fetters. Drink a cold one and make out with Riley. He wanted to become someone else. Grab the golden ring. Or brass bell. Or whatever it was.

He wanted to live and feel again.

LOU SLID INTO THE SEAT and blinked against the sunlight refracting off the metal bleachers of the end zone. Picou and Sally hadn't made it to their seats yet which was fine by her. She needed some time to think. The day had been a whirl of breakfast, lunch and tailgate all paired with the soft sell on the ULBR athletic program. She'd hardly had time to pee.

She glanced about the filling stadium. It was massive. The band trailed down the concrete steps heading for what she assumed was pregame. The cheerleaders gathered signs and poms, while the infamous Gridiron Girls secured capes and filed down toward the field. A black cage containing Champ the Panther started moving around the sidelines, pulled by a large truck. Everyone getting ready, including the Alabama Crimson Tide warming up on the field.

A few choice words flew toward the opposing team, but mostly the crowd seemed to be resting, preparing much like the other parts of the whole process that was a Saturday night football game in the greatest coliseum of the South. Or that's what one of the staff had declared a few moments ago on their tour of the athletic facility.

Lou swiped at the sweat gathering on her brow. The breeze was cool but the sun would be an unwelcome visitor for another hour or so.

A few members of the ULBR football team strolled out from the tunnel beneath her and she couldn't stop herself from looking for Abram.

Abram.

Just the thought of him had her heart quickening. Seeing him last night, his silken words sliding over her, tangling her thoughts into a mess of want and need, had her dreams filled with sweet kisses and…sex in the bathroom? She wasn't sure, but she'd been having sex with him somewhere, his fingers knotted in her hair, when Lori had walked in and caught them. In her dream she'd been mortified.

But also very turned on.

She probably needed a counselor to talk to. Her fixation with Abram and his delicious body had taken over her thoughts and dreams.

"There you are," Picou said, interrupting Lou's fantasy of Abram naked. Dear Lord. She couldn't stop the pink from staining her cheeks. "Caught you daydreaming, didn't we?"

If only you knew, lady.

"Hi," Lou said, standing so Picou and Sally could slide by. "How is your grandmother, Sally?"

"Remarkably better," Sally replied, dropping her bag and program on the seat. She'd already been to the concession stand and balanced nachos in her hand. "For some reason, she feels good. Her blood pressure stabilized and she insisted on being able to go to the bingo game in the parlor of her nursing home."

Picou peered over at Lou. "It was a double blessing because Sally stayed the night at Beau Soleil and got to come to the game. Gives me more time to spend with her."

Sally's face tightened, and oddly enough it looked like Waylon's face when he talked about grades, recruiting or Coach Landry. Stressed.

"I'm glad you both made it," Lou said, sitting back down. "I've been surrounded by guys all afternoon, and Lori left me to go sit with her BFF. She's spending the night at her friend's grandparents' town house, so I'm totally on my own."

"Not anymore." Picou grinned and snagged one of Sally's nachos. "We'll keep you company."

Sally nodded and moved her nachos out of Picou's reach. It made Lou want to laugh because she could remember very well hating when her own mother scooped bites off her place without asking.

"This is my first ULBR game at the stadium. One time we drove to Shreveport when my parents were still alive to see the Panthers play in a bowl game, but from what I hear it's not the same." Lou looked around. Definitely not the same.

Picou looked longingly at Sally's nachos. "It's not. This place gets about as raucous as a liquored-up honky-tonk. Come to think of it, it is a liquored-up honky-tonk."

The older woman wore a bright purple shirt with an ULBR Panther blingy pin fastened to the shoulder. She also wore huge platter earrings with a picture of a panther on each one, which nestled in platinum hair that hung long and straight past her thin shoulders. Her black jeans were tight, and Lou noted there was a good reason Coach Holt had made his way over when the woman beckoned that day at camp.

Picou stood, inserted two fingers in her mouth and whistled.

Lou's gaze jerked to the field as the Panthers jogged on for pregame warm-up. The crowd went nuts. Her eyes immediately sought Abram, but she didn't see him. She did see Waylon in a tight-knit group of recruits moving as a unit onto the sidelines. Walking beside her brother was a cutie in jeans and an ULBR T-shirt. The wattage in the girl's smile as she looked up at Waylon could have powered one of the huge halogen stadium lights. Her brother looked receptive.

Interesting. That might explain why Morgan hadn't been around lately.

"I don't see Abram," Picou said, turning and sitting down. Neither Lou nor Sally had stood when the team ran onto the field, but most of the stadium had. The whole event reminded Lou of the stories of gladiators she'd read growing up. How different was this from the Colosseum? It would be the same roar of a hungry crowd, the clashing of bodies, and a fight till the death, or at least till the clock ran out. Even the panther in the cage moving around the stadium harkened age-old primeval stirrings of savagery—and every one present loved it.

"There he is." Sally pointed, licking cheese off her finger before popping another nacho in her mouth.

Sure enough Abram walked beside another coach toward the sideline. His stride was casual, but Lou saw tension in the way he held his shoulders. Like the beast in the cage, Abram seemed primed to unleash. Odd, but she'd never thought about the coach's mindset leading up to a game. Abram looked as focused as any kid out on the field.

Then somehow his eyes found hers.

She felt heat blanket her, and like the anticipation of the crowd surrounding her, Lou's insides began to hum. She smiled at him. Damn, she was glad he'd scored seats near the field for her and his family. Nice perk.

"Hmm," Sally said with a knowing grin.

Lou jerked her gaze to Sally. "What?"

"I'm beginning to see everything clearly now," Abram's sister responded, with a little self-satisfied bob of her head.

Lou frowned. "Nothing's cloudy."

Picou turned around. "What are y'all jabbering about? Get on your feet. They're about to do the coin toss."

Sally shrugged and stood, looking back at her. Lou felt dread uncoil in her stomach. She hadn't wanted anyone to see what she felt for Abram, especially someone in his family.

But there was no time to dwell on what she wanted people to see or not see.

The Panthers took the field and for the first half, Lou allowed herself to be sucked into the magic that was an ULBR football game on a Louisiana Saturday night. By the end of the half, the Panthers were up by only three points.

As she watched Abram jog off the field, hunger hit her like a linebacker. She couldn't have Abram, but she could head to the concession stand for some peanuts and a Coke. Hopefully filling herself up with food instead of what she really wanted wouldn't lead to a weight problem. She could foresee herself in Overeaters Anonymous. "I couldn't have the man, so I turned to Krispy Kremes to fill my need."

She slid by the other ladies and walked quickly down the steps. She didn't beat the crowd, but she refused to be beat back from this small desire.

As Lou headed back toward the ramp, peanuts and soda in hand, Sally passed her, cell phone to her ear, a grim expression on her face. She didn't acknowledge Lou, but instead strode to the stairwell and leaned against the rough plaster, shaking her head and firing off one comment after the other into the phone.

Lou knew it was none of her business, but something was evidently wrong so she hung out near the ramp waiting for Sally to finish her conversation. When Sally dropped the phone from her ear, Lou knew it had to be really bad news.

"Sally?"

Abram's sister stiffened, her gaze finding Lou. She didn't say anything for a moment, then she beckoned her over.

"You okay?" Lou asked, tucking the peanuts into the crook of her arm and placing a hand on Sally's shoulder.

"No, not really. It's my grandmere." Her voice broke as she wrapped her arms around herself. "Suddenly she crashed. They don't expect her to last through the night."

"No," Lou murmured.

"Oh, God," Sally said, pressing her fingers into her eyes. "I thought she was better. Why did I come here?"

"You couldn't have known," Lou said, awkwardly patting her back. "What can I do?"

"I've got to go. I've got to get to Houma as soon as I can." Sally glanced about. "I rode with Picou, and I don't have my car."

"Let me get her."

"No!" Sally's hand snatched Lou's arm as she turned. "No, I can't deal with her right now. I—I—"

"But she's your mother."

"No, she isn't. I mean, she is, but not really."

Lou shook her head. "You don't mean that."

"I know it sounds horrible, but I can't help it. I'm a fish out of water in that family. I may be that little girl who was stolen away, but I'm not Della. I can't go back and make up for what they lost. I can't. Especially right now. I'm Sally Cheramie and my grandmother is dying. That's the most important thing. So don't say anything. Please."

"I've had just about enough of this, Sally." Picou's voice came from over Lou's shoulder.

Sally flinched as she met her mother's gaze but said nothing more.

"You may not want to accept who you are, but you are my daughter, and I will damn well take you to Enola. Now, here's your purse. The director of the nursing home left a message on my phone when you didn't answer yours in the first quarter. I told her we'd be there within a couple of hours. Let's go." Picou shoved the purse at her daughter.

"Why would they call you? They don't even know you or about all this in my life." Sally glanced about the now-thinning crowd as if looking for help. Or a way to disappear.

Lou heard the crowd roar and knew the third quarter had started.

"Your grandmother figured it out several months ago. Somehow she got my name. We've spoken several times."

"What? Why didn't you tell me? You knew she was sick and couldn't handle knowing I'm not truly her granddaughter. That was mine to tell." Sally's voice rose and a few people craned their heads, pausing to see what was going down in the middle of Panther Stadium.

"Enola called me. We both agreed it would be best to give you time. She wanted to tell you she knew. She said you were tough—she'd raised you that way—but I wouldn't let her. I wanted you to have control, wanted you to decide when the time was right."

Lou started to step back and fade into the background. This didn't concern her, and she had no right standing around listening in on such a personal conversation, but Sally's hand clamped down on her arm.

"I can't believe this. You run roughshod over everyone," Sally said, shaking her head and taking her purse from her mother's outstretched hand. "You know, it doesn't matter. I can't deal with this now. I need to go to Houma."

"So let's go," Picou said, gesturing toward the open stairwell to their right. "And so you know, Sally, you're tougher than what you portray. Enola only refined the steel in you. The Laborde women don't give up, and I won't give up, either. I gave you life, and I love you. One day you will know that."

Sally closed her eyes and sighed. "Just take me to my grandmere."

Picou nodded. "That I can do."

Sally walked toward the stairs, not bothering to look back. Lou didn't say a thing because she thought she might call her a not so nice name. She understood circumstances had been tough on Sally, but they'd been equally tough on the woman standing beside her, not quite defeated but not quite so full of starch.

Picou looked at her. "Will you tell Abram what happened?"

"Of course," Lou said, glancing at the empty stairwell Sally had disappeared down. "Is there anything I can do for you?"

"No, dear." Picou sighed, her blue eyes sad. "I've been telling myself it would take time, and time is all it needs. Enola knew Sally would not give her heart to me easily. She's always been a difficult one."

"But that's no excuse to act like..." Lou's words died as Picou took her hand.

"Dear one, that child has been through something hardly anyone goes through. She's stuck between two worlds. Change is hard, Lou, and some handle it better than others. Some are like you and they take the blows and keep sticking their chin out, and some are like Della, wanting to hide from it all." Picou gave her hand a squeeze along with a gentle smile. "Please tell Abram I'll call him later."

And then Picou disappeared, following after a daughter who didn't want her.

Lou shook her head as an achy sadness washed over

her. She couldn't understand turning down someone who loved you so much. She missed her own mother every single day and would do just about anything to have one more day with her. One afternoon, sipping coffee, talking about funny memories, strumming the guitar, singing her mother's favorite songs while her father backed her up on his twelve-string.

Emotion welled inside her and her throat clogged.

For a moment she stood there and feared she might burst into tears.

But then, as always, practicality settled over her. She had no right to project her longings on to the Dufrenes. No right to judge Sally. No right to even be present in their family melodrama.

Her focus needed to be ten steps up that ramp.

On football.

On Waylon, on Lori, and their futures.

Only then could she get back what she lost long ago—her opportunity to carve a path in the world. It seemed odd to put that stipulation on her life, but there it was all the same. She still had a job to do, and she would accomplish it.

She returned to the stadium and tried to enjoy the second half—and tried to keep her eyes off the sidelines where Abram stood absorbed in the action on the field. Every now and then she checked on Waylon, who really seemed to be getting into the game. Of course, he'd always been an ULBR fan.

But he couldn't choose a program based on being a fan.

Choosing the right school was a process that included academics, playing time, need, depth charts and comfort with a staff and team. The team you grew up cheering for had nothing to do with it—or almost nothing. Recruiting was a science.

But, still, Lou knew Waylon had always set his sights on playing for ULBR, almost every little boy in the state did.

When the game ended, ULBR had prevailed and the mood as she left the stadium to head toward the basketball arena—the spot she and Waylon had agreed upon— was more than jovial. When she exited the stadium, she got turned around. Purple and black swirled around her, pressing into her. She moved to the perimeter and tried to get her bearings. She distinctly remembered the tugboat sculpture in front of the architectural school and knew she needed to head right.

Her phone vibrated in her pocket as she sidestepped a fraternity guy clad in khaki and a tie dancing drunkenly in the pathway.

She withdrew it to find a text from Waylon. Going out with guys. Don't wait up.

She texted back a "stay out of trouble" message before moving away from the crowd and surveying her surroundings. What should she do now? Her time was her own until breakfast the next morning. Abram. She still had to tell him about his sister and her ill grandmere. She had his number on her phone, and though she'd been tempted to call it before, she never had. Better to text. Meet me under the ramp of the basketball arena. Need to talk.

Simple. To the point. Surely he'd come.

CHAPTER FIFTEEN

ABRAM DIDN'T KNOW if Lou would still be waiting. He always had a lot to wrap up after a game. Most of the coaches relied on the grad assistants, but he was particular about things. After the presser, he'd headed back to the locker room, checked his recruits were handled for the evening and then stopped by his office to type up his notes on the game. He had gotten so busy he'd almost forgotten his cell phone.

And she'd texted.

He'd spent most of the night berating himself for slipping in his control around Lou. He shouldn't have whispered that suggestive remark in her ear, but somehow he couldn't help himself when it came to her. She did funny things to his insides.

He grabbed a jacket and slipped out of the offices, tapping a reply in his phone.

You still there?

No response.

Damn.

Wasn't far away so he made his steps long. He reached the now thinned-out Stadium Drive and hooked a left slipping past the panther's habitat, under the ramp to the arena.

"Good game, Coach," someone called.

He raised a hand and scanned the area. Crepe myrtles festooned in hues of gold flickered like fireflies in the north wind while laughter and rap music spilled from the lots surrounding the stadium. Tailgating would go on for several more hours.

But where was Lou?

Probably gone by now.

"Abram?" Her voice sounded like spring rain on cracked earth. He turned. She was perched on a bench near the outdoor track.

"Thank goodness you're still here. I didn't think to check my messages and I should have."

She stood and gave him an unreadable small smile. "I know we're not supposed to have—what is this?— incidental contact, but I told your mother I'd explain to you what happened."

Lou's face was highlighted by the lights of the stadium and glow of the scoreboard and it made her look almost otherworldly. But it stopped with her face. The rest of her was very much of this earth. In fact it was damned real-world and, of course, practical. Some of the women who went to football games tottered around in short skirts and high heels, but his Lou had dressed simply in a purple long-sleeved T-shirt, jeans and running shoes. Comfort seemed to be her goal. "Explain what happened?"

Her blue eyes held sadness and for a moment he thought something had happened to his mother.

"Your sister got a call during the game. Her grandmother took a turn for the worse and the doctors think she won't make it through the night. Picou had to take Sally to Houma. She wanted me to explain…though, come to think of it, she could have called you."

"You would think that, but Picou always has motives. She was born arranging things. In fact, she probably made her parents redo the nursery upon arrival. Something in shades of blue, invoking serenity." He did his best Picou impression on the last line.

She gave another small smile. "She's a force."

"Something else bothering you? Enola Cheramie is a very old and sick woman…it was really a matter of time."

Lou nodded. "I know. I don't know why I feel so depressed. I guess seeing your sister go through something so hard, took me back in time. But even worse was seeing Sally hurt your mother."

He wanted to reach out and touch her, tell her that his mother had an inner toughness that would sustain her, but he also wondered if his mother had reached the end of her rope with Sally. Instead of making it better, Enola's looming death might click a wedge between them. "Hey, she'll be okay. She wants us to be patient with my sister."

"But you should have heard Sally. She said some hard things to your mother, and I just think…" She looked out at the night sky. "I don't know what to think. It just made me sad."

He moved closer to her, picked up the scent of her shampoo on the breeze. She smelled sweet and light like a woman should. No way anyone would believe this woman laced up work boots and donned a construction helmet every day. "Change is part of life. Strange, but if Enola hadn't grown ill, we'd never have found Sally."

Lou didn't say anything. Abram watched her face. Something was wrong. This wasn't the rock-steady, capable woman he'd grown to care for. No, vulnerability shadowed her eyes.

"I don't get it. Sally has this awesome gift bestowed on her and wants to toss it away like it's nothing. Who does that?"

He didn't get why she was so upset about his sister. Then again maybe she didn't know, either. Something else caused this. Had to. Maybe delayed grief. Or the pressure of dealing with two teenagers. "Sally won't toss us away. I've not been around her much, but I know she's a Dufrene. She won't ignore her family."

A sheen of tears had gathered in Lou's eyes. She nodded but said nothing else. Merely stared out at the deep blue horizon.

"Hey, is this about something more?"

She shook her head. "No. I mean, maybe. I don't know."

"Is this about us?"

"What us? There is no us."

He stepped back, ignoring the hurt that had sprung inside him at her words. Ouch.

She turned her blue eyes to him. "I'm so tired, Abram. Tired of not getting what I want. Tired of feeling like I'm always waiting for something. I want to be with you. Why does that have to be wrong?"

He didn't know what to say. He'd never been good at abstaining from anything he wanted, but what choice did he have? To give in to his feelings, sweep her in his arms, and create some sort of future together would destroy too much. He'd worked too hard, slaving over long hours, watching film until everything blurred together, to toss it away so easily. And it wasn't just about him. There was Waylon to consider, the program and his own conscience. "It's not wrong, Lou."

"Yes, it is. I can't have you. Can't have any life I want. Ever."

"We have to wait a little bit longer, baby."

"Why?" Her voice broke and she wrapped her arms around her waist. "The rational me knows we can't be together, but I don't want to be rational, sensible or high-minded any more. My life hasn't been my own for so long. Every day brings more problems—bills, Waylon's rebellious behavior, Lori forgetting every article of clothing she needs for P.E. Every day I climb onto the seat in that piece of machinery and ignore my own desires. I'm sick of it."

He shoved his hands in his pockets to keep from taking hold of her. It had become standard procedure. "I understand."

"No, you don't. You've had love, you've had freedom. You don't know what it's like to be so…alone."

He did, but not the way she meant. He'd never done what Lou had. Made that kind of sacrifice. "I'm sorry."

"Yeah, me, too." A lone tear slid down Lou's cheek.

"Don't," he said, wondering why it literally hurt him to see her cry.

"You know, I didn't even cry at my parents' funeral? I couldn't. I had to be strong for Waylon and Lori. They sobbed through the whole ordeal, but not me. This is how it's been for ten years. Me being strong. Me doing the right thing."

"Lou, it's—"

She swiped at her tears and tried to regain composure. "No, don't give me platitudes. I watched your sister hurt your mother, and all I could think about is what a selfish bitch she is. I know Sally's hurt. I know she's confused. But to deny your mother…I don't get it. I'd kill to have someone love me."

You do.

The words almost left his lips. "Hey, don't cry."

She squeezed her arms around her middle, stifling a sob. "Shut up, Abram."

He couldn't help himself. Before he knew it, Lou was in his arms, and she felt so good there. "Hey, hey."

Her body shook but she didn't make any noise as she cried. He could do nothing more than hold this woman who'd given so much of herself and still had to make sacrifices. He patted her back, rubbing her shoulder as she spent the emotion she'd bottled up for so long.

She cried her tears and he held her, moving into the shadows so that random passersby didn't gawk at a woman crying after a big win. Finally, he felt her relax against him.

"You okay?" he asked after a moment. She fit against him so nicely and he didn't want to let her go just yet.

She nodded and lifted her head. Her eyes were puffy and whatever eye makeup she'd worn streaked down her cheeks. But to him, she looked perfect because she was right where she belonged.

He brushed a light kiss on her forehead. "Ah, baby."

"Just what I thought," a voice said from his right.

Abram turned and found Don Verdun stepping from the shadows with a phone in hand. The smartphone's red light glowed and Abram knew the man had been recording them.

"What in the hell do you think you're doing?" Abram released Lou and moved toward the little man, intent on grabbing his phone and crushing it beneath his shoe. Had Verdun been following him?

"Preserving this beautiful, touching moment. Or should I say revealing moment?" Don said, stepping back quickly as Abram advanced on him.

He couldn't see Lou but he felt her alarm.

"Give me that phone," Abram said, holding out a hand. He half expected the man to comply, but Don merely smiled and shoved the phone into his back pocket.

"I don't think so, Coach Dufrene. There are going to be a lot of people interested in this video. It's evidence. Can't destroy evidence, now can we?"

"This isn't what it looks like. She was upset," Abram said, crossing his arms across his chest and staring down the bug smirking in front of him.

"That's what they all say, but everyone knows your history with Lou Boyd and now I have proof that what I suspected is true." Don moved toward the street encircling the stadium. He was making a getaway, but before he disappeared completely, he turned and looked at Lou. She stood as if her feet were rooted like the ancient live oaks bordering the road, wiping her cheeks. "Nice job, Lou. Screwing the coaching staff might have worked in your brother's favor if you hadn't been caught. Guess using what's between your legs to get what you want didn't work out, did it?"

The growl emerged from Abram's throat without his realization, and his feet moved instinctively. He was about to pound the hell out of the piece of shit scurrying away like the rat he was.

"Abram, don't." Lou's cry was the only thing that could have stopped him. He held up and turned back toward her.

"It will only make it worse. Only make you look guilty." Lou's eyes found his and the sad apology in them was almost more than he could bear.

This was it. They'd been caught together and Don Verdun had the evidence. Tomorrow or the next day, everyone in the state would think he and Lou were having a tawdry affair. Irony slammed into him. All their restraint, all the whole doing the right thing, had been for naught.

He rubbed a hand over his face. Hell.

"Was he following you?" Lou asked, shaking her head. "I mean, he had to wait a long time. Pretty creepy."

"He's opportunistic slime." This was going to be bad. Everything he'd worked so hard for, everything Lou had worked so hard for, would be gone like a puff of smoke. If he could somehow find Don, maybe discredit him? He really didn't know what to do.

"I'm sorry. This is my fault," Lou said, pushing her hair back. Disbelief had etched itself across her face— along with slight panic. "I shouldn't have gotten so upset. He's going to make this look like we were—"

"It's not your fault. I shouldn't have come here to-night. My control is not too good around you."

"But I asked you to come," she said, folding her arms before pressing a hand to her forehead. "I told myself it was because I'd promised your mother, but I know it's because I wanted to see you. I could've called instead."

For a moment, neither said a word. Around them people called to one another, laughing and chattering. The ULBR fight song played in the background—everything absolutely normal around two worlds falling apart.

"They'll make it look bad," he said, wrapping his mind about what was about to go down. "Once the media gets this, they'll have a field day making our relationship look very inappropriate. You need to prepare yourself for hell for the next few weeks, Lou."

"But surely people will see I was upset, and you were comforting me. It wasn't even a passionate embrace— and we won't be lying at all."

He shook his head. "The world has changed. People love scandal, and Don will want to make a splash. Bet that footage will go straight to a guy at *The Advocate* or the doorstep of WBRZ. Then it will hit YouTube, Twitter and message boards."

"We'll do damage control. He can't turn it into something it's not. All we have to do is tell the truth."

If only that were true, but Abram had been in the sports business for a long time, and he knew it would get sensationalized. Rumors of athletes cheating, taking performance drugs, paying for research papers—every little accusation got legs on the internet and on radio talk shows. "It probably won't help. He'll say we're having an affair and most will believe him after seeing that tape."

He scratched his head and thought about how to handle this. It wasn't just about him. This was about ULBR. About his recruits. About Waylon. He'd deal with whatever came his way, but he had to try and protect those who'd played no part in this fiasco. "You may need to hire an attorney."

"Why? I can't hire an attorney. We don't have that kind of money."

"You need someone to protect you. It might get crazy for a while. We're going to deny this, but you're going to be bombarded."

"That's crazy. We're not criminals. Besides, Don may not do anything with it. He may want some way to get his son an offer. He's like that. He's a bit of a blowhard, but surely he wouldn't hurt Waylon or you by making a false accusation. He's got more integrity than that. I hope."

He shook his head. "Coach Holt isn't going to make an offer on the Verdun kid no matter what he had on film or as a witness. Leo basically told the kid's high school coach as much not too long ago. We don't play games with recruits. If we know we won't offer, we cut the kid loose so he can pursue other programs."

Lou shivered. "I can't believe this. Don's going to make it look like I'm some skanky whore trying to get my brother a scholarship. It's crazy. We've never even been together."

"Or it will make me look like a coach so desperate to sign your brother that I hedged my bets with his sister. Neither of us will look good, especially after we openly admitted contact when we first met at Lake Chicot. People saw us there, and the press will throw suspicion on everything we've done to this point. People will remember us talking at the Owls game, they'll question the reason you visited Beau Soleil. Everything will be under the microscope. We have to prepare for it, so find somebody to help you deflect this."

She closed her eyes and then opened them. No more tears. Just regret and perhaps a hint of anger.

"Deny. No matter what anyone asks, Lou, deny. We aren't lying. We've never had sex, we're not in an official relationship, and we've never done anything knowingly suspect. That's what you say. The truth."

She stepped toward him. One, two, three steps. And finally the fourth. It brought her close enough to kiss. "If everyone's going to believe it, Abram, why don't we give them something to talk about?"

Her voice had dropped, intimate and soft. His body responded, his blood heating, desire flaring. He watched her as she nervously licked her lips—a habit that inflamed.

"Take me home with you," she whispered. "If we've got to go down, then let's go down in—" she seemed to search for words "—pleasure."

He wanted to take her up on her offer. God, he wanted

to. She was so beautiful and she made his heart throb, not to mention another important part of his anatomy. They could do it. Leave here, go to his house, spend all night exploring each other, loving each other. It would be so good. He knew it. She may be a virgin, but his Lou was made for loving him. "Babe, we can't."

"You don't want me."

He grabbed her hand and tugged her beneath the ramp. Deep in the shadows no one could see them. Not even a camera. It was dark, intimate, and he waited only a second for her to crash into him.

He clasped her face and lowered his lips, capturing her gasp of surprise with his mouth. Wasting no time, he plundered her mouth, sliding his hands down her body and pulling her tight against him.

She met him full on, opening her mouth, winding her arms around his neck. But he stopped her, grabbing one of her hands and pressing it against the erection throbbing inside his khaki coaching pants.

He ripped his mouth from hers. "Feel that?"

Dumbly, she nodded, allowing her hand to curve against him. He nearly exploded at the warmth, the certainty in her grasp.

"This is even after knowing my coaching career has likely gone down the tubes." He pulled her hand away. "Don't ever say I don't want you, woman, because that would be a lie."

She looked up at him, her lips still glistening from their kisses, and he wondered if he were the dumbest ass in the whole world for not tossing her over his shoulder and taking her home. Maybe she was right. If everyone was going to think they'd been naughty, why not make it legit?

But then he'd have laid his honor out on the field and stomped on it himself.

Both he and Lou had to look at themselves in the mirror each morning. He had to live with himself. If they were going down, he'd do it the Dufrene way. The honorable way.

"Go back to the hotel. Let everyone see you there. Act like nothing is wrong. When you get home to Bonnet Creek, go to an attorney or trusted friend, or see if your boss has a suggestion. Issue a statement to the press when they demand one, then go about your normal life. Go to work, take Waylon on his other official visits, and let everyone see this is nothing to you."

"But what about you? Will you actually lose your job over a hug?"

"I'll handle me."

She frowned. "Are you still going to recruit Way? Is this it? Is this all over?"

"I don't know. I'm calling Leo when I leave here. We'll have to see how the allegations bear out. We can't sweep this under the rug, but we may not get as much play if there is another big sports story to track. Hopefully, we'll get lucky…for Waylon's sake."

"But what about us?" Her words were soft, floating up to him with plaintive, ill-disguised want.

"There is no us, remember?"

Pain flashed across her face, and she looked like he'd kicked her. Yet, he needed to remain stalwart. Couldn't touch her again or he'd change his mind. It had to be this way. They had to drop everything they'd had between them. Only then would they possibly survive the scandal that would break. Don had followed them for a reason, and he'd been rewarded by a moment that had nothing to do with sex. The whole idea of how this would be misconstrued churned acid in his stomach.

"So are we talking…" She swallowed and closed her eyes. "Like never?"

God, he couldn't imagine never having a chance with Lou, but perhaps they'd never been meant for one another. "For now, there can be no us, Lou. Has to be this way. Not for me. Or you. But for Waylon. For the Panthers' program."

She rubbed a hand over her face, and he could see she struggled for a footing. Maybe because seconds ago she'd been in his arms and now he told her she had to go this alone. He hated himself for doing what he did, but it was best for everyone involved. Even Lou herself. "Right. I have to keep the goal in front of me. Waylon and Lori. College. I've got to finish the job."

He stepped away from her though every muscle, every nerve, in his body screamed against doing so. His heart felt shattered and it plain hurt to be Abram Dufrene at that moment. "Good. You've got goals. Keep those in front of you. We'll weather this and everything will work out. Trust me."

She stepped out from the deep shadow of the ramp. "Sure."

For a moment she stood hesitantly. "Go ahead, baby, go back to your hotel. Nothing to hide. Okay?"

She nodded and crossed her arms against the chill of the night. "Okay."

Then he watched her walk away from him, knowing he'd likely not get her back again. Ever.

"Lou?"

She turned.

What could he say to make this better? Nothing. "Take care of yourself."

A sort of fierceness traversed her face. Behind her lay the panther habitat and the beautiful black panther pacing the yard. In Lou he saw the same power, the same restraint. "I will. I always have. Goodbye, Abram."

"Goodbye, Lou."

And then she walked away, gobbled up by the swaying shadows of the oaks. Abram wanted to cry, but, of course, he didn't. There didn't seem to be much left inside him. He lifted his eyes heavenward as if God might help him, but he found nothing but a dark sky, glittering with stars, invoking the inky black of the animal still pacing, with a half moon sitting high behind it.

His world had crashed under a fierce panther sky.

WAYLON WATCHED THE PEOPLE on the dance floor beat the air with rhythmic fists. The music thumped, the DJ had mad skills, the drinks flowed and the girls were smoking hot. What more could a dude want?

Griffin Tate, a big offensive tackle with a mountain of muscles to balance out his impressive gut, passed him another beer. Waylon had already downed two and was getting close to a tight buzz. He'd have to lay off if he wanted to pass the Lou test.

"Dude, that's a nice piece of action right there. Maybe you'll get you some play tonight, brother." Griffin nodded toward Riley. She was pretty spectacular so he ignored the thoughts of Morgan that filtered through. He didn't need a cheater like her, even if she did say Hayden had set her up. She'd gone along with him, hadn't she? Everyone knew you couldn't trust someone like Morgan. Look where she came from. Wasn't her mother sleeping around with a married man? Apples don't fall far from the tree, and lies came easy to girls like her.

Riley glanced over at him and smiled. She stood

with a group of similarly hot girls—the hostesses for the other recruits. He'd seen about eight or nine of the guys he'd been doing the tour with around the club. The others had gone to a different place. Presently, they were at Ringo's, which was right across the train tracks from campus and so close to the river he could smell it on the breeze.

Riley held his gaze.

Was she supposed to do this? Flirt with him? Make him think he's the man so they could reel him in and have him signing on the dotted line?

Probably.

But maybe he didn't care.

He beckoned her to him with a crook of his finger. If she was supposed to make him feel like a king then why not take advantage? But even as he did it, he knew he was being an ass. Guys didn't treat girls that way, not even when their hearts had been torn into and spit upon by another girl mere weeks before.

"You need something?"

He bit down on a suggestive response as images of Lou and Lori flashed in his head. Riley was somebody's daughter. Maybe somebody's sister. He wouldn't want some random dude treating either of his sisters like property or something. "Not really. You're a better conversationalist than Griffin. Plus, you make me look good."

She lifted her eyebrows. "Now that's a pretty nice thing to say to a girl."

"I'm a pretty nice guy."

"Really? You seem all brooding and distant to me. You barely spoke on any of the tours and you kinda had a frowny face. Thought maybe I wasn't doing a good enough job showing you around."

Hmm. He'd never been called brooding. Or distant. Of course, this past year had sucked. Once people had dubbed him a clown. He'd been the most liked camp counselor for his silly antics. Why had he changed? "Lots on my mind I guess."

"Like this recruiting stuff?" She slid onto a stool at the table where he sat.

"Sure, the recruiting is harder than I thought. Coaches calling at all hours, and now I have all these official visits lined up through the middle of January. And my girlfriend and I just split." He didn't know why he told Riley this. He didn't even know her.

"My brother was recruited pretty hard, and I remember how difficult it was on him to choose between two schools. One was ULBR."

"Did he come here?"

"Nope. Went to Florida. At first we were all devastated because my whole family cheers for ULBR. My daddy, well, it broke his heart. But Josh knew what was right for him, and though he'd always liked ULBR, Florida's schemes and the coaches seemed a better fit. He did awesome there though it nearly killed my daddy to put on a Gator shirt." Riley smiled and at that moment he understood why she worked as a hostess. She was genuine, knew football and loved her school. And it didn't hurt she was hot.

"Wait, you're Josh Hamill's sister?"

She laughed. "Yeah."

"He's with Green Bay?"

"Backing up, but working hard to stay there."

"Cool," he said, his gaze straying to her tight T-shirt. A necklace with a small strawberry pendant hung between her full breasts. It turned him on the way it nestled right in that little valley.

"Hey, you know I'm not gonna hook up with you, don't you?"

He jerked his head up. Humor shone in the depths of her eyes. "Uh, yeah. I mean, I didn't figure you would."

"Not trying to embarrass you, but you were staring at my boobs pretty hard. We don't do that here," Riley said, averting her gaze to the dance floor.

He tried not to blush, but felt the heat flood his cheeks. "Jeez, you're blunt. And why wouldn't I stare? I'm a dude."

She looked back at him and smiled. "Sorry. It's just I have two other brothers beside Josh. One is the punter for the Panthers. He's over there hanging with a few other guys." She pointed across the bar.

He turned his head and found Jason Hamill staring at him with a frown. "He knows I'm not touching you, right?"

Riley rolled her eyes. "He doesn't decide who I date or hook up with. None of his business. But this is my job, you know. I don't usually go when the team takes the recruits out. I mean, you're cute and all, but I don't want to be kicked out of the ambassador program. Plus, you're too young for me anyway. I'm twenty."

"I like cougars." He realized he didn't mind not getting any action. He also realized Griffin had set him up. The dude knew she was Jason's sister, knew the rules and knew there would be no scoring for Waylon tonight. "It's fine. I'm just flirting with you. Getting my feet wet again."

"Well, maybe I'll let you give me a little good-night kiss later, you know, since you just lost your girlfriend." She flipped her hair over her shoulder and smiled.

"If you're lucky."

Riley laughed and placed a hand on his arm. "Let's dance, prospect."

He allowed Riley to pull him toward the floor, mostly because he wanted to watch her dance. As he passed the bar, he saw Griffin laughing and punching another offensive lineman on the arm, and it struck Waylon that he really liked being here in Baton Rouge. All the schools had pretty much the same facilities and the same primo coaching staff, so no matter which school he chose—Texas, Alabama or Clemson—he'd get the same chances as he would at ULBR. So it came down to a feeling. Something that nudged him toward the right place for him.

And tonight he was feeling it for ULBR.

It would be the best choice. He'd be close to home. Get a good education. Play on a team contending for a BCS championship every year. And there were sweet, hot Louisiana girls like Riley around every corner.

As he watched Riley sway and move to the beat, he decided he definitely wanted to be an ULBR Panther.

CHAPTER SIXTEEN

One month later

LOU HADN'T UNDERSTOOD the scope of what would happen when Don Verdun unleashed his incriminating video. He'd sent it to a local television station and called a local journalist and given his story replete with rumors about the night at Rendezvous, Lou's relationship with the entire Dufrene family and the reason he knew something had been going on—his son hadn't received an offer and Waylon had.

And the backlash was bad.

As in she could barely get though the day without some reporter or, heaven help her, a sports blogger, calling her house or dropping by the job site. And this was after almost a month of constant abuse at the hands of the media.

Her foreman, Manuel, waved her down as she walked toward her mover on the site they were preparing for yet another bank. "Yo, Lou, got another one of these reporters. You wanna talk to him?"

"No," she yelled across the freshly churned red dirt she'd been working for the past half hour.

Manuel looked back at the pale man punching something into his smartphone. "Hit the road. She don't want to talk."

The man started forward. "Ms. Boyd, you should talk to someone. At least explain your side!"

Manuel clamped a hand on the guy's shoulder. "She said she ain't talking, hombre. Now take your ass back to your rental car and get the hell outta my site."

"Have you had contact with Coach Dufrene? Is Waylon still a recruit for the Panthers?"

"You brought this on yourself." Manuel grabbed the man by his polo collar and dragged him from the site.

"Hey, hey! Get your hands off me!" the man shrieked. "I'm just doing my job."

Manuel released his hold and loomed over him. "Do it off my job site. Lou has nothing to say to you."

"Fine." The man straightened his collar and cast a hateful look toward her. "But you're not helping yourself, Louise Boyd. Everyone thinks you're nothing but a—"

"Don't say it," Manuel growled.

The man clamped his mouth shut and headed toward his economy car.

Lou released the breath she held, waved her thanks to the foreman, and climbed into the cab of her mover. She slid on her leather gloves and fired the engine, finding comfort in the vibration beneath her. She refused to give in to the anger. To the tears.

She should have felt comforted. Her true friends had rallied around her. All the guys who worked with her had chased away the creeps and lookyloos. Tom Forcet had found an attorney to help her fight the rumors. And Mary Belle and the girls had brought food over like it was a damn funeral again.

And in some ways it was. A funeral for her heart.

She hadn't wanted to love Abram, but she'd not had a choice in the matter. Walking away from him that night nearly a month ago had been so hard, but facing her friends and family with the allegations that she'd gained a foothold by sleeping with Waylon's recruiter had been harder, even though she knew they'd stand by her.

But she'd not expected the reaction Waylon had given her—and it had hurt.

It still hurt.

When her brother had gotten back to the hotel room the night Don had filmed her and Abram, Waylon had not bothered being quiet coming into the room, in true male fashion. Hadn't mattered. Wasn't like she was sleeping anyway. He'd snapped on the bathroom light and she'd made the decision to do exactly what Abram had said. Tell the truth.

"Hey," she called as he knocked something on the tiled floor.

He poked his head out. "Oh, you're still up."

She pushed a hand through her hair. "Couldn't sleep."

He rattled around in the bathroom, before coming out in his boxers and an old zydcco festival T-shirt. "The game was awesome, huh?"

"Yeah." She nodded, trying to decide how to tell her brother about Abram and the caught-on-tape incident. She remained silent for a moment. "So what do you think?"

"About what?" He sank onto the double bed opposite her and plumped up a few pillows. The light from the bathroom door cast a beam through the room. Waylon always slept with a light on. Had since he was a little boy.

"About ULBR. It's your first official visit. Wondered what you thought."

He shrugged and settled back into the bed. "I didn't think anything. I know what ULBR is about. It's not like I haven't been to a game before or walked around campus. We come here every year for camps and stuff."

She slid back so her back hit the faux-wood head-board affixed to the wall. "But you're seeing it as a re-cruit now. That's different."

He yawned. "Yeah. I guess. I think I'm pretty set on going here. I like Coach Dufrene and I'll be close to you and Lori."

She winced. He wanted ULBR.

Well, of course, he did. It was the state flagship school, had won several National Championships in the last decade and was just close enough that he could bring her his laundry. "We still have a few other vis-its to make."

"We don't have to go on them. I don't really care."

"Way, this is important. It's not like choosing your socks."

"I know that." He yawned again and pulled the white sheet up to his ears before rolling over. "I've always wanted to go to ULBR and this weekend confirmed it."

Lou rubbed her eyes and tried to think how to play this out. She had to tell him before he saw it somewhere, but what if Don wasn't going to release the video or pic-tures or whatever he'd recorded? Maybe he thought to use it as leverage.

She shook her head. No way. Don would use it to cause Waylon trouble, rock his recruiting process and cast doubt on his family. The man would do anything to get his son ahead—even ruining someone else's life.

"Way?"

"Mmm?"

"I need to talk to you."

"Can it wait?"

"Probably not."

He rolled back over and squinted at her in the faint light.

And then she'd told him. About the near-miss sex-scapade at Rendezvous. About how hard she'd tried not to fall for Abram. About Don and what had happened that night. Waylon listened quietly, not saying a word until she ended her recounting. Then he asked her one question.

"You told me months ago there was nothing going on between you and Coach Dufrene. Did you lie?"

"Not exactly."

"It's a yes or no question."

"Yes, but not in the way you think. It's not a sex thing. It's a—" She stopped talking because Waylon rolled over. He said nothing more to her, nothing beyond perfunctory yes, no, or okay.

And his silence had lasted for weeks.

He'd even kept up the cold shoulder act throughout their whole visit to the University of Alabama in Tuscaloosa and Christmas wasn't looking promising. This weekend they were scheduled to visit Clemson and she wasn't sure if she could handle much more of Waylon giving her a dead stare and ignoring any overtures she made to smooth things over.

After all, she was the one being cast as the slut sister shopping her brother around to the highest bidder. She was the one being stared at in the grocery store, being given disapproving looks from the people she went to church with and dodging every major sports outlet in the country.

And she was the one going to bed every night alone, stewing over what had happened, trying to ignore her broken heart and the fact she'd not had one single call from Abram.

So she tried to ignore her thoughts and instead do her job. That was the one thing she had control over every day.

Just like today—prepping the ground for pouring the pad. Easy peasy to handle. No problem.

Ten minutes into the job, Manuel waved her off.

She pulled off her gloves and cut the engine. Her foreman never stopped her unless there was an emergency, so she knew this wouldn't be some reporter looking for a story.

She climbed down, rubbing her hands over her denim-clad thighs, and headed to where Manuel stood pointing at something on some blueprints. The man in khakis looked aggravated.

"What's up?" she said, doffing her sunglasses. The late-November sun made a harsh glare reflect off the concrete of the lot next to them so she had a pseudo-headache even with the shades.

"School called. Principal Travers has Waylon in his office."

Something sunk inside her chest and the weight that constantly pressed on her shoulders grew heavier than she thought she could bear. "Did he say why?"

"No, but he said you need to come down. Go ahead. I'll get Digger to finish up. Jay will drive you to your car."

She nodded and headed to where the company truck rattled near a Laundromat across the street from the construction site. Several miles later, she slid from the cab, gave the older man who served as transport a wave, climbed into her car and set off for Bonnet Creek High.

As the wheels turned, so did her mind. What had he done this time? Why was he so angry all the time?

What more would she have to endure in raising her brother and sister?

The mostly empty road held no answers.

When she entered the school office, Helen Barham gave her a disapproving stare and motioned toward Harold Travers' open door.

Screw Helen Barham.

Helen had been talking about her at church last Sunday, turning away and making "told you so" eyes at the tittering old wrens clumped together in the worship hall. It had bothered Lou, not because she expected more of Helen, but because she'd always been a family friend.

"Lou, thanks for coming," Harold said, rising from his desk and indicating the seat next to Waylon. Her brother slunk low in his chair, holding an ice pack to his cheek.

"What happened?" she asked, glancing at her brother before meeting Harold's sympathetic gaze.

"Waylon got into an altercation with Brian Meeks before school this morning. They weren't on campus, but were outside Corky's."

"Brian?" She glanced sharply at her brother. "But they're good friends."

Harold cleared his throat. "Well, apparently not this morning."

Lou laid a hand on her brother's arm. "Way, what happened?"

He pulled his arm from her grasp and shrugged, refusing to say anything.

She turned back to Harold and spread her hands. "I don't know what to do anymore. Things have been so crazy lately with all these rumors and allegations. I'm afraid none of us is doing well."

"Understandable, but we don't tolerate fighting. From

what I understand, Waylon threw the first punch, and he's very lucky it wasn't on campus or our security officer would have had to arrest him and take him in. If Brian or his parents press charges, there may be nothing I can do at this point."

Lou swallowed the panic. Everything she'd sacrificed for all those years. Everything she thought he wanted—and she couldn't stop him from chucking it away. "Well, thank you for calling me."

Harold nodded. "I've talked with our counselor, and she's agreed to see Waylon and help him deal with his anger."

Waylon sat up. "I don't need anyone to talk to. Just have Officer Slade take me in."

Lou whirled toward her brother. "Shut up. You'll do exactly as told. You're acting like someone I don't even know."

He turned angry eyes on her. "Oh, yeah? Well, so are you."

She flinched. "Why are you so angry all the time? Because of this whole scandal?"

He broke eye contact. "Why don't you call it what everyone else in Louisiana is calling it? Lougate. Yeah. That's what they're saying. You snuck around and put out for a coach to get me an offer. How do you think that makes me feel, Lou?"

"How does it make you feel?" She jumped to her feet, feeling the anger she'd held in check course through her. She didn't care Harold Travers was in the room. She was tired of this crap. "Try being me. Try being accused of something you didn't do. I never slept with Abram because I didn't want to run the risk of jeopardizing your recruitment, I didn't want Abram to lose the job he loves, and I wanted to get you and Lori out of Bonnet Creek."

"So you could get rid of us?" His words felt like bullets.

"Get rid of you?"

Harold pushed back his chair. "I'm going to hide my letter opener and give you kids a chance to talk for a moment. I don't think I'm needed in this conversation."

He rose, pocketed the brass letter opener and headed for the door. It shut with a soft snick.

"He really took his letter opener?" Lou said more to herself than Waylon.

Her brother flicked his gaze to the door and shrugged. "Guess he thought you might kill me."

"Don't tempt me." She moved her chair closer to him. "Waylon, what's wrong with you? Really? I've tried so hard to give you a place to share your feelings, but you won't. Family pizza night was a fail. My giving you a curfew is a fail. Nothing works. So, please, let's stop skirting the issue. Please."

He turned and looked at her with eyes that looked so much like her daddy's her heart squeezed. "It's about everything in life sucking, Lou. That's what it's about."

"How?"

"Our parents are gone, you resent me and Lori because we held you back, we didn't make the playoffs this year and Morgan cheated on me with that asshole's son. Not to mention, all the programs who've been pestering me now think I'm tainted goods. Lots of suck in my life, Lou."

She slumped back in the chair and tried to rein in the constant despair that had sat inside her since she'd left Abram that night nearly five weeks ago. "Okay, life sucks, but it sucks for everyone at times. That's part of living. And those coaches are still calling, so I'm pretty sure you're not sunk on getting a scholarship. That is, if you can stop getting in fights and acting like a butthead."

"Wow, you're full of good advice, Lou," he drawled.

She clenched the arms of the chair holding tight so she wouldn't smack her brother. "Life hands you crap sometimes, Waylon. Are you going to hold it, carry it with you? Let it stink up your world? Or are you going to throw it aside, wash your hands and keep on going?"

He shrugged.

"I lost Mom and Dad, too. And it hurt, but I didn't have time to break down. I had you and Lori to look after. Do I resent it at times? Yeah. I do. I was your age, Way. I was a senior with a college scholarship in hand. I was you."

His head jerked a little but he still said nothing.

"I understand the pressure you're under, but God gave you a talent for playing football. When you're on that field, you're a genius. Doesn't matter where you go...or how people say you got there, you have the opportunity I never had sitting right in your hand. Schools haven't stopped recruiting you because you're incredible, and people won't remember anything about this scandal once you hit the field again. You can't throw everything away because you're angry at me, or at Morgan or at your football coach."

"Everybody lets me down." His voice was so sad Lou felt tears prick her eyes.

"People are human. They make mistakes. You can't wall yourself away because you make mistakes, too."

He shook his head. "The only person I had left to trust was you...and even you lied to me."

"Oh, please," she said. "Get over yourself and think about someone else for a change."

"What?" He stiffened and set the ice pack on the floor.

"Do you realize what a little shit you sound like?" She stood again because she couldn't sit still any longer. "I didn't do anything wrong. The only thing I did was fall in love. Period. Do you see us together? Do you see me smiling and happy because for the first time in my life I'm in love?"

He looked up at her. "No."

"Yeah, not happening for me, is it?" Her words sounded bitter, but she couldn't help it. She was bitter. Everything she'd gone through felt like it had been for nothing. Her knucklehead brother seemed determined to throw his desirability as a recruit away just to spite her. Proverbial baby with the bathwater. And though he'd not said it, she knew Abram's career was more important to him than her. That's why he let her walk away. He needed damage control. Distance. Nothing more to do with her.

"You want to know the craziest thing?" She didn't wait for him to respond. "I'm still a virgin."

Her brother shifted in his chair. For a moment, she thought he might bolt for the door.

"Yeah, bet you never thought about that. I've never had a boyfriend for longer than a month, mostly because I had kids. Most men don't want a woman with kids, you know? So I spent my nights washing dishes, folding your socks and teaching Lori how to tie her shoes. I finally found someone, Way, and I couldn't have him." Her voice broke and she shook her head.

"Know what? Doesn't matter. I've got to get back to work." She stared at him hard as he sat before her.

He looked ill-at-ease and for once, she didn't care. "Do what you want to do, Waylon. It's your life."

And then she walked out the door, nearly bowling over Helen.

"Oh, sorry, I lost my pencil over here somewhere," the older woman said, pretending to look under a broad-leafed plant.

"Bull," Lou said, shooting daggers at the woman. "You were listening in so you could go spread your poisonous gossip. I hope you heard enough. Should be good conversation for around the coffeepot."

Helen stiffened. "I wasn't—"

"Look, I don't care. Where is Mr. Travers?"

Helen swallowed, narrowed her eyes, looked down her nose and pointed toward the hall.

"Thanks."

Lou walked out, refusing to look back at either the witch or her dumbass brother. Anger had awakened inside her, so it was best Harold took that letter opener.

The principal turned as she approached. The security officer put his hands on his broad hips and looked slightly sheepish.

"Lou, we were just talking—"

"Do what you want to with him. I'm done." She didn't bother stopping to talk with either of them—just kept heading for the exit. Waylon had to have repercussions for his actions. He'd slid by the other times. If they wanted to take him to jail then she guessed they would with or without her consent...or dissent. She had no control over anything anymore, did she?

She stalked to her car, daring anyone to get in her way. She might hit someone. Seriously. She hadn't been this angry since...

Never.

But at that moment, it felt like her world rampaged out of control and it made her plain mad.

"Lou!" The sound came from her left.

She turned to see Amy Landry holding a tray of cookies. Lou tried to head her off by tossing a wave and keeping her head down.

But Amy moved toward her anyway, her little kitten heels clacking on the pavement, her bracelets clinking at her wrist. The coach's wife always dressed like a lady. "Hey, Lou, I've been meaning to stop by and check on you."

Lou didn't want to chitchat. "I'm fine."

Amy came closer, balancing the tray as she tucked a chunk of auburn hair behind her ear. "Are you? I've been worried about you. Guess it's been tough."

You think? Lou wanted to drawl sarcastically but didn't. Mostly because Amy was about as nice as they come. She was the day-care coordinator at Bonnet Creek Baptist and served as an interpreter for the deaf in church. She always smiled, had a soft touch with curmudgeonly old men and had never said a mean word in her life. Plus, her snake of a husband was cheating on her.

"Well, thanks for saying so," Lou said, pulling out her keys and unlocking her car.

"If you need anyone to talk to, you know I'm available. David feels just terrible about this."

I bet he does. "I appreciate your friendship, Amy, but I'm doing okay. After all, those rumors are untrue. I didn't have an affair with the ULBR coach. Merely a friendly relationship. So in this case, where there's smoke, there's just smoke."

"Well, maybe you should say something, Lou. Everybody's thinking the worst."

"I don't care what everyone thinks, Amy. I know the truth. Coach Dufrene knows the truth. I'm doing exactly what my attorney has asked me to do—let him handle it."

"Okay, but if you need anything, let me know."

Lou nodded. "Sure."

"Okay, I'm off to surprise David and the boys with some treats. They feel terrible about not making the playoffs."

Better knock on that door first, sister.

As Lou climbed into her car, she realized even that pissed her off. Landry snuck around, screwing Carla, and he sat prettily upon the dais as the head coach. Everyone in the community thought he was a wonderful Christian family man.

Ha.

She watched as Amy pulled open the door to the school and gave her another wave. Lou slumped forward and pressed her head against the steering wheel, her anger deflating, leaving her empty. How had things gone so wrong? This time last year, things were gravy. Both Lori and Waylon had been happy, making good grades, doing the things they needed to do to be successful.

But you were lonely and unfulfilled.

Yeah. Big deal. Wasn't that where she was now—only ten times worse because Waylon might be in handcuffs as she sat there defeated? Plus, everyone in the state, heck, the nation, thought she was a slut?

Last year she hadn't known Abram.

A lot of good that did her.

She was still alone. Perhaps more alone than ever.

CHAPTER SEVENTEEN

ABRAM LOOKED AROUND his now-empty office with a sort of disbelief. The desk was cleared and all the files boxed and labeled for the next coach.

This was it.

Game over.

And though he had walked around for the past two months numb from the fallout, surrendering his pass codes, cleaning out his office and wrapping up his career as a coach at ULBR hadn't been as bad as he thought. Telling Sue Ann goodbye had been worse. Maybe because she'd cried.

Or maybe it wasn't so bad because it felt unreal. Like a bad dream. But he'd had no other choice but to resign. It had been best for the program, for the players. It had been the right thing to do.

The right thing.

Funny how doing the right thing sometimes brought about unfair repercussions—like stepping down from the job that had been his identity for the past two years.

All because he'd been human. All because he'd tumbled head over heels for a blue-eyed blond construction worker.

Life was weird.

A sound at the door drew his attention. Jordan stood there, looking like he'd been caught in the middle of a lingerie store looking at stockings. Vastly uncomfortable.

"Hey," Abram said, stacking a box of CD cases on top of the pile containing high school scouting reports. "I'm about to head out so I'm glad you came by."

The strength coach shook his head. "Dude, this isn't right. You told Holt, the AD and the NCAA there wasn't anything going on. All they have is a damn video of a hug. I don't get why you're doing this."

"You and I know how this business works. There's a presumption of guilt by the public, and after that whole recruiting service crap, our own administration has damage control on the brain. I had to step down. It was the only way to erase the black eye on the program. Holt's a good man and he trusts me, but his hands are tied. So why make it hard on him? I knew what had to be done."

His friend shifted on stovepipe legs and shrugged. "I don't understand why no one stands up against injustice anymore. You were railroaded by an angry parent who didn't get his kid into a choice program. Why do people always let that crap slide? Why not say 'We trust our guy. We're standing by him.' Instead of smoke and mirrors and then an eventual dismissal?"

"I wasn't dismissed. I resigned."

Jordan leaned on the door frame and snorted. "Yeah, right."

"Here's why. Because the program is above the coaches, above the players, and above even the fans. That's why I stepped down. It's easier this way. Otherwise, the focus goes to me and that distracts everyone. I want to safeguard the integrity of what we've built here…something I helped to build. I'll suffer through a bad reputation if it keeps what I did from being torn down."

"Yeah, the program. I get it. But when does the program elevate itself over doing what is right?"

"Leonard told me he'd stand beside me, and I believe him. But this is my decision."

Jordan remained silent for a moment. "So what will you do?"

Good question. What would he do? He didn't have an answer for that. Hadn't really thought beyond the day he'd walk away from his dreams. And that's what this was—walking away from his future.

It should have had him on his knees.

But he wasn't crawling down the hallway. Not much more could bring him low, not with what he'd endured over the past few months.

It had been hell in Baton Rouge—a town that loved its Panthers, but could be fickle as that very feline and turn against one of their own in the blink of an eye. Kind of like eating its young.

Such scrutiny wasn't easy to live under, especially when it came from those closest to him, but he'd been honest about everything. Starting the night Don Verdun had taped his damning evidence of misconduct. Abram had watched Lou walk away, felt his heart ache with the knowledge she may never walk toward him again, and had called Leonard Holt immediately.

He'd gone to Holt's house and found the Panthers' head coach in a pair of sweats, a glass of wine in hand, and oddly enough, *House Hunters International* on the TV.

Abram had sunk on the couch and held out his hands. "We have a problem."

Leo sipped the red wine, never taking his eyes off the flickering screen. "You said 'we.'"

"Yeah. We."

And then he'd gone over everything that had happened over the past half year, starting with Rendezvous and ending with that evening.

Holt had asked only two questions.

"Did you sleep with her?"

"No, but I wanted to."

"Are you in love with her?"

"Probably."

Then the coach set the wine on the end table and looked him in the eye. "I'll stand by you."

"Good, because I didn't do anything wrong except fall in love. You can't stop your heart when it makes a decision like that."

Leo inclined his head. "No, but most people don't stop their dicks, either. That you were able to do that is impressive. It's damned impressive 'cause I've seen that woman and there's something about her that draws a man in."

Yeah, there was.

Abram sank back onto the leather sectional and rubbed his face. "But it'll look bad. May not be a thing you or I can do to stop it. I'm sorry. This would never have happened if she hadn't cried."

At this, Leo's mouth twitched. "The power of a woman's tears is almost equal to their smiles, not to mention other parts of their bodies."

For a moment, silence descended as the people on TV talked about the tiny size of the half bath.

Leo's voice broke the debate over a bidet. "If you did nothing wrong, it's not a conflict of interest. It's nothing."

"But you and I know once the press gets ahold of this it won't matter. People don't want the truth. They want sensationalism. They want death, destruction and humiliation."

"That's damned cynical."

"But true."

Then Leonard said something that lanced into his soul, both wounding him and healing him.

"Life sometimes takes you down a road you never expect to travel. Some people fight against it, sit down and refuse to move on. They wither and die on the side of the road, heartsick they found the original road closed to them. But others move on, knowing the way may be hard, filled with potholes and things that go bump in the night, but also knowing on a road untraveled there is opportunity. Never know what's behind the next curve. Be the guy that gets up and moves on, Abram."

So Abram had. He spent the next few months defending himself to the administration, avoiding the press, relinquishing his recruits to another coach and focusing on preparing his guys to play in the Capitol One Bowl. The holidays had blurred together with a veneer of happiness. His mother had wiped tears from her eyes while toasting the New Year, her desolation at the bereaved Sally's refusal to talk with her tempered only by Paxton Laborde Dufrene, her one true present, delivered by his sister-in-law on Christmas Eve.

And so the days flew by, each one emptier than the last, because he couldn't bring himself to call Lou.

What did he have to offer? He had no direction. His dreams had been destroyed by the very thing that brought them together. What more could he do to her? His presence in her life would only cement in people's minds what they thought they knew. Of course, he shouldn't worry about what people thought, but that was easier said by people who had not borne the scorn of the general public. He knew Lou had gone through as much as he had. He'd seen what the message boards had said, had seen the implications in the papers, and wondered how she'd been handling all the fallout.

If he could, he'd beat the ever-loving hell out of Don Verdun.

But that, too, would do more damage than good, even if the thought made him feel better.

The wide receivers coach Howie Girard had taken over Waylon's recruiting, and through the older man, he'd learned a few pertinent things like Waylon had gotten into some sort of altercation at school, but since then had seemed a changed kid. He learned the boy had narrowed his choices down to ULBR, Clemson and Texas. He also learned Tom Forcet had sent his attorney to guide Lou through the process. The family had made an official statement denying there was any sort of inappropriate relationship and threatening a defamation suit against Verdun and the media outlets that broke the story. For some reason, it pleased Abram that Lou hadn't played the victim, even if neither of them had addressed the allegations in a public way.

"I'll help you carry this stuff down to your truck," Jordan offered, his voice resigned. "I guess it's the least I can do."

"You could buy me a drink."

"Yeah, I could do that."

"Maybe a scotch. I think I need an expensive double malt."

Jordan lifted the heaviest box and walked out the door past a still-sniffling Sue Ann. "Amend that to just double malt scotch and you have a deal."

Abram picked up the boxes on his desk and followed his friend from the office, giving one last look at the empty room before shutting the door and handing his key to Sue Ann.

She took it, stood and kissed his cheek and dropped back into her cushioned chair. "I won't say goodbye."

"It's the best stand you can make," Abram teased, giving her a smile.

He walked out of the football administration building putting one foot in front of the other, determined to strike out on a new road, even if he didn't know where it could possibly lead.

Even if it scared him—and might not include Lou.

WAYLON STARED at the bare branches dipping over Lake Chicot. The day was stark with bitter wind blowing in from the north. Definitely not a day to be on a lake, but Waylon ignored the cold sneaking beneath his heavy jacket and trudged down the hiking trail skirting the bank of the lake. Dying grasses and vines tangled along the edge of the water, and gray clouds threatened rain that wouldn't fall.

A lone coot hooted as it traversed the waves.

Waylon knew how the bird felt.

He'd come here intentionally to seek some peace. To think.

His father had brought him here when he was young. The memory of his father's voice had faded away, but not so much the lessons his father had taught. Lessons about staying to the path, looking ahead for trouble and wearing mosquito repellant. Funny what a person remembers.

His dad had been a dreamer, and that's what had gotten him killed. He'd dreamed of owning his own business and had gambled everything to make it happen. It had been a calculated risk, but a risk all the same.

What risk would Waylon take?

He had one more week to decide.

Where did his future lie?

Over the past months, he'd done his best to straighten up, which hadn't been easy because being bitter had grown on him like a comfortable sweatshirt. He'd needed no veneer to cover his disillusion, and that felt honest. But after Lou had gone all medieval on him, he'd sat a few minutes in the principal's office and allowed her words to penetrate his armor.

Life hadn't been fair to Lou.

In fact, it had been a lot more unfair to her than it had to him or Lori. He'd always thought she'd gotten the best end of the deal. She'd had Mom and Dad for almost eighteen years while he'd only had seven. He'd been envious of her.

Guess he'd never really thought of Lou as a person. She'd just been Lou. She was the one who fixed things. Who made sure his papers were mistake-free and his cafeteria account full. She'd been kinda his mom and kinda his sister, but not much more to him. He knew what kind of cereal she preferred in the morning, but he didn't know her dreams or her hopes...and had never really bothered to ask.

He supposed that made him selfish.

He paused at a clearing and picked up a flat rock, hurling it, watching it skip on the water four times. It was the same clearing his father had taught him to skip rocks the day after he turned seven.

Dad, what do I do?

He paused for a moment, listening to the wind, but no answer came to him.

Several weeks ago he'd visited Clemson and really liked it. The tight ends coach had played in the pros and had him excited about the possibility of playing for the school. He'd like the facilities and the campus was nice, but South Carolina was far away from Louisiana. He didn't like the idea of being so far from his home.

On the other hand, ULBR was only an hour and a half away—and the Panthers still wanted him regardless of the stupid video that asshat Hayden's father had revealed. Waylon had always wanted to go to ULBR. Had a half a dozen T-shirts and ball caps with the logo on it. Besides, everyone expected him to go to his state school.

But would those allegations follow him? Would he constantly have to answer questions about Lou and why he'd gotten that scholarship?

He figured he would.

Coach Dufrene had stepped down around the time he and Lou had left for the official visit at Clemson, and the news the man had left ULBR had renewed the sadness in Lou's eyes.

And he knew why.

He'd watched the video one night after Lou and Lori had gone to bed. He made certain they were asleep and then logged on to one of the ULBR fan forums and found the link. Of course, he couldn't help but see some of the remarks the posters had made—not flattering toward his sister—and he had to suppress the urge to post something back to the half-dozen morons posting on the thread. Then he'd clicked on the link and saw the truth.

What some might see as sordid proof the coach and his sister had something going on, he saw only as proof his sister loved Abram Dufrene. And most startling of all—the coach loved her back.

Waylon could see it in the way the coach looked

at her, and even though the film was grainy, he could see the tenderness in the way he held her. It had nearly floored him to see the two of them together that way, and some kernel of something he couldn't name had embedded itself inside him.

He'd clicked off the site, but the image of Lou crying and Coach Dufrene holding her had stayed with him. Eventually, over the past few weeks he'd put a name to what he felt: injustice.

All that happened hadn't been fair to Lou or the coach who'd been recruiting him.

He picked up another rock and skipped it along the waves. It skipped once before sinking beneath the choppy waters. Night was falling and soon he'd have to get back home. He had an English test to study for and he'd told Lou he'd change the lightbulb out on the back patio yesterday. She hadn't even fussed at him, which was a miracle, but the last couple of months had changed her.

After his run-in with Brian, he'd gotten his act together. First, he'd talked to the principal and Officer Slade, taking responsibility. Then he'd found Brian and apologized for losing his temper over a silly comment. Then he'd spent two days home on suspension. He'd used that time to catch up on his schoolwork, do odd jobs around the house for Lou and hit his knees and pray for guidance. He'd even gone back to youth group on Wednesday nights. The best thing he'd done was talk to Morgan and admit he'd been partially at fault for their ruined relationship. They weren't back together, but he could at least tolerate seeing her in the hall.

He hadn't bothered returning any of Cy's texts. He figured Cy had gotten the message. Waylon had closed

that listless, dark chapter in his life, and it felt good to
let Cy, Rory and freaky Leesa fade away.

Finally, things started to click.

But no matter how much better he acted, Lou had
sunk deeper into herself. On the outside she seemed fine,
strong even. On their trip to Clemson she'd laughed,
smiled and acted much as she had before, but he could
see the cracks. The far-off looks. The way she flinched
when the new ULBR coach called to chat with him.

Right now they were in the middle of a dead period.

No more calls.

No more hassle.

Just time to decide where he'd sign when he climbed
onto the stage at Bonnet Creek High School next Tuesday morning. When he announced on ESPNU what
school he'd chosen, signed his letter of intent and faxed
it to the university.

Only problem was he didn't know which school that
would be.

He'd hope to find the answer here in this place he'd
roamed as a child, in this place his father had loved, but
nothing had been revealed to him.

Just more static in his life—something he'd grown
accustom to hearing.

Lou HAD SPENT several sleepless nights, and it showed
in the mirror. That morning Waylon would sign his letter, and finally the recruiting process would be over.
That idea should have blanketed her with relief, but it
didn't. She was too tense to feel anything other than her
nerves on high alert.

Mostly because Waylon still wasn't talking.

Usually family knew. They were in on the debate,

weighing the pros and cons, pacing the floor, grappling with the gut-wrenching decision. But obviously Waylon hadn't gotten the memo.

So she and Lori had decided they would force him to tell them last night. Lori had baked cookies with colored chocolate candies in all the school colors he had on his list. Of course, she had gone heavy on the purple. Lou had made chicken enchiladas—the only thing Waylon said she was good at cooking—in preparation for a night of talking about choices and about what the morrow would bring, and she didn't get out her recipe for nothing.

Lou recalled last night's exchange.

"Yeah?" Waylon had called through his closed bedroom door when she'd knocked.

"Time for dinner."

"I grabbed a burger after I left Brian's house. I'm good."

"Will you open the door?"

The door opened and her brother gave her a quizzical look. "What's up?"

"What do you mean 'what's up'? You know what's up. I made dinner and Lori baked cookies. Don't you want to talk about this? About tomorrow?"

He shrugged. "Not really. I made up my mind earlier today and I'm good with the decision."

Lou felt Lori creep up behind her.

"Well?" her sister said.

"Well, what?" Waylon asked, stifling a yawn.

"Aren't you going to tell us what you've decided?" Lou asked, crossing her arms.

"No."

Lori kicked the door frame. "No? What do you mean 'no'?"

Waylon mimicked Lou's stance, crossing his arms over his broad chest and giving his best glower. Lou tried not to notice how messy his room was. For goodness' sake, there was a damp towel on the carpet along with shoes, boxers and an old gym bag. "I'm waiting to tell everyone tomorrow. I want it to be a surprise for everybody."

"But we're your family," Lori yelled, kicking the jamb again.

"Stop, Lori. Are you insane?"

"No," she said, "but you are! Why won't you tell us what you're doing? That's stupid. We're your family."

"So you said already." Waylon leveled his hazel eyes at them and stood akimbo. "But I'm not telling you what I've decided."

Lori narrowed her eyes. "Oh, you think you're such a big deal. Like I care where you go throw a stupid ball? Whatever."

Then she stalked away.

"For your information, I catch the ball. Not throw it," Waylon said.

Lou didn't turn around to watch her sister stomp dramatically toward the living room, but by her brother's twitch of lips she figured Lori had given him the finger.

"Are you sure you don't want to talk about things?" Lou asked, trying for some gravity. "Regardless of what Lori just said, it is a big deal. This is your future."

He gave her a little smile. "Exactly. My future. I'm not trying to be an ass or anything. Just want to make it fun for you and Lori."

"Fun? Really?"

He laughed. "Come on, sis. How often are you really surprised in life? Humor me. This whole process has been long and hard, and even though it's screwed with our lives more than I care to admit, I want this to be totally my decision."

Lou opened her mouth to argue, but then closed it. It was his decision. "I can't believe you're holding out on us, but fine."

He nodded and then grabbed her, giving her an uncharacteristic hug. "It's all good, Lou. It's all good. I'm feeling great about tomorrow, but right now I want to get some sleep."

She squeezed him back before releasing him. "Okay, maybe I'll save you some enchiladas."

"I love you, Lou. I really do. I know this whole year has been a bitch, but you've stuck by me all the way, and I appreciate that."

For a moment she couldn't speak. Her throat was raw with tears and something felt all cloggy in her chest, too. "Who are you?"

"The guy I should have been all along. I'm sorry, Lou."

She managed to hold herself together and gave him a nod. He grinned and shut his door with a soft click, leaving her wondering what the devil had happened.

Back in the kitchen she'd shed a few tears—and then grown a little aggravated she still hadn't found out where her brother was headed for college.

And she hadn't heard from him all night. Not until this morning when he bellowed about being out of deodorant. She loaned him some of hers, which didn't make him happy, and then he disappeared again, locking his door. She still couldn't believe there would be a press conference to cover his announcement. That recruiting had come to this boggled her, but all over the country ESPNU and online sports sites would be covering National Signing Day.

At 9:00 a.m., Waylon appeared looking remarkably calm.

He nodded at her. "Let's do this."

So they headed for the high school and Waylon's uncertain future.

Problem was, Lou still had no clue where that uncertain future lay.

CHAPTER EIGHTEEN

THE ADMINISTRATION HAD set the press conference in the gym and had arranged for a pep rally. Cheerleaders bopped around in short blue-and-white skirts and the dance line had already performed a rousing jazz routine to an '80s rock classic. Lou thought it a bit overdone, and even Waylon looked sheepish about the abnormal amount of attention. She figured it was one of the bigger things to happen to the small school. They'd once had a National Merit Scholar, and one kid a few years back had gone to Arkansas on a full track scholarship. So she supposed having ESPN run a feed into Bonnet Creek merited something other than a normal signing.

The gym filled quickly and the principal climbed up on the small platform holding a podium and a table with five ball caps sitting in front of Waylon's designated spot. Next to him would be Brian Meeks, who had already given his verbal to Louisiana Tech a few months back, but would still share in the festivities. Principal Travers went through a spiel about proper behavior before handing the reins to Coach Landry.

At this point, Waylon was instructed to mount the few stairs and take his place at the table. Lou and Lori wouldn't go up, merely stand close by.

She noticed Waylon, who'd been so confident earlier, looked a little anxious. He followed his friend Brian up the stairs and they both settled into their chairs. Even Brian looked intimidated.

Coach Landry looked over at both boys. "I know most of you know Waylon Boyd. He's been our bread and butter on offense for several years. Next to him is Brian Meeks, another standout who will go on to represent the Owls at Louisiana Tech next season. I can't tell you all how proud I am of these two fellows."

Hearty applause broke out and several cheerleaders did high kicks and wiggled spirit fingers. After everyone settled down, the coach went down a laundry list of rules for the press conference, trying to ensure all went smoothly.

Five minutes later, the local cameramen crowded around the stage as Brian signed his LOI. The applause was thunderous when he stood up and pulled off his jacket to reveal a Bulldog jersey under his shirt. Even Waylon laughed when his friend got the sleeve caught on the edge of the podium and nearly pulled the wooden lectern into Principal Travers's lap.

"Okay, folks. Now we're moving on to Waylon Boyd. We all know his statistics, what he's done for the Owls and the choices sitting before him, but what we don't know is where he'll be lending his talents next year. Waylon?"

At that point, they waited on the red light from the camera guy from ESPN. When it appeared, the guy pointed to her brother.

Tension filled Lou as Waylon leaned toward the mike and Lori gripped her hand. Here it was. The moment they'd been waiting for all year long.

Waylon cleared his throat. "Um, I want to thank the school, my friends and family for all the support this past year. It's been a hard year for me and making a decision about where to play has been pretty tough. A lot of schools wanted me which was a true honor."

He cleared his throat again. "But before I talk about my selection, I wanted to say something to all of you about something that's been weighing on me."

Lou swallowed and looked at Lori. She looked confused—and slightly apprehensive. Everyone else in the gym seemed to lean forward in the bleachers. Even the cameraman jabbed his finger at his assistant. Tension thickened.

"A few months ago, there were some questions about my sister and a coach from ULBR."

Oh. No. Lou felt her stomach contract. What was he doing?

A buzz erupted over the crowd assembled before they quieted at Waylon's raised hand.

"Just bear with me because this needs to be said."

Silence descended and Lou wondered if her toast and over-easy egg might come back up.

"I know many of you saw the video some jerk took of my sister and Coach Dufrene, and a lot of you jumped to the conclusion that something more was happening than a normal recruiting relationship…and you were right."

Lou felt her mouth drop open as eyes shifted to her. Even the damn cameraman moved his camera to her. She closed her mouth and swallowed hard, zipping her gaze to her brother. He looked at her with eyes that revealed nothing.

What was he doing? Was this some sort of punishment? Her heart raced and she felt heat flood her cheeks.

"I saw the video, too," Waylon continued, before licking his lips, "and where most of you saw something wrong in that embrace, I saw something right."

Coach Landry shifted on his feet and Lou wondered if he might rip the microphone from her brother. She half wished he would.

"You see, I saw what Lou had been trying to hide all along, and it wasn't some crazy, screwed-up affair with Coach Dufrene. I saw they'd fallen for each other."

Air whooshed from her lungs and she thought the gym floor might come up to meet her. She swayed and Lori clasped her hand even tighter.

Waylon moved his gaze to her. "That wasn't fair to you, Lou."

She shook her head, but couldn't find any words.

"See, I have a problem with everything everyone was saying because they don't know you like I do. They don't realize that when you were eighteen you gave up your life to take care of me and Lori. They can't see what an awesome sister you are. How moral and good you are. How you taught us right from wrong…and how you denied yourself love to do the right thing for me."

Lou felt tears slide down her cheeks and could only managed to whisper. "Way."

"They took something genuine you felt for someone and made it tawdry. That's a word I learned for the SAT. But the thing is, I know you didn't do anything that would hurt me. You never have."

She shook her head and swiped at the tears.

"Because both you and Coach Dufrene did the right thing, you both lost and that's not fair."

The buzz in the gym had become a dull roar and all eyes were on her, not her brother.

Waylon tapped the microphone. "I had some deep thinking to do on this whole deal, and a few days ago, it occurred to me that if I went to my state school, things would never die down. I have always loved the Panthers, like most of you do, but when I put things down on paper and then did a gut check, I knew it wasn't the place I belonged. It was my safety net."

Lori whispered, "Oh, wow."

He charged forth. "I found a place where I know I fit. So today, I want you all to know that I'm choosing to attend Clemson University. This fall I'll be a Tiger in South Carolina."

The gym erupted. Some clapped. Some booed. Everyone started talking at once.

Lou merely stared as her brother picked up the orange-and-purple ball cap and placed it on his head. He grinned and stood to shake Brian's hand. They gave each other a bro hug and then Coach Landry moved forward to shake Waylon's hand.

"Lou?" Lori asked softly, jiggling her hand.

Lou rubbed her eyes and looked at her sister. "Huh?"

"Shouldn't we go hug Way?"

At that moment Waylon broke his handshake with the coach and leaned over and spoke into the microphone. "And another thing, Coach Dufrene, if you're listening, I think the best find you ever made in Bonnet Creek is still here. Don't let her get away."

And suddenly people starting standing up and clapping. Their broad smiles and nodding heads registered in her mind at the moment she took her first step toward the brother who already headed for them.

He didn't hesitate. He swooped her into his arms for a hug, lifting her from the floor.

"Way, why did you do this? You wanted ULBR."

"Nah, I liked Clemson all along, but I was afraid

to leave. I'm not afraid anymore. You shouldn't be, either, Lou."

"But—"

"No buts." He set her on her feet and grabbed Lori who smiled like Christmas had come late. He whirled her around and laughed.

Lou stood rooted to the spot where he'd dropped her.

She couldn't believe what he'd done. It blew her mind.

"Lou, would you consider giving an interview to ESPN regarding your brother's commitment? Also regarding his message to all those listening about your relationship with Abram Dufrene?" It was the cameraman's assistant. The camera bobbed toward her.

"I don't have a relationship with Abram," she said more to herself than to the cameraman.

But even as she said the words, something bubbled up inside her, spilling over into the desert of her soul. The feeling flooded her, soaking her in sweet hope. *What if?*

"Ma'am?"

She shuffled backward. "Um, excuse me. I need to get some air."

Waylon set Lori on her feet and before he was consumed by well-wishers, leaned over and whispered in Lou's ear. "Go. Go get your dream."

She blinked once before spinning away from the stage, leaving Lori and Waylon to accept the congratulations bearing down on him from teachers, faculty and staff. She even caught a glimpse of the mayor pressing flesh with the principal.

She didn't stop, not even when Mary Belle waved frantically at her. She headed for the back exit, the one that would take her to the parking lot. She burst through the doors and into the crisp February morning, hands trembling as she pulled her phone from her pocket. It had vibrated once as she headed toward the double door, indicating a text message.

It was from Picou. Abram is at Beau Soleil. Don't break any speed limits.

Lou laughed, maybe somewhat hysterically, and shoved her phone back into her pocket, pulling her car keys from the other pocket of the new pants she'd selected for the press conference. She'd lost so much weight that she'd had to buy new ones along with a new rose sweater that made her skin glow in spite of the bags under her eyes. She looked at her car sitting in the parking lot.

Should she take the gamble?

Her mind flipped back to Waylon and his eyes as he berated the people of Bonnet Creek and the media for their conclusions about her.

She pushed the button, unlocking the car, the beep-beep echoing the trepidation in her heart.

Find her dream.

She could do that. And the first step was going to the man who was an integral part of that.

ABRAM SHUT OFF THE TV in the kitchen where he sat eating cinnamon rolls Lucille had made that morning. The housekeeper had gone into town and his mother was nowhere to be found—and he really wasn't looking to find her.

I don't have a relationship with Abram.

The same words uttered by Lou many times before. But why did this time feel so final?

Maybe because it was true.

And Waylon? The boy's courage amazed him. He'd

sat there in the spotlight and berated the world for believing the worst. The boy had stood up for love.

Amazing...but maybe a waste of breath.

When he'd left ULBR and Baton Rouge looking for a
break, he'd come to Beau Soleil—the place he'd grown
into a man. He'd hoped coming here would give him
better direction, and on some level he'd lapsed into a
fantasy, dreaming of Lou calling him and telling him
nothing else mattered but being with him. But after a
few days he realized it was stupid to expect her to call
him, especially after he'd sent her off to suffer through
this mess on her own. He'd told her it was over and had
left only the slightest sliver of hope they could ever have
a future together.

That road had been closed down.

He'd have to find a new one to travel.

Abram shoved away from the table and dropped the
empty plate in the sink. He'd put on five pounds staying at Beau Soleil and he needed to go for a run. Two
days ago he'd interviewed for the head-coaching job at
Bayou Bridge High. He was overqualified for the position, but still felt nervous about hearing from the school
board and principal regarding the job. He'd never taught
high school and the position required he teach World
History. He hoped he could handle it because suddenly
it had become very important to him to be named head
coach. He and his agent had parted ways over a month
ago when he'd refused a coaching gig in California at
a Division II school. He'd put his eggs in this basket
and hoped he didn't end up scraping yolk off the floor.

If it didn't pan out, he'd do something. Coach Holt
had told him he'd help him out and talk to some schools,
so he could always call in that favor. Or look for a new
agent.

But in the back of his mind he wanted to stay near Beau Soleil.

Wanted to be near Lou.

Wanted a chance at something he'd not tasted in a while—true happiness.

"Oh, you're still here," his mother said, padding into the kitchen in a pair of yoga pants and a long-sleeved matching top. Her hair lay in a fat silver braid and her forehead was sheened in sweat. "You know, yoga would do you a world of good. I noticed your flexibility wasn't so good."

He frowned. "I work out every day. Well, at least I did."

Picou grabbed bottled water from the fridge and pointed at the empty pan of rolls. "Might want to lay off those, too."

"Really, Mom? That's what I wanted to hear. I'm unemployed, lonely and living with my mother. Let me have some pleasure in life."

"Poor pitiful you. You'll have a job by week's end. That I know. You still have a house in Baton Rouge. Besides, I'm working on the lonely part."

An alarm sounded inside his brain. "Don't. I can handle my love life on my own."

"But she's such an interesting girl. I know you'd like her."

"No." He jabbed a finger at her. "I'm going out for a run. If my phone rings, take a message. Might be the school board."

"Do I look like your secretary?" She gulped down water, wiping her lip with the back of her hand. She sat the bottle on the counter, placed a hand on her hip and looked hard at him. "You look more pathetic than you did yesterday. Everything okay?"

How could he tell her Lou had put a nail in the coffin with her denial on national TV? "I'm good. Still trying to deal with my life going down the shitter."

"Language, please."

"Sorry."

"I think you're bouncing back well. After all, unless you were merely going for prestige, you'll still get to coach, to make a difference in the lives of young men. In fact, you may find your true place in life where you least expected it."

Abram shrugged. "I won't lie. I wanted to work my way up the coaching ladder. Be a head coach in a Division I school. Still, I'll be fine as long as I can still coach guys and impact them in some way. And, it will be nice to sleep in my own bed rather than on the couch in an office."

"You'll still live in Louisiana. Near me."

He laughed. "Yeah, living with my mother. That's what it's come to. Maybe I should go ahead and move in with you, Mom."

"Absolutely not." Picou headed toward the swinging kitchen door. "Go forth and rebuild your own life."

He shook his head. If only it were that easy.

He headed up the stairs to change into some shorts and a long-sleeved tee. Maybe a run would clear his head and give him direction. Or maybe it would give him release from the pressure of having no direction.

At the very least he'd burn off those cinnamon rolls.

LOU NEARLY MISSED the turn to Beau Soleil, she was so busy planning what she'd say to Abram when she saw him.

What would she say?

Sorry I haven't called?

Sorry you lost your job?

Sorry Waylon signed with Clemson?

Sorry I gave up on love with you?

The gates nearly jumped at her as she took the corner, and she turned so sharply the car nearly scraped against them as she pulled into the drive. She tapped her brakes and took a deep breath.

Okay, easy, Lou. This is Abram. This is the man you love.

But her words didn't stop her heart from galloping or her stomach from churning.

She pressed the brake, bringing the car to a complete stop and then drummed the steering wheel with her fingers. "Should I do this?"

Her voice sounding in the car startled her. The hour-and-a-half-long drive had been too quiet and had given her too much time to talk herself out of going to Beau Soleil.

What if he didn't want her?

The thought had crossed her mind more than once—okay, a lot—over the past few months. Maybe she'd only imagined his heart was involved. Maybe it was merely a lust thing…and a man could fulfill that need with another woman easily. Or at least a man who looked like Abram could.

Dear Lord, what if he'd already moved on?

That would royally suck to pull up into his world again and find him taken. But then again, Picou wouldn't have sent her that message, would she?

Too many questions and the answers lay ahead of her in that rambling plantation house with peculiar charm and addictive men. She jabbed her foot on the accelerator and the car leaped forward, nearly hitting a blur of blue coming around the corner of the abnormally long drive. She slammed on her brakes and the car skidded in the gravel, striking something.

The thump of a body hitting and falling had her throwing the car into Park. "Oh, my God!"

She'd hit someone. And whoever that someone was had been thrown into the brambles on the side of the drive. After throwing open her door and climbing out, she caught a flash of color to the right of the wheel well. She left the car idling and ran around the front end.

"Damn it."

Abram sprawled out in a tangle of vines and brush. His shirt clung to a barbed vine, lifting the hem to reveal spectacular abs. Her mouth went dry.

She'd hit the man she'd come here for.

"Oh, God, are you okay?" she asked, hurrying to where he lay, picking at brambles caught in the weave of his shirt.

"Ow!" He rolled to his bottom and winced before moving his arms and legs, checking that they worked. "I'm okay."

"I'm so sorry. I didn't see you."

"Lou?" He looked up at her with incredulous green eyes. "What the hell are you doing here? It's signing day."

"I know."

He flipped over and then sprang to his feet, dusting the bits of leaf off his athletic shorts. "So why are you here? Is something wrong? Or are you trying to kill me?"

"Of course not. I wasn't paying attention. Instead I was thinking so hard about what I wanted to say to you that I almost, um, killed you."

He shook his head and blinked his eyes rapidly. It was

cartoonish and normally would have made her laugh, but this was no laughing matter. Nor was it a smiling one.

He blinked one last time. "What you wanted to say?"

She licked her lips, taking in how good he looked. He'd put on a few pounds and looked super fit if not a little pale from the winter—or maybe the fact he'd lost his dream job for no good reason. "Um, yeah, I came here to tell you…"

And then she couldn't remember what she'd practiced in the car. Something about how they'd squandered a chance at love but still had an opportunity to overcome all the obstacles they'd had before them, and then something about Waylon bringing her to her senses. But after having nearly run him over, that sounded stupid.

"Uh, well, I had this whole speech planned out about how we sort of let this thing between us, you know, fall away. I thought we could maybe talk about—" she swallowed "—something more."

"Something more?" he repeated, rubbing a hand through his short hair. "Like a relationship? Or a friendship?"

Oh, Lord, she was screwing everything up. She wasn't good at words.

She flapped her hands. "Oh, hell."

She moved as quick as Waylon ever could and launched herself into his arms, wrapping her legs around his waist and landing a kiss somewhere near his mouth.

Lucky for her, he caught her cleanly or they might have landed in the thorn-covered vines again. He moved so it was his lips she kissed instead of a spot sort of near his lips.

Lou went for it, tugging his head back, deepening the kiss so it was a slow, wet one just like Kevin Costner had suggested in one of his countless baseball movies.

And it was wonderful. Like candy at Christmas. Or like a jazz standard on a rainy night. Or like a hot, hard man doing sweet, delightful things with his hands.

Which he was.

Finally, she broke the kiss and leaned back to look at him. "I didn't have the words."

He smiled. "I think I like you tongue-tied."

She didn't let go of him. Instead she squeezed her legs harder, hugging her to him, laying her head on his shoulder. "I missed you."

His response was to hold her tighter and kiss her cheek. She smelled that familiar scent she'd missed— some kind of sporty aftershave and quiet confidence. That was Abram—and all she'd ever want in a man. "You can set me down now. I forgot I hit you with my car. Are you hurt?"

"No, and what if I don't want to let you go again? What if I just hold you here forever?"

She sighed. "We'll get rained on, and eventually get hungry. And I know I've lost weight, but I'm pretty sure your arms will get tired."

He set her down. "Ah, Lou. Ever practical. You just suck the romance out of things."

Well, that hadn't been her intent. "Maybe I need someone to show me how romance works. The last date I went on the guy made me go dutch."

He laughed. "That's wretched. A travesty. And what the hell are you doing going out with some other guy?"

"Trust me when I say it was a mistake." She darted her gaze to where a blackbird hopped on a naked branch of the tree behind him. She didn't want to look him in the eye, just in case he blew her off. "So you think you're up for the job of teaching me about romance?"

He tucked a strand of hair behind her ear and tapped

her chin so that she was forced to meet his gaze. In his eyes she saw such sweetness and her heart contracted. Warmth filled her as he whispered, "You came for me. Do you know how romantic that is?"

She felt her eyes fill, reflecting tenderness. "I never wanted to go in the first place."

He lowered his head and kissed her and she tasted forever in his kiss. She slid her hands up and around his shoulders and tangled her fingers in the short hair at the nape of his neck. He felt so warmly masculine, so very right in her arms. She thought she might stay there forever. Rain and hunger be damned.

Abram slid his hands up her back and wrapped his fingers in her hair, forcing her head back. He broke the kiss, tipped his head back and looked at her. Suddenly she felt like a heroine in one of those Regency romances she had stacked on her bedside table. Like her dreams might be coming true.

His gaze caressed her and she couldn't help the smile that curved her lips. "Hey, we kissed out in the open and there was no one to catch us. Bummer."

He chuckled, releasing her hair so he could move his hands to cup her face. Something about the way he held her made her feel treasured, and it had been forever ago since she felt so cherished. "Been lots of irony in this whole thing, hasn't it?"

She nodded, but didn't relinquish him. Felt too nice having her fingers all over him. "Like I'm pretty much the sluttiest virgin in all of Louisiana."

He bent his head and dropped little baby kisses along her jaw, nuzzling her neck, nipping her earlobe. "I like slutty virgins though I can't say a part of that will remain true for very long."

"You're going to take away my sluttiness?"

She felt the rumble of laughter in his chest as he lifted his head and pulled her against him. "Underneath that serious demeanor, you've got a wicked sense of humor, woman."

She arched an eyebrow and grinned.

His eyes became soft as spring grass. "Stay with me, Lou."

"I will, I want to build something with you, but there are considerations…like Lori, my job and my house in Bonnet Creek, so literally, I'll have to leave you."

"I know that, but I never want you to close a door on us. No more walking away."

She shook her head. "That's why I drove like a bat out of hell to get to you. I want a new beginning with you with nothing in between us. It won't be perfect, but I think what we have is worth a do-over."

He closed his eyes and took a deep breath. When he released it, she felt the cleansing…the relief, and it shook her to her core. This man wanted her. This man loved her.

Finally, her day had come.

He opened his eyes and smiled. "I think I found my new road."

"What?"

He kissed her quickly and turned her toward her car. "I'll explain later, for now I'm just happy to be in this moment. Happy you came to me."

Twining his fingers with hers, Abram tugged her back toward her still-idling car. She glanced up at him, his brown hair dappled with the winter sunlight, his cheek scruffy with a two-day beard, and said, "There is a lot to be sorry about over this past year, but I'll never be sorry I walked into that honky-tonk, found a pretend date waiting for me and rekindled something within me that had lay dead for so long. And I'll never regret falling in love with you."

He stopped. "You're in love with me?"

She nodded. "I thought that was understood."

He snatched her from where she stood, hauling her into his arms. "I love you, too."

And then he kissed her again.

Forever echoed in his kiss.

Lou tilted her head back and laughed. "This is wonderful. So, so very wonderful."

"And special," he added. "Don't forget I told you to wait for someone special."

She lowered her chin. "What are you talking about?"

"That night on the pier when you told me you were a virgin. Remember? I said don't give it up to me, some random stranger, but wait for someone who means something to you."

Lou felt joy bubble up inside her, following swiftly by red-hot desire. "And to think he's one and the same."

"I better get you back to Beau Soleil before your first time is on a pile of brambles near an old graveyard."

Lou shook her head. "No way I'm having sex in your mother's house."

He eyed her car. "Think you can turn that car around quickly?"

"You're not serious? What about your mother? What would she think if I didn't come inside to say hello?"

He made a confused face. "She doesn't even know you're here."

Lou started laughing. "Who do you think told me where you were?"

"My mother called you?"

She shook her head. "No, texted me."

He started laughing, lifted her and swung her in a circle. "You're the interesting girl?"

She couldn't stop the laughter. "What are you talking about?"

He set her down, kissed her and said, "Just before I left for my run, she told me she'd found me an interesting girl. I thought she was trying to set me up, but she meant you."

"Come to think of it, the first time I met her, she told me I was interesting. Then she told me she dreamed about me and that I would be important to her family. She said I led someone out of the woods." Lou looked around at the naked trees enveloping them.

Abram hummed the *Twilight Zone* music before saying, "You know, I didn't know I was lost until I met you. My world felt rock solid, but far less interesting, not to mention lonely. I had this goal in front of me, something I thought meant more than anything, but sometimes dreams divert in the most interesting ways. I found you, a new career that I'm surprisingly excited about, and I'm truly happy."

Lou felt the same way. For years her goal had been to get Lori and Waylon raised and successful so she could go back in time and recapture her old dream, but life had changed her and she could never go back to being that young, bright-eyed freshman. Somehow in setting her goal so solidly in front of her, she'd forgotten that the joy was in the living—and the surprises life held.

Abram was the best surprise she'd ever had.

"I'm happy, too, and excited about the future in a way I've never been before."

She reached her still-idling car and turned toward him. He braced both arms on the frame of the car, capturing her in his arms. "Me, too. So as to our future, do you think you can pencil in a date with the Coach?"

"Like when? And are you still a coach?"

"As of ten minutes ago, I'm the new coach of the Bayou Bridge, and, I think tonight will do fine."

"But it's Tuesday."

"The best day to start a new beginning."

Lou smiled, cupped his face and bestowed a kiss that held all her desire, passion and love on his very delicious lips. "Bring a condom."

He smiled and nipped her ear. "I'll bring a whole box."

* * * * *

COMING NEXT MONTH
from Harlequin® SuperRomance®
AVAILABLE AUGUST 7, 2012

#1794 ON HER SIDE
The Truth about the Sullivans
Beth Andrews

Nora Sullivan wants justice for her murdered mother and will do almost anything to make that happen. Even if it means consorting with the enemy's son, Griffin York. She can hold her own against the too-tempting man...or can she?

#1795 WITHIN REACH
Sarah Mayberry

If anyone ever needed a friend, it's Michael Young. Suddenly facing life as a single father, he's struggling. Thankfully he has Angie Bartlett to keep him grounded. But as his feelings for her change, he could risk ruining everything.

#1796 MAKING HER WAY HOME
Janice Kay Johnson

It's a nightmare. A few moments of inattention and Beth Greenway's ten-year-old niece has vanished. Worse, instead of looking for her niece, Detective Mike Ryan seems to be focused entirely on Beth!

#1797 A BETTER MAN
Count on a Cop
Emilie Rose

Roth Sterling couldn't get out of his hometown fast enough. Now he's back—this time as the new police chief. When he left, he burned a few bridges that need to be mended. And first up is Piper Hamilton...the woman he's never quite forgotten.

#1798 IN HIS EYES
Going Back
Emmie Dark

Hugh Lawson can't believe it. Zoe Waters has returned, ready to run her grandfather's vineyard. The old attraction is still there, and it isn't long before Hugh discovers that what he thought he knew about her may have been a lie.

#1799 OUT OF THE DEPTHS
Together Again
Pamela Hearon

The perfect photo will land Kyndal Rawlings the perfect job. But when the attempt gets her trapped in a cave with Chance Brennan, the man who broke her heart, she'll need all her strength to resist him. And to deal with the consequences if she can't.

You can find more information on upcoming Harlequin® titles, free excerpts and more at www.Harlequin.com.

HSRCNM0712

REQUEST YOUR FREE BOOKS!
2 FREE NOVELS PLUS 2 FREE GIFTS!

Harlequin®

Super Romance®

Exciting, emotional, unexpected!

YES! Please send me 2 FREE Harlequin® Superromance® novels and my 2 FREE gifts (gifts are worth about $10). After receiving them, if I don't wish to receive any more books, I can return the shipping statement marked "cancel." If I don't cancel, I will receive 6 brand-new novels every month and be billed just $4.69 per book in the U.S. or $5.24 per book in Canada. That's a saving of at least 15% off the cover price! It's quite a bargain! Shipping and handling is just 50¢ per book in the U.S. and 75¢ per book in Canada.* I understand that accepting the 2 free books and gifts places me under no obligation to buy anything. I can always return a shipment and cancel at any time. Even if I never buy another book, the two free books and gifts are mine to keep forever.

135/336 HDN FC6T

Name _____ (PLEASE PRINT) _____

Address _____ Apt. # _____

City _____ State/Prov. _____ Zip/Postal Code _____

Signature (if under 18, a parent or guardian must sign) _____

Mail to the **Reader Service:**
IN U.S.A.: P.O. Box 1867, Buffalo, NY 14240-1867
IN CANADA: P.O. Box 609, Fort Erie, Ontario L2A 5X3

Not valid for current subscribers to Harlequin Superromance books.

**Are you a current subscriber to Harlequin Superromance books
and want to receive the larger-print edition?
Call 1-800-873-8635 or visit www.ReaderService.com.**

* Terms and prices subject to change without notice. Prices do not include applicable taxes. Sales tax applicable in N.Y. Canadian residents will be charged applicable taxes. Offer not valid in Quebec. This offer is limited to one order per household. All orders subject to credit approval. Credit or debit balances in a customer's account(s) may be offset by any other outstanding balance owed by or to the customer. Please allow 4 to 6 weeks for delivery. Offer available while quantities last.

Your Privacy—The Reader Service is committed to protecting your privacy. Our Privacy Policy is available online at www.ReaderService.com or upon request from the Reader Service.

We make a portion of our mailing list available to reputable third parties that offer products we believe may interest you. If you prefer that we not exchange your name with third parties, or if you wish to clarify or modify your communication preferences, please visit us at www.ReaderService.com/consumerschoice or write to us at Reader Service Preference Service, P.O. Box 9062, Buffalo, NY 14269. Include your complete name and address.

HSR11

New York Times **bestselling author**

SUSAN MALLERY

is back with a charming new trilogy!

**Three California cowboys are about to find
love in the most unlikely of places...**

| Available now! | July 2012 | August 2012 |

Read them all this summer!

www.Harlequin.com

PHSSMT2012R

*Angie Bartlett and Michael Robinson are friends. And
following the death of his wife, Angie's best friend, their
bond has grown even more. But that's all there is...right?*

*Read on for an exciting excerpt of WITHIN REACH
by Sarah Mayberry, available August 2012
from Harlequin® Superromance®.*

"HEY. RIGHT ON TIME," Michael said as he opened the door.

The first thing Angie registered was his fresh haircut and
that he was clean shaven—a significant change from the
last time she'd visited. Then her gaze dropped to his broad
chest and the skintight black running pants molded to his
muscular legs. The words died on her lips and she blinked,
momentarily stunned by her acute awareness of him.

"You've cut your hair," she said stupidly.

"Yeah. Decided it was time to stop doing my caveman
impersonation."

He gestured for her to enter. As she brushed past him
she caught the scent of his spicy deodorant. He preceded
her to the kitchen and her gaze traveled across his shoulders before dropping to his backside. Angie had always
made a point of not noticing Michael's body. They were
friends and she didn't want to know that kind of stuff. Now,
however, she was forcibly reminded that he was a *very* attractive man.

Suddenly she didn't know where to look.

It was then that she noticed the other changes—the clean
kitchen, the polished dining table and the living room free
of clutter and abandoned clothes.

"Look at you go." Surely these efforts meant he was
rejoining life.

He shrugged, but seemed pleased she'd noticed. "Getting there."

They maintained eye contact and the moment expanded. A connection that went beyond the boundaries of their friendship formed between them. Suddenly Angie wanted Michael in ways she'd never felt before. *Ever.*

"Okay. Let's get this show on the road," his six-year-old daughter, Eva, announced as she marched into the room.

Angie shook her head to break the spell and focused on Eva. "Great. Looking forward to a little light shopping?"

"Yes!" Eva gave a squeal of delight, then kissed her father goodbye.

Angie didn't feel 100 percent comfortable until she was sliding into the driver's seat.

Which was dumb. It was nothing. A stupid, odd bit of awareness that meant *nothing.* Michael was still Michael, even if he was gorgeous. Just because she'd tuned in to that fact for a few seconds didn't change anything.

Does Angie's new awareness mark a permanent shift in their relationship? Find out in WITHIN REACH by Sarah Mayberry, available August 2012 from Harlequin® Superromance®.

Copyright © 2012 by Small Cow Productions PTY Ltd.

HSREXP0812